EVERLASTING

BOOK SEVEN of *THE STARLIGHT CHRONICLES*

C. S. Johnson

To Get *Awakening* (A Special Christmas Episode of The *Starlight Chronicles*) as a bonus for picking up this book,

Click Here

Download It At:
https://www.csjohnson.me/awakening

For Sam, until we meet again.

THE STARLIGHT CHRONICLES

Check out *Reawakening* (A Rebirth Episode of The *Starlight Chronicles*), a short story that takes place before Book 7!

4

☼<u>1</u>☼
Beginning Again

For the fourth or fifth time in less than an hour, I looked down at my legal pad, only to realize I had no idea what was going on.

My office seemed too bright. The lights seemed too sharp. I glanced around as the client in front of me continued to babble on about some financial legal nonsense.

Everything else was in its place: My various diplomas and certificates, celebrating my undergrad and graduate degrees, hung on the wall, proudly and prominently displayed right across from the entrance; my desk was off to the side, facing the wall, with the window behind me; my books were stacked in precise order on the bookshelf, tucked in with some of my awards. Among them was my newest one, the one from the Pittsburgh Law and Order Association, declaring my position as "Best Associate Lawyer of the Year" that arrived just before Thanksgiving last month.

Outside, the streets of my adopted city were hobbled with people looking for warmth and a cozy corner to cuddle up in, all while the snow continually dumped down out of the sky.

Nothing was out of place, not even the typical, dull-looking client in front of me.

No wonder I was bored.

The room was a temple to law and intellect, and I'd made sure to erase quite a bit of my heart in the process of setting it up.

No wonder that, instead of taking notes, I'd been doodling.

Despite the fact I had suddenly caught myself not paying attention to my meeting (again), I smiled thoughtfully, almost longingly. *Raiya used to do this same thing in Martha's class,* I recalled.

Instantly, as though I'd touched some mental flame inside of my mind, I flinched. *Where in the world did that thought come from?*

I didn't like to think of her anymore. Not if I could help it.

Of course, now that I was completely against thinking about her, my mind wasn't listening to me, and I wasn't sure I could help it.

I didn't have to glance at the calendar on the wall of my office to know more than seven years had passed since that day.

Seven years. *Seven years.*

Seven years, and I still crumbled as I remembered Raiya's body as it collapsed against mine, still sucked in my breath as the last breath of her words passed me by, still felt the dying chill of the fire-feather she'd tucked into her hair as it flicked into darkness.

Seven years, and it was still much too painful for me to acknowledge that the only person I'd ever loved more than myself, I was unable to save.

"Sir?"

I nearly jumped out of my seat as I realized that I was still in the middle of a legal hearing. "Yes?" I straightened up in my seat, trying to look nonchalant, and, as was my usual, managed to succeed enough to get out of any possible trouble.

"Are you all right? You look … troubled," my client, Mr. Brown, muttered reproachfully.

I put on my most winning smile. "I'm perfectly fine, Mr. Brown. I am just making some extensive notes on your business concerns so we will be ready with the rebuttal at the end of the trial." I tucked the drawing up against my chest, making sure he couldn't see it, just to be on the safe side.

Mr. Brown visibly relaxed. "Oh … well, good." He nodded. "For a moment there, I could've sworn you started daydreaming."

I almost shouted, *"Lawyers don't daydream!"* It took a surprising amount of self-control not to.

Instead, I laughed cordially. "No, no, sir, not at all. I assure you, I am the most capable lawyer available for handling your case. I know what is needed to get the job done."

"See to it, then," Mr. Brown said as he looked at his watch. "Well, I best be off for now. I'm to meet my wife for dinner."

"Well, don't keep her waiting on my account." I smiled. "I'll get your files pulled and we'll be ready for court as soon as the judges assign a day for it."

"Good to hear."

"Thank you for your time. Don't worry about anything. I'll have your case wrapped up in as little time as possible."

"I'll send you your retainer check in the mail." He grinned. "With a nice Christmas bonus, just to make sure you know how I appreciate your dedication."

And then Mr. Brown picked up his hat, put on his jacket, and walked out the door.

When he was gone, I just rolled my eyes. I hated representing people who weren't concerned so much with justice as with getting out of justice, but I had to do my job. I supposed.

I didn't like to think about that too much either.

When I did allow myself those small moments of reflection, I longed for another life. But I could hear a certain annoying voice in my head, chiding me for making life one big to-do list.

Then I quickly squelched my desire. I would, to this day, never admit to Elysian, my old "pet" dragon from years ago, was right. Not if I could avoid it.

I began to pack up my stuff for the day. I had my own dinner plans for tonight.

One of my best friends from my hometown of Apollo City was coming in to see me, and I wanted to have some time to prepare for the unpleasant lecture I was sure to receive.

My eyes fell to the notepad drawings I'd created while Mr. Brown was droning on and on about the unfairness of his situation, the integrity of his investment portfolio, and how his company was no doubt infiltrated with spies who had set him up to look like an embezzler.

My face softened for a moment, as the picture staring back at me was of a lovely young woman with wings fluttering out of her head. Even though the picture was not in color, I knew her eyes were the shade of the most vibrant spring violets, and her hair was the color of Christmas gingerbread. And even though the picture was not supposed to be real, the watchfulness and steadfastness of her eyes were more than mere reflections.

I sat down in my chair and looked at the picture glumly. *When did I get so good at drawing?* I wondered to myself.

I'd been only working as a lawyer here at Pharris & Dahlonega for … was it a year, already? Surely, I hadn't been doodling for all that time.

And when did I start allowing myself to think of Raiya again?

Of course, it's entirely possible I never really forgot her, I mused, *since she was the—No! I'm not going to think about it!*

I silently chastised myself as I packed up my things. Thinking about her only made it worse, I knew.

I barely remembered graduating from high school at all. When I looked back at my pictures from that time, I could tell part of me was not there.

I didn't have any pictures from the summer after I graduated. All I could remember was looking for her and not finding her, and having to drag around this emptiness in my chest all the time.

Thankfully, I'd transferred out of Apollo City College's dual enrollment program, and actual college began soon enough. I'd whisked myself away to Pittsburgh, to a new city, to a new home, a new school, and new distractions.

But no new self to go along with it. I was still in love with a memory.

Anger and sadness pushed through me; I shoved the doodles into my briefcase and slammed it shut. *I'll deal with those later. I can't think of this now. I have stuff to do …*

Once more, all of my secret longing, all of my hurt and anger, all of it was swept away under the carpet of scheduling.

"So, you're a bonafide Steelers' fan now, huh, Dinger? That's great." The man sitting across the table from me laughed heartily.

I smiled at him; he was one of my oldest friends, Mikey Salyards. "Come on, why wouldn't I? They are among the best teams in history."

Mikey stopped laughing and turned more somber. "You've changed a lot, I guess."

"I haven't changed, Mikey. I'm still the best of best of best."

If anything, I thought, *it's Mikey who's changed since high school.* The awkward teenage years and the pressure of always being in my shadow had dispersed to reveal a strong, confident, and capable (looking) person underneath. It was almost a shock for me to see my old friend looking so different.

The weird-looking beard didn't help, I silently decided. It reminded me too much of his father, and Dante Salyards was a man I was more than happy to forget.

Mikey cocked an eyebrow at me. "Maybe in your field of law," he said. "But you couldn't hold a candle to me when it comes to coaching or gym class."

"I could probably handle the PE, but I doubt I would handle the sixty-some immature teenagers running around a gym after snorting sugar," I conceded after careful thinking.

"Aw, it's not that bad," Mikey said. "There're only about forty-five students. Apollo's a pretty small district, actually."

We began laughing as our dinners came.

"Thanks for treating me, Dinger," Mikey said, cutting up the medium-rare, freshly harvested, lightly seasoned teriyaki steak before him.

"No problem. I suppose it's worth it if you're going to travel six or seven hours in the car to come and see me."

"You know," Mikey said in a careful tone, "you could make the trip shorter for me if you wanted."

11

I flinched. I should've known that was coming.

I side-stepped the subject. "How does Gwen feel about you coming all this way out here?"

Mikey caught on pretty quick and grinned; I was still as hardheaded as always, and he knew it. "She's fine with it. I think she'd come herself if she wasn't so worried you'd throw her out or something."

"I wouldn't do that to Gwen," I said with a huff. Goodness knows I had more reasons to hate Mikey than Gwen, and I had agreed to meet with him.

"Well, she'd probably feel more than a little awkward with the whole high school thing, too," Mikey admitted. "She is doing well though."

"Really? How nice."

Mikey frowned at my tone. "I know you're still sore at her for what happened to you, but you can't keep this up, Dinger."

"She attempted to blackmail me, before she tried to stop me from … " I shook my head, but my fists clenched. "And she blamed me for getting attacked."

"She was confused at the time."

"Please. Don't give her an excuse."

"Get over it. You didn't even love her. You were just mad she got in the way. And besides, you had—"

"Shut up. I don't want to talk about it."

"You had Raiya—"

"I told you, I didn't want to talk about it!" I slammed my fists down on the table, hard.

So much for self-control.

Mikey frowned. "Come on, Dinger! It's been years! You *still* can't talk about it?"

I gritted my teeth together. "I *don't want* to talk about it. And frankly, you're a gym teacher, not a therapist. If I wanted to talk about it, I would hire one of those to sit around and question me."

"Hey, I'm a coach, and I have to deal with my students' problems all the time," Mikey said. "I'm good at handling problems. And besides that, you should talk about it with someone. There might be a clue in your information."

I froze. "What do you mean?"

Mikey smiled; he seemed to be glad he'd finally arrived at the point he'd wanted to bring up all evening. He leaned closer and said, "Weird stuff's happening again."

"What do you mean, 'weird stuff,' Mike?" I asked carefully.

Did I really want to know? I didn't think I did. The last time "something weird" had happened, I needed to transform into Wingdinger—oh, God, how I cringed at the very thought of that stupid name—and had to save the world.

Mikey sighed. "Dad's back in Apollo City. I heard from Jason he came by, and he was asking for me. And you."

I said nothing, only remained motionless. Mikey's dad was not really a pleasant memory to either of us. If he was back in town, something was certainly up. And it certainly was going to be unpleasant.

After all, Dante Salyards was not a man who would take anything like supernatural trouble lightly. During his last stay in Apollo City, I knew Mikey's dad had seen a good extent of what trouble the supernatural could do.

But still, that selfish, peace-seeking center inside of me wanted this to be fake. So I showed no emotion or reaction as I asked, "What does he want?"

"I don't know what he wants," Mikey admitted with a shrug. "But if he's looking for both of us, I'm pretty sure it's not to give us an award or any money. Trouble's coming."

"How would you know for sure?"

Mikey frowned. "Come on, Dinger, don't get like that. We have to do something."

"You mean *I* have to do something, don't you?" I snorted into my drink.

"Well … yeah. I came all the way out here to see you and talk about it."

"I can't just get up and leave, Mikey," I told him. "I have a job. I've been working with the firm for a while now, and if I needed to take time off, I would've had to put it in months ago."

"Can't you take a leave of absence?"

"I can't just go, I just told you."

"You have to!"

"Why? Why should I?"

"For Raiya."

"Shut up!" I reached across the table and grabbed a hold of Mikey's shirt. Death was staring through my eyes as I growled, "Don't mention her to me. She's dead."

"Are you sure?" Mikey asked. We'd caught the attention of quite a few people by this time.

"What? What do you mean, 'Are you sure?!'" I nearly shouted. "I was holding her as she died!" I cringed as I looked down at my hands; they tingled at the memory of Raiya as she shuddered and breathed her last breath, her blood mingling with my tears … I felt shame-faced as I recalled asking her—begging her—to come back, to stay alive, to stay with me … and how, all of a sudden, she was gone. We were gone.

"But … she wasn't human, remember?" Mikey whispered uneasily as he glanced around to see that some of the people nearby were still looking at us. "Maybe she didn't die, maybe she just … went somewhere else."

Why had I never thought of that?

I was taken aback. Was it possible? Was it true?

Maybe Raiya hadn't died. It was possible—after all, I believed more unbelievable things; I'd *seen* more unbelievable things.

But I shook my head as the last remnants of my daydreams melted away in the cold light of reality. "It doesn't matter. If she wasn't dead," I said slowly, "she would have come back to me."

I might have believed it, but I still felt dumb for saying it.

"Maybe she's trying, and you're just not there." Mikey raised his eyebrows, no doubt silently congratulating himself on his advanced logic.

It was enough to get me to release him.

I allowed Mikey's remark to settle in my mind. It didn't make any sense. Why would she come back now? What else was going on? I wondered this and questioned Mikey on it.

Mikey took a bite of his steak and said, "Like I said, there's a bunch of unexplained events going on … and Dante promises it's not even half of it. I can't explain it, but you're not there and Raiya's not there—"

"You just said she wasn't dead!"

"Hey, give me a break. Rachel would be the first one to know right? And Jason hasn't said anything about her saying stuff like that."

I remembered the bright-eyed redhead who ran my favorite coffee shop when I was in high school. Years later, I still had nothing to compare to Rachel's food. Even the steaks and lobster fillets I billed to my bosses were unable to fill the longing my stomach carried since I moved.

"How is Rachel?" I asked, deciding I'd had enough of the gloomy topics.

Mikey shrugged. "She's fine. Pregnant, actually."

"Oh? Really?" Images of a recent dream popped into my head. A little girl with red hair, smiling as she chased a smaller boy with brown hair and matching violet eyes. Rachel's children? Is that whose kids those were?

It was possible, I supposed.

"It's a girl, they know that much," Mikey continued on, not realizing I was caught up in my own thoughts. "She's due in the spring; she and Lee announced it at their anniversary party this summer."

"Do you think she'd really come back?" I whispered softly.

Mikey sighed. "Let's change the subject. Here." He pulled out an envelope. "I was going to mail this, but it's okay to give it to you now."

I opened it and quickly scanned through the letter. Then I went back and read it again, properly this time, just to make sure I understood it. I groaned to myself, but put on a smile for Mike. "You and Gwen are getting married, huh?"

"Yeah." There was nothing but joy in his big, goofy grin.

So I humored him. "That's great, man."

I humored him, and he caught me. Mikey laughed. "Come on, you're going to have to do better than that."

"You can't blame me for not being excited," I snorted. "This means I'll have to go back home."

"And not to mention be my best man," Mikey added.

"Are you kidding me?" I felt oddly conflicted. Like I should agree to it, but I would rather stick needles in my eyes or puke up a pig.

"No. I'm asking you to be my best man."

"Okay, sure, I suppose." But this better not be a lot of work, I added silently.

"Great!" Mikey grinned. "Wedding's in two weeks, so I'll be looking forward to my bachelor party—"

"Two weeks? What do you mean, two weeks?" I looked down at the invitation again. Yep, two weeks. "I can't get off from work just like that."

"Ah, don't be such a sour-butt, Dinger. Everyone else is coming. Besides, you can't really like your job that much."

"Huh?"

"I saw you when you came in. You're tired and exhausted, and probably sick, too. You don't seem to care, either. I can tell. We've been friends a long time."

"That's not the truth."

"It's a good part of it."

I grumbled, caught. It had been forever since someone was so good at reading me. "That's not the whole picture."

"What else is there? Is Charlotte still giving you grief?"

I moaned at mention of her. I put my head in my hands. "You've got a point there, I suppose."

Charlotte was one of the first friends I made in college. I remembered only introducing myself to her because I'd thought, foolishly, she was actually Raiya. Charlotte had the same long, reddish-brown hair as Raiya, and looking at her from behind, I was too hopeful to be cautious.

But Charlotte had been more than gracious to me, even helping me get my current job at her father's law firm, and we were friends—but that was the problem, for her, of course.

She'd been bugging me lately with hints of how we should be dating. Or married with seventeen children and living down in the South with her mother's side of the family. I wasn't sure which she wanted, but I was terrified to discover the specifics.

"You don't have to bring her to the wedding." Mikey smirked.

"I wasn't going to. But she did get me the job at her dad's office. That's why I don't think I can just get off."

"Come on, surely he'll be okay with it."

"I'm not worried about him. It's my other boss, Pharris, who's the real piece of work."

"Piece of work" was the kindest way of putting it. How do you explain to scientists that you've found the missing link between humans and the Tyrannosaurus Rex? Everything from her meticulous, over-gelled bob to the edge of her gilded fingernails screamed dinosaur DNA. If that wasn't enough, her attitude and tone sealed the deal.

"Just ask," Mikey said. "And if you can't get off, well, just quit. You don't like it anyway."

"I'm good at it."

"So what? You need something in your life that you love."

"Look, just get off my back, will you? If a miracle happens and I can get off work, I'll do it. But short of that, you'd better call up Poncey."

Mikey grinned, and for a moment, I had to laugh; Mikey looked just like his high school self, with food stuck in his teeth, his smile wide and innocent. "If that's the best I can get from you for now, I'll take it. Besides, given our history, I'd say a miracle is right around the corner."

"Ha, ha, yeah right." I rolled my eyes. I'd forgotten how to believe in miracles.

☼<u>2</u>☼
Old Pains

Surprisingly, I survived the rest of the dinner with Mikey, as did our friendship. If there was any casualty, it was my appetite. And that was a shame, as the restaurant was a top-rated steakhouse in the city, with one of the most renowned bartenders.

I headed outside behind Mikey, thankful I could just walk him to his car, say good-bye, and make promises to come visit that I wasn't planning on keeping. Then I could go home, get some work done, and go to sleep.

I'd learned over the years the comfort of an empty home. My attempts to get over high school and celebrate my many accomplishments had produced some incredulously horrifying memories.

"Well, it was great seeing you, man," I told Mikey as he pulled out his keys.

"Hey, wait. I have something for you."

I nearly groaned. *Wasn't the wedding invitation bad enough?* Naturally, I was upset I would have to go back home. Though, in all honesty, Apollo City was far from home for me these days. I'd adopted Pitt as my own, and for the most part we worked well together.

"What is it?" I asked. "It's not a copy of Gwen's new book, is it? Because I don't think I finished the first one."

Gwen had majored in theater studies in college. I knew she was teaching at a kids' workshop in Apollo City. She also worked with Central, helping out the drama department, ACHE, when it came time for their performances. But on the side she'd written a few kids' novels, a series called *The Soldiers from the Stars,* about a couple of teenagers who have to save the world from aliens and survive high school at the same time.

Yep, she'd more or less taken my life and made it into a simplistic parody. I read the first one, but I wasn't really impressed with it. After seeing how she portrayed me, I didn't know if I should be insulted or flattered. Given our history, I had a feeling she was, in her own way, trying to apologize to me.

It was a stupid way to apologize. It was also a stupid way to try to rebuild a friendship. But, considering my distance, and my actions, I felt, on some level, maybe that was precisely why she did it.

So, naturally, I didn't say much about it. I decided to ignore it. *If only Mikey would let me forget it completely …*

"No, Gwen's finished the series," Mikey said. He frowned. "I thought I gave you the complete set."

"Oh, really? Okay then." I shrugged. "What do you have for me? It's not an early Christmas gift, is it? Because I didn't get anything for—"

My voice broke off as Mikey pulled a wrapped present out of the car. It was a picture frame, and a sudden rush of awareness hit me so hard I stopped breathing.

"It's not a Christmas present," Mikey said. "It's more of a late gift. Rachel heard I was coming to see you while I was going to my teacher's conference here, so she asked if I would take it to you. She found it while she was cleaning out the house and thought you should have it."

"Cleaning out the house?" I repeated, barely able to process what he was saying.

Mikey gently placed the frame in my hands. "Oh, yeah, I guess I didn't tell you," he said. "Grandpa Odd's been officially declared dead, you know, instead of just missing, so Letty inherited all his money. Turns out he had a pretty sweet fortune at his disposal, so Rachel upgraded her business … "

I didn't listen to him as he told me about Rachel moving her coffee and catering business uptown and putting her original coffeehouse, Rachel's Café, up for sale. I was too busy telling myself that I was happy for her. And it wasn't like I was surprised to hear about the money. Grandpa Odd—or rather, Draco—had been alive for hundreds of years on Earth after he fell from the Celestial Kingdom. I wasn't surprised to hear he had a lot of money, and I was even happy for Rachel, who had struggled for a long time to balance her family's checkbook.

I think the thing that made me the most upset was hearing she was selling the coffee shop. I'd taken a very small amount of comfort in knowing it was still there, even after I stopped going and left Apollo City.

Mikey continued to talk, and I continued to mostly ignore him. The weight of the painting settled into me as I held it, making me think of a time when its painter did too. My heart began to beat between my ears as the coldness of western PA whipped around me, adding to the warmth I felt as I held onto my frame. My illusions of comfort were disappearing, quickly and sharply.

As Mikey finished up his story, I forced myself to breathe again. The stress lessened, ever so slightly, and I was able to focus again.

"Sounds great," I muttered, hoping that would allow me some wiggle room in the conversation.

"Yes, she's very happy about that," Mikey said. "It works out for me and Gwen, too. She insisted on catering the wedding for free, as a gift to us."

"You can't pay for your own caterer?" I scoffed.

"Hey, not all of us are making the big bucks as city lawyers," Mikey said with a grin.

"Psh. I don't make *that* much." I waved it off, even as I knew I was lying. I actually probably made more than even he thought I did. My own lawyer-mother, Cheryl, was more than ecstatic when I told her about landing a job with Pharris & Dahlonega, one of the most influential international business and corporate firms in the city, and I was getting a much better starting pay than the average newbie on the block.

I was happy enough about it. My job, along with the pay and prestige that came with it, was the only real reason Cheryl accepted me staying in Pitt to work. Her own law firm in Apollo City was taking off, and she had hinted more than once she would love to have me come back and join the ranks.

I had a lot of things I had to tell myself to be happy about.

"That's actually part of the reason we thought we'd do a Christmas wedding," Mikey explained, as he stood there, with his car door open, as I stood there, with Raiya's painting in my hands. "Lots of sales going on during the holiday seasons."

"I imagine more people are able to come, too, since even I'll be out of the office that day," I mused aloud.

He nodded. "Exactly. Why do you think I was able to get Poncey to come? You know his business flew him out to Germany last week."

I grinned, thinking of my sidekick companion. Just like Mikey, I was almost surprised how much of a leader he had become. "He's got a gift for negotiation," I remarked.

"Yeah, how else did he get his wife to marry him?" Mikey laughed. "She's way too hot for him."

I laughed, too, but I was relieved when an awkward silence came over us, and I could go.

"Well," I said, "thanks for … this." I gestured toward the painting.

"No problem," Mikey said. "I'll call you tomorrow, okay? Maybe we can do lunch, if my stupid teacher's conference will let me escape early some, huh?"

"Maybe," I agreed, trying to be cordial, even if it killed me by that point.

Mikey eventually left, and I waved as he drove away.

Then I shuffled to my car, stuffed the painting in the back, and drove to my own apartment, trying not to think too much about Mikey's gift. It was too tempting to think about pulling over and just dumping it somewhere where I didn't have to see it.

There was a small push in the back of my heart, and I was doubly tempted to do just that, out of little more than spite.

A vision of Raiya's face, crumbled and angry, popped into my mind. I couldn't do it after that. I didn't even know which one of her paintings it was, but I knew she treasured them all.

It was unnerving, realizing there was a way to love her—and hurt her—from the other side of the grave.

Some time later, I found myself sitting down on my couch. I ran my palms over the surface of the gift, feeling the coarseness of the staid, brown wrapping paper. Underneath, it was smooth, with no bumps; I knew Rachel had likely had it framed.

I'd always admired Raiya's work. *Hadn't I been doing just that, I thought, when she saw me for the first time on this side of Time?*

Images of another realm, the brightness and brilliance of a cosmic sea, flashed before me.

I pushed the vision aside vehemently. "I need to get a drink," I said aloud.

I'd had a couple of roommates while I was at college, and even some after. It helped with the rent, and it was nice to have someone else to make sure I never ended up lying in a ditch somewhere, drunk or otherwise.

But my last roommates, a pair of brothers, Ravi and Dinesh, had moved out when they'd been offered jobs down in D. C. We still kept in touch, and they still called me for legal insight more often than they'd ever admit to their bosses.

But for the most part, I was alone, and in many ways, I was even less than alone.

After getting a full glass of wine in hand, I finally managed to pull off the paper.

"Huh." I frowned. *It wasn't the one I was expecting.*

Raiya had done several paintings for Rachel's Café, and I was full expecting something with a phoenix or a dragon on it, for me or Elysian; I also thought it easily could've been a van Gogh picture. Where else would someone like Raiya get "Starry Knight" as her superhero name?

Instead, the picture before me was a weird portrayal of a something like a supernova; it wasn't realistic at all, but pictured more like a stained glass window. "What is it?" I asked aloud, not expecting an answer.

My memory decided to help me out, much to my displeasure.

"A neo-expressionist supernova," she said.

It was the last picture I'd seen her work on, the one she'd been working on the week before …

Before …

Geez, I can't even think *the words.*

"Who does this?!" I yelled. "Who can't get over someone who died *over seven years ago?!*"

It was insane. *Insane.* It was stupid, too. There was nothing I could do about her. Nothing! I had to move on, and I kept trying, and trying, and meanwhile all the rest of the universe seemed content to pull me back into a vicious cycle of hating myself, hating her, and hating my fate.

"Why are you doing this to me, Adonaias?" I moaned. My head fell into my hands. "Haven't you made me suffer enough? Isn't it enough that she's dead? No, of course not. You have to keep me unsatisfied and humiliated and alone, too, always questioning my sanity or my stupidity, don't you?"

I glared out my window, searching for the face of the Prince of Stars, even if I hated him.

He didn't seem to stop anyone else from suffering. There was no reason to think I was any exception. I thought about the different things I'd done over the years to forget everything. The girls, the prescriptions, the addictions; the lies, the half-truths, the "my truths." Exercise, meditation, consultations, depression. Throwing everything I had into my job, my degree, and my friends' lives. All to find some semblance of one of my own, where it did not touch anything outside of the physical world.

All for naught.

Certainly, nothing stopped the flood of memories that poured out from just *seeing* one of her paintings.

"Augh!" I screamed as I threw the painting away from me. "I can't take it anymore!"

The *trinkle* of broken glass seemed to break through my heart.

I looked over at it, only to see a large web of broken lines cutting through the heart of the painting. It seemed I felt its pain as my own.

I drew in a deep breath, trying to steady myself.

Very carefully, I propped the painting up against the wall by my door. I decided I didn't want to be alone, here, tonight.

I grabbed my keys and headed out, headed for any other place other than where I was.

THE STARLIGHT CHRONICLES

☼3☼
New Pains

Prrrinng! Prrring!

My office phone rang, and it might as well have been a full-fledged demon from the old days, from all the power the sound had behind it. I felt pure pain rush into the middle of my forehead, and I groped for the disconnect button.

My head was pounding as I laid it down on my desk, reveling in the small relief the cool surface had to offer.

I could barely see out of my eyes. The lights were too bright and too sharp again.

I need to get a light dimmer, I thought. *I could probably hide my condition a bit better if I had one.*

And I did need to hide. Today wasn't one of my better days; my clothes were wrinkled and unkempt, my leather shoes were cracking from shuffling around in all the wet snow, and my hair was sticking up in a strange way—strange enough that it wasn't immediately overlooked by my older colleagues as one of those "young people" type things, anyway.

I think I forgot to brush my teeth, too. That would account for the foul taste in my mouth.

Maybe I could get off work—leave early, or something.

I didn't want to go back to my apartment. Raiya's painting was still out in the hall, and I felt weak.

I *hated hated hated* feeling this way. I hated feeling I wasn't capable of handling something in a mature, poised manner. Not something like that, anyway.

There was also the matter of cleaning up the mess. I didn't want to have to sweep up the tiny bits of broken glass. In my current state, I didn't really trust myself to do a good job. It was something better left to my cleaning service.

But I didn't want to end up labeled "weird" or "depressed" or "eccentric" by my coworkers. I was sure they had enough labels for me, considering how many of them I'd managed to outperform over the last several months, despite the days of my varied appearances.

There was a knock at the door, and I let out a curse at the sudden, loud interruption.

"What is it?" I snapped, jerking upright in my seat.

The door opened just a peek, and I didn't have to ask to know who it was. I groaned to myself.

"Come in, Charlotte," I grumbled.

"Hey, Alex." She greeted me warmly, and even though I'd been going by my middle name for the last several years, I wondered who she was talking to for a longer moment than made me feel comfortable.

One of the more important things I'd been able to do since moving away from Apollo City was go by my middle name. "Hamilton" was a novelty in college, but in the lawyer business people prefer "relatable" names.

"So, um, are you okay, Lexy?" Charlotte asked, her face still half-hidden by the door. "I heard you, uh, had a rough night."

"I'm fine," I bit back. "And stop calling me Lexy. You knew when we were dating that I hated it then. There's no reason to think I would like it better now."

She opened the door completely. The first thing I noticed was that she'd cut her hair. The golden brown locks fell down to her shoulders now, making her look both younger and older at the same time.

Good, I thought. Maybe it was a sign she'd given up on me.

When I first met Charlotte, I couldn't stop staring at her hair. It was nearly the same color as Raiya's, and the length was close to the same, too. Part of me had wondered if Charlotte had been sent as a stand-in for Raiya after she died. I mean, Mary had taken that role once before, and our classmates didn't notice. Maybe Charlotte was supposed to be something of the same for me?

It didn't take me long to doubt it. Even now, I couldn't believe I ever thought that was a possibility to begin with. In recent months, I'd begun to hate it, especially after Charlotte pushed me into dating her.

I only went on a couple dates to get her to stop asking me, cajoling me, and synching my schedule up with hers. It was properly horrifying. I certainly saw the light, but she willfully remained blind to our incompatibility.

Maybe getting her hair cut—something she knew I wouldn't necessarily like—was a sign she was ready to give up, and we could go back to being friends.

"Daddy was trying to reach you," she said.

Ugh. What does he want?

I looked at her expectedly.

"He said your case for the Wilsons was moved up to this afternoon," Charlotte said. "And he said I was going to be your partner in court today. He wants me to work on my presentation some, and he says you're the best we have when it comes to closing arguments."

I bypassed the compliment. Likely it was true, but I didn't think Mr. Dahlonega had actually said it himself. "It's this afternoon?" I glanced at my calendar. *I guess Mikey and I aren't going to be meeting for lunch today.*

"Yes." She took a tentative step inside the room. "Would you like to go to an early lunch with me? Daddy said it was okay if we went early so you could set up."

"I would appreciate it if you didn't call Mr. Dahlonega Daddy," I said. "I know he's your father, but it's not very professional. Even if you are a junior lawyer here, same as me."

Charlotte frowned. "So I guess that's a no to lunch?" she asked, her voice tight.

"I can't make it today," I said. There came a point when I was pushed that I would do the right thing and push back passive-aggressively.

Pain shot through my eyes and dashed out my temples. It was time to push back, period.

"So it's more of a no, thank you," I clarified. My breath sucked in as I began to rub my forehead. "I have a huge headache this morning." I stood up and grabbed my papers, then stuffed them into my briefcase less than carefully. "I'm going to go home, grab some medicine, grab some coffee, and then I'll see you in court."

"Fine." Charlotte's eyes dropped to the floor. "I'll see you at one o'clock."

"Sharp," I agreed as my head reeled in pain once more.

I headed down for the parking deck and nearly limped to my car as my head balked at the cold, December air. Some part of me did believe I would've felt better if I'd been able to drive my motorcycle, a Dragon XL 2200, instead of my car.

But as I pulled into the small parking lot by my apartment complex, I decided that it was a good thing I didn't drive the motorcycle.

For one, I didn't want to be dead. My whole body ached, and my eyes winced at the midday light. The winter "wonderland" around me didn't help, with the layers of snow bouncing sunshine, sparse at it was, back into my brain.

For another, I didn't want to be reminded of Elysian any more than I wanted to be reminded of Raiya.

I stumbled into my door, nearly tripping over my own feet.

I can't wait to get to bed. This whole day needs a complete do-over.

Getting back home and settling in for an hour or so before I went back to court would help me.

But just like the day a meteorite decided to come crashing down into my world back in high school, life had other plans for me that day.

I opened the door and walked in, slipping as my shoes stepped right in the middle of the small puddle of smashed glass behind my door.

"What in the—?!" I cried, my palms catching me before my face hit the floor, only to realize there were suddenly a dozen and a half lacerations on both hands.

Blood seeped out instantly, as I swam to get out of the glass shards. I got up and headed toward the kitchen sink, spitting out cuss words left and right.

It was as I was wiping the soap off my cuts that I realized something was off about the situation.

I'd broken the glass on the painting, but it hadn't splattered out everywhere, especially not by the door.

I glanced over by the door. The picture frame was not only smashed, but it looked like the glass had been blown out from the other side.

That's when I began to hear the whispers.

"That's got to be him."

"He sure doesn't sound like one of us. He's got no control over himself. He can't even control his language or his mouth."

"We still have to ask him. He's the one who has the—"

"That could be a mistake, easily."

I grabbed a knife and made my way out to the hallway. "Who's there?" I called, ready to defend myself.

The voices quieted, and I could hear the pitter-patter of running feet.

"I heard you," I said. "And I know you heard me."

I waited for a long moment, before I sighed. "I'm not interested in playing hide-and-seek with a couple of thieves, but I'll warn you I trained—"

After a *whoosh* of movement, there they were.

They were smaller than I expected.

A boy and a girl appeared before me, dressed in normal-looking kids' clothes. The boy was a bit younger and a bit shorter. He had brown hair and blue eyes; the girl was clearly his sister. She had the same eyes, but they were a shade darker. Her hair was cut in one of those "trendy" fashions, I guess, because it was uneven on either side. Not a bad look, I decided, but it seemed too adult for a girl I would have pegged for fourteen.

"What are you doing in here?" I grumbled. "You're not the neighbors' kids, are you?"

"No," the girl said. "We are—"

"We're here looking for someone," the boy said.

"Lucas, stop interrupting me," the girl snapped. "I'm the older one, so I'm in charge."

The boy, who I assumed at this point was named Lucas, glared back at her. "That's how we got into this mess, Lyra. You shouldn't have been messing with stuff, or we'd still be home, and Mom'll kill us when we get back!"

"You were the one who actually made the bottle break," Lyra shot back.

My headache, while it had dulled some since I got home, flared back to life. "Alright, stop," I ordered. "Geez, and you were complaining that I don't have any discipline."

They both looked at me, slightly shocked, but it was enough to get them to stop arguing.

"Good," I mockingly praised them. "Now, tell me why you're here before I call the cops."

They both glanced at each other. I had the feeling they were communicating with their own language, and at the moment I hated it.

It's time to kick them out, I decided.

"Okay, never mind." I reached out and grabbed their shoulders, careful not to hurt them, but still wanting to show them who was in charge. "I don't need any cookies, I'm not buying anything for fundraisers, and you really should get back to school so they can call your parents to come and get you."

"Stop it," Lucas grumbled, trying to subvert me.

"We need help," Lyra insisted.

"I already told you, I'm not interested in buying whatever it is you're selling," I snapped. "Especially since you managed to bust into my apartment. You should be glad I'm not calling the cops on—"

"We're looking for someone known as 'Wingdinger,'" Lucas shouted over me.

I paused. And nearly fell over.

It took me less time than I expected for me to shout back, "Well, you're going to be looking for a long time, because he's dead. He died a long time ago."

"He did not," the boy argued. "That was the cover story for SWORD."

My hands dropped from his shoulder. I was surprised to see they were shaking.

"Who told you that?" I asked, as a sinking feeling took hold of me, one that was different from my other ailments this morning.

"My dad."

"Your dad tell you about Santa Claus and the Tooth Fairy, too?" I shot back. It was instinctual for me to fight back; both as a lawyer and as someone who didn't want to lose the argument (so about the same thing, I guess). But Mikey's news, about Apollo City, and about his dad, terrified me.

Lucas stuck his tongue out at me. "I'm ten years old," he announced proudly. "I know Santa Claus and the Tooth Fairy aren't real."

"You still cried when you found out," his sister muttered beside me.

I turned to face her. "Let's not antagonize him, okay?" *Lucas was just a little bit younger than Adam*, I realized. It was close enough. Adam had just turned twelve some number of weeks ago. Hadn't my assistant sent him that check?

Lyra folded her arms across her chest in reply. "We wouldn't even be arguing if you would just help us."

I could only hope that dealing with Lyra wasn't as difficult as dealing with the boys.

"If I'm going to help you," I said, going through the script I used with my clients, "we should get to know each other first."

"Who are you?" Lucas asked.

"I'm ... Alex," I said, deciding that's how I would introduce myself to their parents when I met them and told them I could easily sue them for breaking into my apartment. "I'm a lawyer. This is my apartment."

"I'm Lucas," the boy said, not realizing I'd already been able to figure that out. "And this is my sister, Lyra. She says she's in charge, but she's not even two full years older than me. That's not so much. I can take care of myself."

"Since you're able to take care of yourself," I said dryly, "let me go ahead and correct you on your assumptions. Women are in charge, no matter what." (I decided I would tell him later that it was better to just let them think they were.)

That line was enough to get Lyra to soften. Her eyes warmed up to me immediately, even if her stance was defensive.

I almost felt myself softening toward them at their silliness. But recalling the nature of their "visit," I pushed that instinct aside. "Now, what are you guys doing looking for Wingdinger?"

"We need his help to get back home," Lyra said. "He's the one who has the portal."

"What portal?" I frowned. I didn't have any idea of what she was talking about.

"Yeah. How do you think we ended up here in the first place?" she asked.

"I think you broke in, or let yourselves in, assuming I forgot to lock the door." I sighed. "How long have you been here, anyway?"

"Just a few moments," Lyra replied.

Looking down at the bloody mess on my hands, I rolled my eyes. "I guess you were the ones who ruined my picture frame?"

True to kid form, Lucas puffed out his chest in proud denial. "No," he asserted. "It was like that when we got here."

"If it makes you feel better," Lyra said to me, "we landed on the glass, too." She held up her spotless hands.

"Well, at least you didn't get hurt," I said.

She frowned. "Yes, we did. Look."

I glanced back, non-interested, when I saw it. There was a faint glow around her hands.

"Oh, geez," I sputtered. "You're … you're, uh, that word." *It's perfectly reasonable that I've forgotten Star language after all these years.* "You're Starlight Warriors."

"Duh." Lucas rolled his eyes. "How else do you think we knew about SWORD and Wingdinger?"

Lyra, on the other hand, perked up instantly. "You're a Star, too," she said. "Aren't you?"

"No, I'm not," I grumbled. *Not anymore.*

"How else would you know about us?" Lyra asked. "It's a secret."

"Are you ever going to stop asking questions?" I groaned. *No wonder I never wanted kids.*

Lyra put her hands on her hips. "Are you going to help us get home or not?"

I rubbed my eyes, trying to process it all. "I need a drink," I muttered. The last twenty-four hours had not been kind to me, and it didn't seem like it was going to get any better.

"I heard drinking's bad for you," Lucas said.

"Context matters." I grabbed another bottle of wine out of my cabinet.

"How are you going to be able to help us if you're drinking?"

"If you're a Starlight Warrior, you know about miracles," I retorted, taking a large gulp, right out of the bottle. "Besides, I'm not sure I *can* help you, let alone *will* help you."

"My dad says that all Stars should help each other," Lyra argued.

"Well, your dad sounds like an idiot," I snapped back. "Especially since he should know that Stars *don't* all help each other."

"My dad is *not* an idiot!" she yelled.

Instantly, the force behind her words blew power past me. My bottle was blown out of my hand, and my kitchen shook from her outburst.

Instantly, I cursed at the shattered glass, but I was appropriately terrified and appalled. I had removed as much supernatural activity from my life as I could. It had been awhile since I'd seen any; I'd forgotten it all, and how disconcerting it was to see it.

I grabbed a paper towel and began cleaning up. It was only when I heard the boy's small sniffles in the next room that I stopped.

They're just kids. And it looks like they need help getting home. I better be nicer to them. I wouldn't want their parents trying to sue me.

Especially if they did know about things like Starlight Warriors and SWORD. That could be dangerous. The last thing I needed was to run into SWORD again.

I walked into the living room, looking for Lyra. I didn't have far to go. Lucas had his arm protectively around Lyra. I almost smiled at the picture they made.

"Lyra's just coming into her second level of power," Lucas said, rushing to explain his sister's misbehavior. "She doesn't have a lot of control over them yet sometimes."

"Shush, Lucas!" Lyra snapped. "He doesn't need to know. He's just a stranger." She glared at me, making me feel even more uncomfortable. "And a mean one, at that."

"Look, I'm sorry," I said, the words feeling crusty as they came out of my mouth. "I don't know if I can help you. Let me think of a plan."

"I want my mommy," Lucas whispered, still whimpering.

"Come here." I knelt down next to him and opened my arms. Without a word, he came running, as if it was the most natural thing in the world. Just as if it was the most natural thing in the world for me to wrap him up and hold him tight.

It has been a long time since I've seen Adam, I thought. Maybe I missed him more than I let myself realize.

"We need your help. You wouldn't just toss us out, would you?" Lucas asked.

"No," I said, already wondering if I was going to regret it.

"Are you going to help us, then?" Lyra asked. She remained skeptical.

I admired her for it; it was a smart move. I wasn't entirely sure of how I could help them.

They needed to get home, and I didn't know much about finding people's parents. I worked with international regulations and finances. Family law was more of Cheryl's forte.

"Tell me what happened," I said. "How did you get here?"

"We were playing with our mom's stuff," Lyra admitted. "It had some trace elements of Time's power in it. We got sucked in and that's how we ended up here."

"Time's power?" I asked.

"You know. Lady Time."

"Alora?"

"Duh," Lucas said.

I frowned at him. "You're killing me with that routine, kid."

He stuck his tongue out at me and then went to go sit on the couch. He laid his head down on the pillow and curled his legs under his chest. "I'm tired," he murmured.

Lyra sighed. "You don't have time to be tired, Lucas."

"My mom would be able to help you," I said slowly. "She works as a lawyer. I think she has some experience working with families."

If nothing else, she should still be able to connect with Dante, I thought bitterly. *He might be able to help us get these kids back to their parents, whoever they are.*

He was the one who told me before, years ago, that there were other fallen Stars on Earth. Surely he'd have some idea of whose kids these were, and where they were located. SWORD struck me as the kind of company that would tag people like animals if they could get away with it.

"When can we leave?" Lyra asked.

"Let me make a few calls," I said, wondering if I could get a moment to take some medication. I had a feeling Cheryl was going to flip when I talked to her.

Of course, that was assuming she answered her phone. She didn't do that much when I was a teenager, and I doubted she would be more reliable now.

"I'm hungry," Lucas said.

"Okay," I said slowly, telling myself to take this stuff one step at a time. "Let me see about making some lunch for us, too." I nodded toward the mess on the floor. "And I should probably get this cleaned up before you get hurt again."

"I'll help with that," Lyra said.

"I don't think so," I said. "You could get hurt."

She looked down her nose at me. "I have healing powers," she said, almost rendering me silent in how much she reminded me of Raiya in that moment. "I don't need to worry about that, even if I have trouble controlling them sometimes."

She's a little spitfire, I thought with a smirk. "Fine. The broom's in the closet over there." I turned to Lucas. "So, Lucas, want to help me in the kitchen?"

He grinned and came dashing over to me. "Alright!" he cheered. "Food time!"

I laughed, barely realizing that my headache had gone away.

THE STARLIGHT CHRONICLES

☼ 4 ☼

Lady Boss

After a late, modest lunch of chips and grilled cheese sandwiches, Lucas and Lyra went down for an accidental nap.

I was calling my mom's office for the third time when I noticed they'd curled up on opposite ends of my couch, cuddled under my throw blankets. They were fast asleep, and it was only two o'clock in the afternoon.

I suppose it's not every day that you get transported around the world and into a stranger's apartment.

I didn't mind. They were pretty interesting kids. I mean, as far as kids go, I supposed.

Lucas liked sports and animals. He told me he missed his pet back home as I gave out the cookies I had stuffed in the back of my pantry. He said his lizard had a soft spot for sweets.

Lyra was in love with music. She managed to find the built-in sound system I had installed a few years ago and turned it on. I was surprised to find she liked the orchestral arrangements. Her mother, she said, was teaching her the violin.

I didn't get too much information about their parents before they fell asleep on my couch. I knew they were Stars. Their dad was a teacher, and their mother worked at a hospital. I also learned that they had several other brothers and sisters—they were only two out of nine, to be exact,

49

which told me all I needed to know about their parents—and they were the youngest.

Once they fell asleep, I watched them for a while, transfixed by the absurdity of my situation, and even more so by my reaction to it.

I should have been running from this. I should have been kicking them out, calling the police, and getting my own nap in peace.

I didn't want to even think about being a Star, let alone getting involved with other people who were. But these kids—*kids*—charmed me and managed to make me want to help them.

And I had agreed, even if I didn't have a solid clue just how to do that.

Lyra muttered in her sleep and turned over onto her other side. Her brown hair was splayed out across my throw pillows. Lucas was a stomach sleeper; he had pulled one of my throw pillows nearly over his face.

I decided not to worry about it. Surely, Cheryl would know what to do.

As I moved into the study, I glanced at the time.

Immediately, my heart began to stutter.

It's two-thirty!

I had to present a court case.

More than an hour ago!

I grabbed the phone and dialed Charlotte's number. I was surprised to see I had several missed calls from her. Was my phone on silent?

She didn't pick up when I called her back.

What is wrong with people today? I wondered, tossing the phone down on the counter.

As I did that, there was another knock on my door.

I opened it to see Charlotte glaring at me. "There you are," she exclaimed, exasperated. "Where have you been?"

"Just here," I said. "And hey, can you keep your voice down some, please?"

"I don't particularly care if your neighbors hear how much you've managed to screw things up this time," Charlotte said.

"Well, this time it's about a case, not about our relationship," I pointed out. "So you should care more about what they hear this time."

"Ugh! You're just saying that because you don't like to argue."

Really? You think I don't *like to argue?* I sighed. Maybe it was true when it came to her. Usually, Charlotte was a bit of a pushover. It was only times like this—times when she was angry—that she was harder to deal with.

"Besides," she marched on, "the music's on in here." She huffed as she read the title. "Weren't you the one who told me last year that the orchestra was for losers?"

"I would've said anything to get you to stop asking me," I told her. "And I do really need you to keep it down. It's not the neighbors I'm worried about." I nodded toward the room. "I had some unexpected guests this afternoon."

Charlotte glanced into the room. "Children? Are those children?"

"Yep. I don't know whose they are," I said. "They're lost. They were just here, so I thought I'd call my mother—"

"You didn't call the cops?"

"No." I sighed. It was hard to explain that it was a delicate situation, with Starlight Warrior connections. I didn't talk about my past as a rule.

"Well, thanks to you, I had to take over the case. The Wilsons were so mortified, they're asking for their money back."

Dread sank into me. Despite being just a "simple" fraud case, the Wilson deposit was a hefty one. It would be a big loss to the company. (That was part of the reason I'd been assigned to take care of it.)

"Come on," I said, trying to shrug off my shame. "It's a just a fraud case. You couldn't present it on your own?"

"Daddy says I struggle with performance anxiety." She lowered her gaze to the ground, before skirting around me.

"Would you stop calling him that?" I rolled my eyes. I had a feeling she didn't struggle with just performance anxiety;

there was probably a whole slew of problems I didn't want to even contemplate.

"Well, he is my father," she said, "and he's your boss. I called in and told them what happened. He's not happy, and neither is Pharris. She wants you to come and see her. Today. ASAP."

"Great," I muttered. I tugged Charlotte's arm, towing her toward the door. "Go ahead and tell her I'll be in before the end of the day. You can tell Sue down in HR that I'm taking a sick day, too."

"You don't have any more days left," Charlotte said.

"What? Why? I haven't taken off since June."

"Sue's been docking your pay every time Pharris doesn't think you're working hard enough. She says that you piddle around a lot."

I groaned. "Well, I guess I'll have to see about filing a lawsuit of my own while I'm down there. Good-bye, Charlotte."

I slammed the door in her face before she could object. Not that I thought she would anyway. For a lawyer, she didn't seem to be very forthright about exercising her options.

"Well," Lyra said. "That didn't go well."

I rolled my eyes before turning around to see that the almost-teenager was just behind me. "You don't need to eavesdrop on my conversations," I said.

"You hurt her feelings."

THE STARLIGHT CHRONICLES

"I've had a rough day."

"Is she your girlfriend?"

"Aren't you being nosy?"

Lyra pursed her lips together, making herself look more like an adult. "No," she said. "I'm just trying to point out that you should be more kind to people."

"I can tell you're an idealist when you talk like that. You talk of how things should be, not as they are." I sighed. "I have to go into work. She's not my girlfriend, okay? I mean, we dated a few times, but that's not … " I was surprised to see Lyra's eyebrows arch. *She's only … what, twelve, right? Why is she making me so … flustered?*

"When will you be back?" she asked.

"I don't know. But not too long." I sighed. "Look, just stay here and watch over your brother. Turn on the TV. Help yourselves to whatever you want in the fridge … "

I mentally decided it wouldn't hurt to lock the liquor cabinet before I left. Even if Lucas was smart enough to stay away, I didn't want temptation to be a problem while I was out and minors had free rein of my apartment.

Grabbing a pen and a paper, I jotted down my cell phone number. "Here," I said, holding it out to Lyra. "Take this. Call me if you need me."

"Okay."

Now she looked so young when I saw her. I almost wanted to shake myself. *It's not like they're your kids, and it's not like it's your fault they're in this situation. Get a grip.*

But still, I gave her a quick pat on the shoulder on my way to the door. "Everything will be alright," I told her, my voice nearly cracking at the familiar adage.

She brightened instantly. "Okay."

I left before I could feel even more hapless.

I was surprised to find that Charlotte was gone; for some reason, I wouldn't have been surprised if she'd waited for me out in my apartment parking deck, just to make sure I was actually coming, and also to give me some more mopey stares.

It was less than an hour later that I arrived back at the office.

"Alex! Get in here," came the call, and I drew in a deep, steady breath.

Mary Kaye Pharris didn't get to be the partner at a prestigious law firm specializing in international and corporate finances by any amount of sheer luck. From her several diplomas and certificates, I knew she was a hard worker, and I could respect that.

It was more her attitude that I hated when it came to dealing with her. Her hair was a bob, short and prim, and she wore a lot of Chanel suits. She was starting to get up there in years, but if people could get fingertip implants, I would say that she had. Her fingernails were always meticulously polished in bold colors. I had the feeling, and some of my coworkers did, too, that she'd secretly been trying to get Mr. Dahlonega to marry her since his wife left him just over a decade before.

She took off her glasses and looked at me. "So, there he is, the great Hamilton Alexander Dinger."

"You're my boss," I said, "not my mother. There's no reason to middle-name me."

Her smile was bitter. "I'm glad to see that Charlotte got my message and gave it to you."

"Did she give you the message I had for you?" I asked.

"Why, no. No, she did not."

There was something absolutely sinister about her smile. It was perfectly straight and perfectly white, but it just seemed like she was gritting her teeth throughout her time dealing with me.

Pharris was the living reminder to me that it was sometimes easier to deal with demons than it was to deal with people. She was the person who taught me Elysian had been right; humans do have more power, because they have choices. Pharris seemed to use all of her choices to make my life miserable.

Perhaps *more* miserable.

"Well then, let's start with you and then we'll move onto me. What can I do for you?" I asked. "I have a bit of a … family emergency today, so I will be leaving soon."

"Oh, you'll be leaving?" Pharris practically cackled with glee. "I was about to suggest it myself."

I had a feeling I knew why she was excited all of a sudden. She wanted to fire me, and I'd finally given her proper cause.

Ever since I'd earned "Daddy" Jeremiah Dahlonega's approval on my own, aside from Charlotte's influence, it seemed a lot of my coworkers had been waiting for Pharris to make her move. I found out about four months after being hired that she managed to scare off a lot of the better workers. They quit in droves since she was taken on as partner.

Mr. Dahlonega was a big dreamer, a big idealist, and had a relatively "bubble-esque" approach when it came to seeing the world. He wasn't able to see Pharris was a talent-killer, and he wasn't able to see the dirtier sides of people. It was part of what made him a great defense attorney. It was also part of the reason several white-collar crime lords were walking free in the city streets.

Pharris knew this and took direct advantage of it. But I was tired of playing her games, and I suspected a lot of my coworkers were, too.

This was the wrong day to pretend to be better than I was.

"I hardly think missing one court hearing is enough justification for getting me fired," I told her bluntly. "Especially after all the other cases I've saved for you."

"When you work here, it's not about performance," Pharris countered easily. "You signed the employment agreement. This is an at-will employment. We can let you go for any reason, and missing a court hearing happens to be a valid reason."

"You've been having Sue mess with my HR records," I said. "Charlotte told me, and I have a witness to the conversation."

She momentarily faltered, but evil never dies or shuts up when it's supposed to. "I docked your hours because of your rather lackadaisical work ethic. Time theft is a real issue in the workplace environment."

"So is a high turnover rate of employment, and bosses with questionable work ethic requirements."

I could defend my work records; my cases would speak for themselves. I knew I had a higher success rate than most of my coworkers, and I was at the top of my game for the city lawyers.

She put her hands down on the table between us, her fingernails sharp and all of them, seemingly, unconsciously pointed at my heart. "Be that as it may," she said, "I'm more focused on your habits at work."

"Then you'll need to address them with me, specifically," I said. "Docking hours because you don't think I work hard enough is against the law—something you should know. I could easily sue you for it."

"And I could sue you for harassment," she shot back.

There it was—the crack in her voice. She was fighting a losing battle, and she knew it.

"So which is it, then?" I asked. "Are you going to sue me or fire me?"

"Both!" she exclaimed.

"You can't." I smiled. "Mr. Dahlonega has the final say on whether or not to fire me."

"He's right, Mary Kaye."

We turned around to see Daddy himself as he waltzed in. "I was just looking for Alex," he said, nodding to me. "Y'all want to come into my office, or are y'all comfortable where we're at?"

"I'm comfy," I said. In situations like this, it's always best to set the terms of everything you can, including the environment. Besides, there would have been nothing more pleasing to me than to see Lady Boss get demolished and overruled in her own office.

"Good, good then. Well," he said, "Alex, you let me down today."

"I know, sir, but as I was trying to explain to Ms. Pharris here, I had a bit of a family emergency."

He sighed. "Family's family."

I shot a quick, nonchalant look of victory toward Pharris.

"Which is why, Alex, you should be more than understanding about what I'm going to say next."

Huh? What?!

I turned to him, fighting to keep a stupefied expression off my face. "Yes, sir?"

"I'm going to put you on administrative leave for a month," he said.

"What? Why?"

"I talked with my girl today, and you've hurt her real bad," Mr. Dahlonega said.

"If she's crying because I don't want to date her—"

"She's always been hung up on you, son."

"I don't want to date my coworkers," I muttered. "Charlotte has always known that."

"Well, she was in tears earlier, and it's a father's job to act."

"Act on what? You can't fire me because I won't date your daughter."

"Exactly. I'm putting you on leave for missing the Wilson hearing. " He twirled one end of the salt and pepper mustache on his face. "She's my only daughter, son. I suspect you'll understand when you're married with a girl of your own."

I gaped at him, shocked. It was hard to think of anyone I knew who put their family before business. It was practically wired into my DNA.

"Sir," I said, trying to think of a compelling argument to combat this, "let me—"

Pharris jumped on my hesitation. "Well, Alex, that's just horrible! How could you have ever mistreated our sweet Charlotte around the office here?"

"I *didn't*. She was the one who was too easily offended by my rejection of her," I snapped back at Pharris.

It was ultra-irritating to see the smirk on her face.

"I know, son." Mr. Dahlonega looked at Pharris. "Mary Kaye, would you please pardon us for a moment? We've got to have a talk, man to man, if you catch my drift."

"Sure, Jeremiah," she crooned, practically dancing out of her desk chair.

I had to wonder if she thought he was going to punch me or something. I wondered if that was what I thought, too.

But the instant the door closed, Mr. Dahlonega smiled. "There, that's better."

"If you're not going to punch me," I said, "she'll probably hate you later on for that 'man-to-man' comment."

He waved his hand in the air. "You know I'm never worried about all that stuff," he said. "The good Lord will protect me from Satan's wrath on the Day of Judgment, and if that's true, then I have no reason to fear Mary Kaye's raging in the meantime."

Hearing him more or less say Pharris was a step up from the devil almost made me laugh.

"I do not want to worry about my girl," he added, quickly wiping away any chance I had at levity. "Charlotte's my baby

THE STARLIGHT CHRONICLES

girl, and I know she's up here because she's got aspirations of being a good lawyer."

"She seems like she's improved since last year," I said, trying to be as fair and helpful as I could.

"There's no need to be brown-nosing, son," he said. "I know what kind of books my daughter reads and what kind of movies she spends my money on. She wants to be married and have kids and go on long vacations."

I definitely agreed with him there.

"I've been hoping the world would help her see the truth— that this is a nasty business, and one that's not suited for a lady of her temperament."

That was definitely surprising.

"The truth is, if you're not interested in marrying her," he said, "you're just going to become a scapegoat here."

"Sir?"

"That's why I'm going to give you a month's leave," he said. "Paid, of course, though there's no overtime. I'll also reimburse you for whatever Mary Kaye did to your past wages, though I'm putting the overtime cap at sixty hours per week."

Eighty would've been more fair, but I didn't argue with him as he told me about how he already had Charlotte getting his cases reassigned to some of the other staff lawyers.

At the end of my questions and his information, he smiled kindly at me through his big mustache. "Now, go on and take care of your family," he said. "I'll take care of mine."

"What happens after the month's up?" I asked.

"Hopefully, my baby girl will find a way to either get what she wants from somewhere else, or she'll find out for sure if she's got what it takes to be a good lawyer. Either way, with you removed from the picture, she will come to the decision on her own. We can talk options when you get back."

I stood up, walked over, and shook his hand. "I think you're a good father," I told him.

Mr. Dahlonega nodded. "I sure hope I am. This is painful, Alex, my boy. I love you like a son, and truth be told, even Mary Kaye knows we'll take a hit the instant you decide to leave us."

"Thank you."

"Expect your check in the bank by the end of the week." He tipped his head to me and then headed out.

I stood there, in Pharris' office, and felt the coming conundrum. I was overjoyed I wasn't getting fired, despite Pharris' efforts to destroy me. But I was also perplexed, because I was pretty sure I'd just witnessed a miracle.

THE STARLIGHT CHRONICLES

☼<u>5</u>☼
Old Enemies

Well, I guess I'll have to go to Mikey's wedding now for sure.

As I parked my car and headed up to my apartment, I thought about calling him up and letting him know, but I decided to hold off on it for a little while. If I could get him to feel bad about the sacrifice I made for him, I would milk it.

Hey, he'd been trying to guilt me, bribe me, and coerce me into going back to Apollo City since I left. Mikey could use a little bit of justice himself, and even then, I was still going to be the more merciful one between us.

All thoughts of Mikey were hurled aside as I took out my keys. I had all the time and resources I needed to take care of the kids now, and I was happy about that.

"Lyra?" I called as I opened the door. "Lucas? I'm back."

There was no answer.

That's not *good.*

"Hello?" I walked past my kitchen, wondering if they'd managed to break something or if they'd found a way to transport themselves out of there.

For a small moment, I felt a rush of disappointment. That in itself was shocking. Apparently, I'd genuinely wanted to help them.

I pushed through the shock and felt a rush of determination. *Surely they're just playing in my spare room?*

65

I turned into the living room and stopped.

Dante Salyards was sitting on my couch, a small cup of coffee in his hands.

Across from him, Lyra and Lucas sat on the loveseat, both of them silent. I could almost see the ripples of fear and uncertainty coming off their faces.

"Hello again, Hamilton," Dante said, as though we were regular friends and he'd just seen me last week at a football game or something. "Or should I go along with your coworkers and call you Alex now? I know you hate Lexy, so I won't even ask about that one."

He set his cup down on the coffee table.

I cracked my knuckles, both in warning and preparation. "Dante," I grumbled.

"Yes, it's good to see you, too," he said. "I have a proposition I'd like to discuss. I'm sure your young charges will want to hear it, too. Please, come and join us."

I fought the urge to go over and punch him. *Later*, I told myself. *He would see it coming too easily this way.*

Instead, I walked over to where the kids were sitting and sat down next to them. They shuffled toward me, almost hiding behind me on either side of my body.

I hoped they couldn't feel my own hesitation. Mikey's dad was the last person on the face of the earth I ever wanted to see again, and even that was being generous.

Thankfully, I managed to outwait Dante. It didn't take as long as I thought it would.

"So," he said, "you never did answer me. Hamilton, or Alex?"

"Hamilton is fine," I said. I glanced over at Lyra; she seemed confused at the change. I made myself promise to tell her about the name situation later. "That's what you know me as."

"I know you by another name as well," he reminded me.

"That name died with Starry Knight," I replied quietly, getting angry. "You saw to that."

"Fair enough." He crossed his legs and lounged back in the cushions. "So, Hamilton, how would you like to do me a favor?"

"No."

"You haven't even heard the terms."

"There is literally nothing you could do to me that would make me work for SWORD."

"I'm surprised you didn't realize it," Dante said, "given your expertise in semantics and the law. I didn't ask you to do a favor for SWORD. I'm asking you to do a favor for *me*."

"If you're worried about Mikey," I said, "he's a grown up now. I'm not going to help you get on his good side."

I suddenly recalled what Mikey had told me the other night. "Stuff" had been happening in Apollo City.

"I'm not here to discuss my son, nor am I going to comment on his impending wedding," Dante said.

"I would hope you'd have the good sense to stay away from him."

"I do," Dante assured me. "Mikey's moving on, and so have I."

"Good."

"I know I have very little room in his life."

Correction: You have no *room in his life, period. I'll see to that.*

"Come on," Dante said, "I know we were never on the friendliest of terms, but surely you wouldn't say we were adversaries?"

"I recognized it too late, just how terrible SWORD was," I said. I thought about the time Dante appealed to Mikey by getting a Sinister to take Gwen's Soulfire from her, and about the time he captured me, and the time he captured me and Starry Knight. Most of all, I thought about how they failed to save Raiya, at the end of our last battle. My hands tingled again, remembering her. "I'm not making that mistake again."

"Then I'll say it again: I need a favor from you." Dante took another sip from the coffee. He raised his eyebrows. "I'm surprised you don't order Rachel's blends. She sells them over the Internet now, you know."

I hadn't thought about doing that. Not seriously, anyway.

"But then," Dante drawled on, "I suppose you wanted the chance to completely sever your ties from your teen years, didn't you? Understandable, if somewhat regrettable."

My fists clenched at his words. I felt my fingernails digging into my palms as I tried to tell myself to wait for the best moment to punch him, rather than the moment I wanted to. Which was the one right now.

"Here's my favor: I need you to break into one of our bigger black sites," he said. "There's been some issues with SWORD in Apollo City lately. I'm afraid since the death of Ogden Skarmastad and his 'heirs,' there's been a brewing power struggle to control the company. Something has happened that's broken the system."

"What is it?"

As soon as the words were out of my mouth, I nearly cursed again. I mentally consigned my curiosity to hell.

Dante smiled. "You know as well as I do that there are some fallen Stars who worked for SWORD," he said. "The meteorite falling—what? Ten years ago? Nine?—caused a bit of a kerfuffle among ranks. Our leader, exasperated, had all of them eliminated as a result."

My eyes widened in surprise. Even for a morally ambiguous organization, that seemed a bit extreme. But then, I knew what others would do anything for power.

"You can see the trouble. Now, we have an issue. The meteorite's origins have been traced to its original Star's position."

Raiya's star.

"There's a black hole there, according to our charts," Dante continued. "And that would be fine—if SWORD's leader didn't want to gain control of it."

"You can't control a black hole," I scoffed.

"Well, we weren't supposed to be able to open a portal into the void inside the earth and get a full glimpse of hell, either," Dante replied.

I said nothing to that. He was right, unfortunately.

"What makes you think I can help you?" I asked him. Lyra and Lucas both glanced at me, and I wondered if they were beginning to think I was being mistaken for some kind of Starlight Mafia boss.

"You're a Star," he said simply. "And you're familiar with the meteorite case."

"Psh. That's nothing," I grunted. I shook my head. "I haven't used my powers in years," I told him. "I no longer carry the Emblem of the Prince." I held up my blank wrist as proof.

Years before, there had been a four-point star on my wrist, colored the same as blood, and when I pressed it I was able to transform into my superhero self.

Now, I wanted nothing to do with it; I didn't even want the memories tied to it.

"That's nothing," Lucas said. "Here, give me your hand."

He took it before I gave it, and pressed into my wrist with his small fingers. A flare of light spindled out, and I felt the titanic clash of power as the mark, briefly, faded in, before it vanished once more.

Lucas frowned. "I guess it really has been years," he said. "You don't seem to be connected to it."

"It went away," I snapped at him. "It went away, and I didn't go crawling after it."

"More like you turned your back on it," he retorted.

This kid has an attitude problem. Maybe it would be better for me to hand them over to Dante while he's here.

"It doesn't matter," I insisted. "I don't want to help SWORD *or* Dante."

"I told you," Dante said, "someone has figured out how the black hole can compromise Time's power. Don't you know what this means?"

"The end of the world?" I guessed.

"Exactly!"

I rolled my eyes. "It's always stuff like that," I said, "and it never happens."

"That's because it's stopped by the people who can stop it." Dante frowned at me. "When things don't work the way they should, bad things happen."

Hearing Elysian's words—and one of his favorite phrases he used to guilt me into doing stuff all the time—was the last straw; I could almost feel my temper igniting.

"I know you've made yourself welcome here," I snapped angrily, "but I need you to leave now. You're not actually welcome."

"Well." Dante huffed. "That's a shame. I would've thought you wanted to go and see Starry Knight."

There was no use waiting for it anymore.

I jumped to my feet, catapulted myself over the coffee table, and punched him right in the jaw.

All those kickboxing classes finally came in handy.

As he reeled from the first blow, I pulled him back and hit him again and again. It was only when I saw his nose bleeding that I stopped and allowed myself to catch my breath.

"What do you mean, go and see her?" I roared. "She's dead!"

Why did I have to keep telling people that? Why did I have to keep hearing myself say it?

"Stop being an idiot. SWORD has her body," Dante told me as he pulled out a handkerchief and held it to his nose. "They want to break open Time so they can get to the River of Life and gain immortality. With her body, they have control of her residual power."

I found myself breathing deeply. "They didn't bury her?"

"No." He shook his head. "Even if she is gone, there are trace elements of her power in her body."

Remembering we had an audience, I called back to Lyra and Lucas. "Kids, go to my bedroom and turn on the TV in there for a bit. You don't need to hear any of this."

I was shocked when they actually followed my orders.

When I could hear the television on in the other room, I turned my full attention to Dante. "What kind of sick organization do you work for?"

"I can assure you they aren't selling her organs."

"Well, that just makes me feel *so much* better," I snapped.

"There's a big black market for that," he reminded me. "It should make you feel better. It means they've kept her safe."

Safe in the enemy's fortress. I grimaced. I didn't want to think of that.

I also didn't want to think of Raiya again. I didn't want to see her. I tried to divorce the idea that it mattered what happened to her body, now that she was gone.

But I couldn't. I never truly had peace with her death, and now I had to fight for her body and my soul at the same time. It would be painful. It would be hard. But it was the right thing to do.

If nothing else, leaving her body in SWORD's control, especially if what Dante was telling me was true, was clearly the wrong thing to do.

"Fine," I finally said, already feeling like this was going to be the worst Christmas vacation ever. "I'll help you. But I want something in return. I want you to help me find their parents," I said, jerking my thumb in the directions of the two kids, "and get them back home, safely. And then I want you and SWORD to leave me and my family alone, forever."

"Deal," Dante said. "But you have to complete my mission first. We don't have a lot of time, and the situation could easily get out of hand, fast. Even some of the citizens seem to be getting more nervous by the day."

I thought about what Mikey had told me. Were there more demons attacking the city, hoping for an easy victory? Or were they just settling down quietly, hanging out like leeches on an unsuspecting host?

Either way, I didn't want Lyra and Lucas around to face it. "It would be easier to do my job if the kids went home first," I said.

"It would be easier to do my job and get them home if you saved the world first."

I glared at him, before glancing back toward my room. I could see Lyra and Lucas as they ducked back from the cracked doorway.

Considering Lyra and Lucas were Starlight defenders, maybe it was for the best that they were here.

I don't know much about what is happening in Apollo City, but it would be nice to have allies again, I thought, almost wistfully. I would just have to be careful and make sure they knew not to tell their parents what they did when they made it back home.

Especially since it seemed like any number of evil people and their plots to destroy the world were involved.

"When can you leave for Apollo City?"

"Give me some time to get them ready and pack," I said. "And then tomorrow, I'll head home."

"Then I'll expect you to be ready tomorrow."

THE STARLIGHT CHRONICLES

☼6☼
Old Places

"Are we there yet?"

I gritted my teeth as I pulled off the highway exit, heading toward Lake County.

"We're almost there," I barked back at Lucas, who had asked if we were there yet about forty million times already.

"You said we were almost there ten minutes ago," Lyra pointed out.

"And we're still technically almost there," I argued. "We're actually even closer than 'almost' there."

"But—"

"I don't want to talk about this anymore," I yelled. "Find a new topic, please."

They were both quiet for a long moment. I preemptively rejoiced, hoping against all hope they would both just shut up and leave me alone.

"Alex?"

Alas, silence was not to be had.

"What?" I gripped onto the steering wheel more tightly, preparing myself to be annoyed.

"Is your name really actually 'Hamilton?'" Lyra asked.

"Yes," I said. "It was my mother's idea, not mine, let me assure you."

"That's Lucas' middle name."

"Is it?" I frowned. I didn't know of any other fallen Stars who were living on the earth. Not any that introduced themselves to me with that label, anyway.

"It is," Lucas agreed.

"So you really are Wingdinger then, aren't you?" Lyra asked.

"I *was*," I told her. "I wasn't lying when I said he died. SWORD put that in the newspapers."

"Do you know all about Starry Knight then?"

I nearly swerved off the road at her question. "I don't want to talk about her," I said as evenly as I could.

"Why not?"

"Because. It's too painful," I told her honestly. It was even more painful now, on some levels, because I was going to have to sneak into a SWORD black site, recover her likely-decaying body, and bury it properly myself. And I had to do this, of course, while trying to stop myself from jumping into the grave after her. It was going to be trying, harrowing, and likely expensive.

There goes that Christmas bonus of mine. If the Wilsons didn't take it first.

"I wish Aeolian was here," Lucas said. In the rearview mirror, I could see he was doodling in the condensation on my car windows.

"Who's Aeolian?" I asked.

"He's my pet." Lucas sighed. "He's funny. He'd be all up for an adventure. He gets bored easily."

I remembered him saying things about his pet earlier. "You said he was a lizard, right?"

"Most of the time."

"Most of the time?" I frowned. "That's weird. What do you mean—" I stopped.

These kids were Stars. Surely they didn't have …

"He's a changeling dragon," Lyra explained. "But he's too small. He's not very old yet. We just tell our friends he's a rare lizard because reptiles are the easiest forms for him to take."

"He's still cool though," Lucas said. "He can move his tongue like this." He stuck out his tongue and pointed it upward, almost like he was trying to lick his eyes.

Which, I remembered clearly from when Elysian would do just that to annoy me, was probably what he was doing.

I was feeling increasingly uncomfortable with the conversation.

"Well, okay then," I said. "New subject. Who wants to stop for dinner? I highly recommend we do, since I wasn't able to get a hold of my mom, and she's probably got a weird chef or two running around the house."

As the two of them began to battle it out over dinner options ("Pizza!" and "No, spaghetti!"), I wondered to myself all over again.

What am I doing?

I'd spent the greater portion of the last decade of my life fighting to get away from my past. I'd moved, made new friends, graduated college, graduated law school, and did a lot of other stuff, too.

Yeah, I didn't have any real "peace," but you lose your girlfriend and the love of your life the way I did, and you probably wouldn't have peace either.

The only semi-logical coherent thought I had about it was that this was a way to move on. Running from the past didn't make it easier to lose. Maybe if I confronted it, maybe if I saw her body, and maybe if I stopped SWORD from devolving further into a power-hungry organization bent on controlling power around the world, I would feel better about living through her loss.

That made more sense.

This is only a way to appease my survivor's guilt, I told myself.

Seemingly hours later, with a bag full of Italian goodies, we arrived at my parents' house.

It was strange, seeing the old place. In the winter sunshine, I could tell the house itself was more worn than it used to be. Cheryl and Mark, for all their meticulous—well, Cheryl's anyway—caring, could not stop the passage of time when it came to aging houses. Even the gardens seemed to be more untamed than I remembered.

"This is where you live?" Lucas asked. "It's huge!"

"This is where I *lived*," I corrected. "It's my parents' house."

"Cool!"

Even Lyra, the pickier of the two, seemed happy. "This seems nicer than your apartment," she said.

"You didn't like my apartment?" I arched an eyebrow at her.

"It was okay. This is bigger. I like bigger."

Damning with faint praise, this one, I thought, even as I smiled. "Come on, let's get inside." I glanced out the window at the sky; it was filled with gloomy-looking clouds, serving as a welcoming committee of sorts. "It looks like rain's coming soon."

Since it was near dark, the lights were on, and I felt a rush of feeling at home as I recalled walking into the house late at night, likely past curfew, hundreds of times.

I was surprised to see my key still worked. Some days I didn't know why I had even kept it, but I supposed it was for days just like this one.

Lyra and Lucas shuffled in after me as I walked into the house of my childhood, already dropping my backpack and briefcase by the door.

"Those need to go up to your room, Hamilton," Cheryl called from her office.

"This is the first time I've been home in years, and you're already yelling at me?" I called back.

She came out to see us, a smile on her nearly unchanged face. In all the years I'd been gone, my mother had remained largely the same. Her suit, still on from her hours at her law firm, was impeccable, and her hair was still tightly secured, not a hair out of place. But just like the house, there was little to be done about things that insisted on aging.

There were small lines by her cheeks, and the bags under her eyes seemed larger than the ones she had the last time I saw her. Her hair, while it was perfect in style, had a few strands of gray sticking out against the brown and blond highlights.

She leaned forward and gave me a kiss on the cheek. "I was happy to get your call," she said. "And I'd be happy to help with your project. I even took off half a day from work tomorrow."

A rarity, indeed—or perhaps another change.

"Well, that's good," I said. "I have some things to do, so I'll need your help with the other stuff."

"Hamilton," she snapped. "Don't talk about children like that. No need to call them 'stuff.'"

"We're not children," Lucas insisted. "We're almost adults."

"If you're not an adult, you're a child," I told him. "Whether you like it or not."

"Am not," Lucas said, sticking his tongue out at me.

"I'm almost a teenager," Lyra insisted, joining in on the arguing.

Cheryl, in her typical mom way, waved the matter aside. "Well, if you're all adults, you'll be able to eat the dinner I had Louis prepare."

"Louis?" I asked.

"He's my new chef," Cheryl said. "He's an expert in French food."

"You're eating French food?"

"Exclusively. French women don't get fat, you know," she said, already turning toward the house. "Now, let me notify him we're about ready, and then I'll take these two and make sure the guest bedrooms are ready. Hamilton, I assume you can handle setting up your own room?"

"My room's still here, right?" I was suddenly feeling worried.

"Yes, but your brother has been looting through your stuff more often than I think you'd like."

"I don't know why he would be bothered by it," Adam said from the top of the stairs. "He's rich now. He can buy more stuff anytime he wants, and he can go eat out anytime he wants."

I turned to see my little brother as he came sauntering down the stairs.

I barely recognized him as the little boy who'd go running up to Raiya, calling her his "angel" when he was younger. His black hair was a lot like mine had been at his age, sticking up in different places, trying to be "cool." His brown eyes were a replica of Mark's, and he seemed to have the same sense of ennui I'd managed to present to the world when I was a teen.

Of course, the French food probably helped with that, I thought with a grin. "Hey, Adam."

"Hey, Hammy," he said, his voice clearly teasing in a welcoming way as he waved at me. "Thanks for the check last month. I think I forgot to tell you. I used it to buy some new sports gear. Coach Shinal said he's going to be running me for the junior varsity next year."

"Good choice," I said, leaning over and giving him a hug.

Despite the "cool dude" attitude, I felt the familiar rush of pleasure and contentment I'd always associated with him as he hugged me back.

Cheryl beamed. "Adam, these are our guests," she said, gesturing toward Lyra and Lucas. "I trust you'll help me make them feel welcome here this week?"

"Sure, Mom," he said. He sent me an eye roll when she wasn't looking.

"I'm Lyra, and this is my brother, Lucas."

"Cool," Adam said. He frowned. "You seem familiar to me."

"Are you a Star, too?" Lyra asked.

"Of course he is," Cheryl interrupted. "He's already skipped a grade and he's going to be on junior varsity football team. And that'll help him get a scholarship to Pitt, just like Hamilton."

Adam and I grimaced at the same time, most likely for different reasons.

"How are things here, beside that?" I asked Adam as Cheryl hurried Lucas and Lyra up the stairs.

"Good," he said. "I'm heading out to go hang at a friend's house. Be a pal and tell Cheryl for me, will you?"

I grinned. "You know you're not supposed to call her that."

He rolled his eyes. "You did the same thing when you were my age, Dinger."

"I prefer Alex now, actually," I said.

He shook his head slowly. "You keep doing that," he said. "It's never worked, you know. You're still Hamilton to the rest of us here."

"Of course I am," I said. "But if you're going to call mom Cheryl, then at least change my name, too."

"I still prefer Wingdinger, believe it or not," he said.

I groaned, this time angry. "Don't call me that."

"Why not? I always liked it. And your dragon did, too. He's the one who called into the news station for that contest, you know."

"What?"

My memory of my teen years was intentionally foggy, but it always amazed me how anger could easily clarify a lot of it.

Adam laughed. "I was home with my old lady nanny, and she was sleeping as she was watching me and the news. I saw him come down, dial the phone, and ask for the same news channel we were watching. He then told them that he wanted to enter your name into the 'Name our City Super' contest. It was only years later that I managed to put it together."

"*That's* how I got stuck with 'Wingdinger?'" I clenched my fists. "It's a terrible shame Elysian's dead, or I'd kill him all over again."

"He's not dead," Adam said. "Or at least, not anymore."

I frowned. "What do you mean?"

"I mean, I dream about him sometimes," Adam said. "And Angel, too."

"You mean Raiya?" My heart stopped.

"Oh, yeah. I guess that's her real name." At the look on my face, he began to shuffle away from me. "Anyway, I gotta go, man. Nice seeing you. Remember to tell *Mom* I'll be back soon, okay?"

Before I could ask him anything further, he sped away.

The little schmuck.

I realized a moment later why he had left, as Mark came into the room. "Hamilton. You're home."

"Dad."

I was shocked to see him. If my mother had managed to defy the odds against aging, my dad must've picked up her slack.

His hair was nearly all gray, and he was wearing glasses. I had to remind myself that staring was rude.

But I wasn't the only who needed to be reminded of that. He stared back at me.

"How are you?" I asked, my voice almost cracking.

He shook his head. "I have to go," he said, backing away. "I'll see you later."

I finally started to see what Mikey was saying about me moping around. Suddenly, I wanted to scream, *"It's been over seven years! You can stop acting weird now!"* at Mark.

That's what I wanted to say. I think it would have been better than what I did say, which was, "Okay, bye." Even it if was a bit harsher.

I glanced at the grandfather clock in the living room. Despite the long drive, I had to go. Dante had made arrangements for me to meet with him. I glanced down at the piece of paper he'd passed to me, with the address on it.

If I was going to uphold my end of his bargain, I had to leave.

THE STARLIGHT CHRONICLES

☼<u>7</u>☼
Deceived

I slid down the alleyway behind the entrance to Shoreside Park, undetected. As I made my way among the shadows, a small burst of pride settled inside of me; it had been years, after all, since I had to go hunting for supernatural trouble, and the fact that I had lost little, if any, of my original talent, made me very happy indeed. Even if my knees had cracked a few more times than I wanted to admit.

Upon further reflection of the reasons why I was there in the first place, I snuffed out the pride inside of me. There was nothing to be happy about in this case—nothing at all.

I was glad it was dark, and not just any dark—the cloudy overcast hugged me close, keeping a cloak of protection around me. If I had been a *normal* human being, I might have been afraid. But I'd never been normal, and I was especially nothing close to it.

Even if I had tried to be normal for most of the last several years now.

Darkness had somehow become more comfortable to me. It became a place where my true self could hide, comfortably, and no one around me was any wiser.

As I walked into the park, I could easily make out the outlines of all the familiar places of my childhood and my teen years. Even in the fog, I could see the rounded roof of Lakeview Observatory, which had been a home of the meteorite that had crashed into the city, destroying my life, and leading it down a path of further destruction.

Behind me, I could see the new extension of the park, where the old Rosemont Academy once stood.

Further over and beyond the trees, I could see the marina, and on the other side I knew Rachel's Café remained, even if it was now closed and boarded up.

For me, this place was a graveyard of sorts.

I was glad when I reached the marina, even if there were more lights around.

"There you are."

I heard Dante's voice before I saw him. He came out of the fog and shadows, and for a moment I wondered if he had been following me.

"I was beginning to think you wouldn't come," he said.

"I said I would come," I grumbled. "Besides, you have your part of the bargain to uphold, too."

"I haven't forgotten," Dante replied.

"Okay then. Just tell me the plan so I can get out of here," I said.

"We're here," he said. He nodded toward Lake Erie.

"There's a black site under the lake?" I asked. "Is that even allowed? I mean, wouldn't the government object to that because of the EPA or something?"

"It might surprise you—or not—to know that various governments besides Apollo City have hired SWORD before. This is part of our pay, unfortunately. Rather than money, we are given space and anonymity."

"I guess people will always want land," I murmured, thinking of a movie I'd seen a long time ago.

"Exactly." He nodded. "You know, you're lucky SWORD didn't try to get you to join when everything happened here all those years ago."

"I wouldn't call it luck."

He nodded. "I guess I can understand. Sometimes I think about how my life would be different if I hadn't been hired."

"Mikey's life would've been better."

"No one can say that for sure," Dante said with a shrug.

I narrowed my gaze, allowing myself to see his emotions. It took longer than it normally did, but after a moment I saw them. The little wisps of color flared off him, saturated with regret and self-loathing.

Appropriate.

"At least you wouldn't have had to deal with me," I told him.

"You're Mikey's friend, and Mark's son. Our paths would have crossed eventually, though likely not to the same end or degree."

I sighed. "I don't really care. Let's just move on, okay? How are we going to get inside?"

"All SWORD members have a secret code that allows them access to the site," Dante explained.

"Alright then. Let's go find the entrance and get going." I grimaced. "I really, really don't want to be here."

"Then I suspect this will make it worse."

Before I could react, lightning lashed through my body. I yelled as I fell over, stunned by the pain and the betrayal. "What are you doing?" I hissed.

"Capturing you, of course." Dante's brown eyes gleamed as he brought a Taser down on me once more.

Though it had been years since I'd felt it, my body reared in agony and determination to get away.

"I've forgotten how fun it is to shock you," Dante admitted. "You were always a punk kid."

"Why are you doing this to me?" I whimpered.

"Gotta make it look convincing, you know." He grinned. "And I'll admit some of this is for punching me earlier. I'm not a man who forgives easily, Hamilton."

"I'm not either," I muttered back, before he brought the weapon down on my head. I fell limp as the world darkened once more.

I didn't know how much time had passed when I woke up, but I had a feeling it hadn't been long.

I could hear the whispering of small waves above my head. Without opening my eyes, I tried to get an idea of where I was.

The first thing I noticed was that I was moving. I was being carried on a stretcher. There were four people, two in the front and two at the back, and they were all walking forward. I didn't know who they were specifically, but I made a vow to specifically go out and find Dante when this was all over and pay him back for his treachery.

I should've known.

I should've known this was coming.

The old disappointment, the blindsiding power of betrayal, bit into me, deeply and bitterly.

How was it possible that in seven years, I'd gotten *stupider* when it came to trusting SWORD? I hadn't been that smart about it to begin with, true. I could chalk that up to teenage naivety. But this …

This was after years of working in law, too. It was even worse, because of the majority of people I knew who worked in law tended to be among the most paranoid about trust and commitment.

I can't believe I thought he would help me. Immediately, I decided that I would break out of here, destroy this place and everyone in it, and then I would find a way to get Lyra and Lucas back to their parents, no matter how long it took. Getting Dante out of the picture was key. Keeping him out, one way or another, was the goal.

Before I could imagine wringing his neck, one of my escorts spoke up. "Agent Salyards said he needed to be treated before we took him to the Matriarch."

The Matriarch? Huh?

Another one of the guards grunted in reply. "We'll take him to the medical ward on level three—"

An alarm started blaring. Sirens went off, and even though I hadn't yet opened my eyes, I could see the emergency lights flaring all around us.

"Code Security Alpha," a voice called.

The escorts started running. Before I knew it, I was dropped off, carelessly, and they began to scurry away.

I tentatively opened my one eye. The lights were still flickering, and with the headache, and the aches and pains from Dante, I was more than ready to break a few of them just to get them to stop.

"You're awake?"

A woman came up behind me; I assumed she was an agent, but I still felt a little bad when I grabbed her.

"What's going on? Tell me," I demanded.

She paused. "We're under attack," she finally said. I could barely hear her voice over the sirens.

"From who? Who even knows you're down here?" I yelled over the alarms.

"It's an inside attack," she called back. "All the sections are shutting down. Now let me go. I have to get to my post!"

I watched as she headed for an opening, one that led down a hallway. She keyed in a number on a lock and a door began to slowly close downward.

As soon as I realized what was happening, I knew I was trapped.

Dante's going to die. I'll kill him for this.

If I survive, I added silently to myself.

I swore under my breath and peeled myself off the floor. I needed to finish the job I came here to do.

"Why did I ever agree to this?" I muttered to myself, ducking around another corner as a number of guards ran past me in the opposite direction.

Fortunately, none of them seemed interested in stopping me. I took this as a good sign, and I took that as a sign I was crazy.

"You there!" a voice called out to me. "This way!"

Up ahead of me, I saw another troop of guards. From where I was, the guy didn't realize I wasn't one of them. He

95

probably thought I was just another agent. "What is it?" I called back.

"Break in the med ward. Something's going on in the freezer," he called. "We need to get down level and stop them before they dismantle the entire morgue."

Freezer? Like, where they keep the dead people's bodies? I frowned. *Was it possible someone else was here to steal Raiya's body, too?*

"Which way?" I called back to the guard.

He turned and made his way over to me. "You're not one of us!"

"No, but you will be hearing from my lawyer," I promised, giving him a swift roundhouse kick. He doubled over and I tried to get away.

He managed to grab my ankle, and I went flying fast into the floor.

I wriggled my foot free of his grasp and then kicked him hard, hoping that the blow to the face would be enough to knock him out. "Let me go," I yelled.

My wish was granted as I heard his unconscious groan.

I felt his hands fall off me, and I managed to claw myself back up to a standing position.

"Deep breath," I told myself.

I could honestly say I hadn't had a workout like this in years—you know, one where I had to really, actually fear for my life.

It took me more than a few deep breaths before I was ready to go on.

Steady once more, I headed off.

Some of the guard's companions turned to face me just as I reached them.

"Stop," one of them said as he made a grab for me.

I twisted away and then wondered if I could bluff my way out of fighting them. They outnumbered me by more than my karate and kickboxing classes at the college had prepared me for, no question.

"I'm here to help," I said, trying not to have a panic attack or giggle nervously or give myself away. "Stand down!"

"Are you an agent?" one of them asked.

"Uh, yeah," I said. "I'm new. Just signed on. What's happening?"

"This is the emergency protocol for a Code Security Alpha," one of the other guards said. She pointed down another hall, where, if I could just clear out the sirens, I could hear a whisper of small explosions. "We're here to wait, until we're called to battle or we're called to evacuate. The last group just went in moments ago."

"Where's the boss?" another guard asked.

"He, uh, got hit with something back there," I said. "Totally knocked out. Where is the med ward?"

"It's down that hall," the lady guard said. "It's been attacked."

"Where's the freezer?"

She frowned at me. "Why do you want to know?" she asked.

"So I can help."

"Everyone here helps."

"I want to help *more*," I clarified, hoping she wouldn't think she was stupid. "You know, see if I have any beginner's luck."

She looked at me quizzically and then shrugged. "The freezer's down a level," she said. "It's only accessible from the ward."

"Got it."

A grumble came out of the hallway from behind us. "Hey!"

Uh-oh. Looks like the boss guy woke up!

I managed to grab one of the guards' Taser guns and slip away, then I hurried off down the hallway. They were momentarily too confused to stop me and, fortunately for me, too well trained in following orders to follow me. They had to wait, and wait they would, it looked like.

As for me, I wasn't thinking out any specific plan. I was just trying to survive, first of all, and then, second of all, do my job.

As I got closer to the med ward, it was clear I would have to focus on the first part more than the second.

There were bodies, bodies I didn't know if they were dead or unconscious or just mangled, but they were lying all around. I didn't stop to take a look, and I didn't want to. I hurried forward and kept my eyes alert for any unexpected movement or attack.

The doors to the med ward, or what I assumed used to be the med ward, had been blown away so hard I could see indents in the walls across the hall. They were under burn marks and a layer of dusty debris.

I stepped inside the room, preparing for the worst. I was only comforted by the fact that at least the alarms were more muffled here, and I had enough space left in my mind to hear myself think.

"What happened in here?" I awed at the damage. "It looks like something exploded … "

Dante had mentioned that the leader of SWORD—who I guess was the one known as the Matriarch—had killed off her Star employees. Was it possible she'd missed one?

Out of all the room, only one bed stood still intact. I made my way over to it, still cautious.

There were papers, all scattered and burning. Two IV bags of medicine were there, torn open and leaking. I picked them up and smoothed out the plastic.

"Versed?" I read aloud from the one package. I looked at the other one. "Propofol?"

Sometimes I wished I had some of Mark's medical training.

Before I could lament my situation further, I heard another loud banging, followed by a frustrated scream, coming from below me.

Catching sight of the doorway, I sped toward it, the borrowed weapon, which I had no real clue how to use, held in front of me as a last-resort type of defense.

Another round of banging made me flinch as I approached the door.

"Morgue." The word was swinging loose, now half-hanging above the door, where it had probably been anchored securely only a few moments before. This was the freezer that my earlier escorts had mentioned.

Another scream came from the room, and I saw a flash of brilliant light bomb out.

"Well," I muttered, "that answers one question." I was, in fact, dealing with a Star.

There were more sounds now, ones I could make out despite the continuing muffled sirens—metal crashing, glass shattering ... and a woman, weeping.

The banging stopped, the crashing halted, and the smashing ceased. But the crying continued.

Maybe she's out of power. And any other weapons, I thought.

Either way, I didn't have a lot of time before the rest of the black site caught on and found us.

I eased into the room.

It was a mess. Two desks were toppled over. A myriad of morgue doors were smashed in; several had been opened, and their contents remained. I could still see shadows inside others, and instinctively I cringed.

My heart ached. How was I ever going to find Raiya's body now?

The weeping continued. And then I heard the broken whisper all the way across the room.

"I'm sorry I couldn't save you."

My heart jolted, reeling from shock. I had trouble breathing as a new sense of numbness took over me. Music, music that I hadn't heard in years, came sailing back, sweeping me away from the rest of the world.

I felt my stolen weapon slip out of my hand; I barely heard it clatter to the ground.

I watched, transfixed, as a shadow detached itself from the corner of the room when it stood up and faced me. When her eyes—the same violet eyes that had haunted my memory for the last several years—turned to rest on me, all or any doubt I had left in my mind fled from me. I felt my eyes tear up, as though I'd been slapped in the face.

At that moment, mountains crumbled, thunder broke through the heavens, and a wave of warmth tore through the walls of ice inside my heart, breaking the spell of loneliness cast on me all those long years.

That was when I knew she was real.

"Raiya."

☼<u>8</u>☼

Blindsided

I could've stared at her forever. There was a part of me that didn't want to believe this was real. There was another part of me that couldn't deny it was. And then there was yet another part of me that wanted to know how this could've happened in the first place. All the possibilities paralyzed me.

Trust, but verify.

I didn't want to. I didn't want to be wrong. It would just kill me if I was wrong.

Ultimately, it was a good thing that my curiosity still demanded a short leash. I stepped forward.

"Raiya." Her name escaped me once more, more at my soul's compulsion than either my mind or my body's.

I saw her eyes narrowed, both in frustration and rage. "Who are you?" she asked.

Her voice was slightly different. It sounded deeper than the voice I remembered, even though it still carried the same music.

"Is it really you?" I asked, tentatively taking another step forward.

"Stay back," she ordered. A small bubble of power appeared in the palm of her hand, glowing with fury.

Despite my shock, I almost smiled. It was really and truly her. She was my Raiya.

103

It was then that I noticed she was holding something. Several somethings. There were several medical packs in her hands, all no larger than a sandwich bag.

Was she looking for food? I wondered.

Taking another look at her, I couldn't have blamed her if she was. She was wearing a hospital gown, but it did little to hide how emaciated her form had become since … I didn't really want to think about the last time I'd seen her.

Her hair was long, longer than it had been when we were together last time. Her feet were bare, and there was blood running down her one calf.

It was her face that finally caught and held my gaze.

It was the same face, the same beauty that I'd known all those years ago. But it was much more stark, much more clear, and much more sad. The angles of her face were sharper, gaunt with dark memories and a lack of sunlight. She hadn't aged with the passage of time, I realized, so much as with the experience of pain.

I was still in pain, too, as I was puzzled, really, as to why she didn't seem to recognize me the way I'd recognized her.

"Tell me who you are," she commanded, this time more forcefully.

"It's me," I said quietly. "Don't you remember me?"

When she only narrowed her eyes more, I sighed. I had to get her out of here. I could worry about this another time.

"I'm not going to hurt you," I tried to assure her. "How could I?"

"Very easily," she shot back.

"No," I breathed. "No, I couldn't. Are you sure you don't recognize me?" I took another small step forward.

"No." Her answer was quick, and it cut me to the quick. Some part of me felt like crying.

I gave her a shaky smile. "It's me," I said, my voice barely a whisper. "Remember? I'm Ham Dinger."

I waited for her to respond to me, the way she had all those years ago. *Goodness knows I never thought I'd be so happy to be called "Humdinger" again.*

But she said nothing. She just glared at me, with fear and distrust in her eyes.

"We're friends," I told her, finally. *Something must've gone wrong*, I thought. Maybe they'd drugged her or something, and she wasn't able to recall anything.

Fear seized my heart all over again. What if she never remembered anything? What if she never remembered anything ever again, about who we were and who we could be?

I finally reached her. She seemed taller than I remembered, but she was still the perfect size for me; just from looking at her, I could tell her chin would still fit perfectly into the crook of my neck. I held out my hand. "Please, trust me."

"I don't trust anyone," she retorted.

If there was anyone who could convince her she was wrong, it was me. Not for nothing was I Pittsburgh's best associate lawyer.

"What about Adonaias?" I asked. "What about the Prince of Stars?"

She faltered at that.

"Don't you trust him, Raiya?" I asked.

She hesitated. "I do, but you don't," she finally said.

I frowned. "How would you know that?"

"It's not hard to see."

Good, this is good. She's talking. I had to tell myself all these lies, all these good things to refrain from screaming.

Thankfully, I was interrupted. I could hear footsteps hurrying down the stairs behind us, and they were rampant with relentless anger.

I knew I had to hurry. "Come on. I'm here to get you out of here." My throat clogged up as I added, "You told me that you would be waiting for me. Here I am."

Raiya's eyes seemed to dull, clouded by confusion. "Why didn't you come sooner?" She clutched the bags she held against her as a fresh batch of tears escaped her.

Before I could do anything else, a new round of guards appeared at the door.

It was time to go. If we could; it seemed I'd only blinked, and we were suddenly surrounded.

I stepped in front of Raiya, shielding her from their view. "Stay close to me," I instructed her.

"Do you even know what you're doing?" she asked.

Her tone reminded me of how she used to chastise me after the early battles with the Sinisters and their minions. Before I could argue with her, a guard stepped forward. "That's him!" The leader of the guard I'd managed to knock out was leading the pack. "Get him!"

"No!" Raiya cried out behind me. I felt her power hit me, hard. I fell over, hitting my face on the floor, and I felt the power of her partial supernova crush into me.

This is too familiar, I thought as I inched my way toward her. *Even without remembering me, she still thinks it's her duty to protect me.*

As her power pummeled into me, and all around me, I scraped myself off the floor.

I had to push back a smile. I hated myself for it, but I was thrilled to be back again, back in the middle of her power, where time had no say in how we felt or what we did.

I tried to grab a hold of her shoulders, moving closer to her as her power grew around us. As I reached out, my hands took hold of her arms, and I felt her grasp on the different bags in her hands weaken.

I wondered if I would get a chance to kiss her again, just like the last time we were stuck in one of her supernova power bubbles.

Before I could pull her close to me, she froze. "No," she said, the terror as clear in her voice the first time we wound up together. Instantly, her power ceased.

Thankfully, it had been enough to render the guards useless and blow a nice-sized hole into the ceiling. I could even make out the sky from where we stood, thanks to the gaping hole her power had left behind.

"Good job," I said.

"Get back." She stepped away from me. "These are mine," she said, indicating the bags. "You can't have them."

"It's okay," I said, holding my hands up in defeat. "But I need to get you out of here. Will you come with me?"

She scowled, and I wondered if she had always been this much of a skeptic.

Finally, she softened. Just a little. "Alright."

She agreed, just in time. Above us, several floors of broken beams snapped free, sending a wave of building scraps fluttering down all around us. I glanced up and saw the sides of the different floors waver dangerously.

We don't have much time. This place is going to cave in on itself.

Raiya looked at me. "It's going to collapse," she said, her eyes wide with shock.

THE STARLIGHT CHRONICLES

"Yep." I said nothing else as I led her through the site, trying to retrace my steps as we moved through the building. We managed to outrun several other evacuation teams, and hide when we couldn't outrun them.

It wasn't long before Raiya slumped against a wall, breathing hard. I could see she was shaking, and I didn't blame her. Water from the lake was leaking through the various nooks of the building, and we were beginning to get wet.

I didn't think it would help much, but I took off my jacket and placed it around her shoulders. "Here," I said. "This might help."

She gave me a small smile, and I just about melted. "Thank you ... what did you say your name was again?"

"Oh, uh, Hamilton." It took me longer than I wanted it to for me to give her my name. I turned away from her, pretending to wipe the sweat and water off my face to hide my disappointment. "Are you almost ready to go again? We don't have much time."

"I haven't moved like this in a long time," she said, almost as if she was answering the question I'd been meaning to ask.

"Do you remember who you are?" I asked. "How you got here?"

"Yes and no," Raiya said. "I remember who I am, what I am. But I don't remember much about coming here."

"Do you know how long you've been here?"

She shook her head.

"Do you know anything about a black hole?" I asked, deciding there was no point in getting myself disappointed anymore. It would have to be business, from here on out, until I had her safely outside this prison.

She shook her head slowly. "No," she said. "At least, nothing for sure."

"What do you remember?" I asked quietly, hopefully. "Can you tell me?"

Raiya's eyes filled with tears. "Pain," she said. "And so much more than pain."

She slumped over, sitting with her bags tucked on her lap, her head resting in her hands. I came and sat beside her, wrapping my arm around her.

"Everything will be alright," I said, choking on the words all over again. *I* didn't actually know that, and it was beginning to get on my nerves that I thought it at all still. Especially given the circumstances.

Oh, yeah, sure, I had Raiya back. But not all of her; I had a shell of her former self, one who was weak and distrusting and in need of a security blanket comprised of plastic bags she'd stolen from the morgue.

She glanced over at me. "Are you sure *you* know that?" she asked.

I flustered instantly, almost guiltily. Memory or no memory, Raiya was still good at calling me out.

So I did what I did best. I changed the subject.

"Time to go," I said. "We've rested long enough. The guards will still be looking for us."

"I know." I was surprised as one of her hands came up and caressed my cheek.

The shock of feeling her skin on mine again ached through me. That, coupled with her gentle smile and sad eyes, made my heart lurch inside of me uncomfortably.

"Thank you for saving me," she said.

"I didn't save you," I replied somberly. "I'm just getting you out of here." I took her hand and tried to pull her up. "Come on. Let's see about finishing the job."

"Don't!" Raiya jerked back from me.

"Don't what?"

"Don't grab me like that. I have to hold onto these." She gestured toward the bags. "They're mine."

I frowned, trying not to snort disdainfully. "What's inside that's so precious?"

Her face crumbled as she looked down at them. "They're mine," she repeated, this time with a hard edge to her words. "I have to protect them."

"Okay," I murmured, still somewhat confused. "I won't touch them, but we need to go."

There was a loud rumbling noise, and it made me nervous. As kindly as possible, I hurried Raiya along.

It was only when I heard screams and looked back to see the long hallways caving in, that I began to panic.

"Hurry!" I urged her onward. She seemed to catch the fervency behind my message, since she spurred onward.

"Hamilton," she gasped as she fell forward.

I caught her and saw no choice. I picked her up, and, angry at how light she felt, carried her close to me. Raiya didn't fight me; she tucked her bags between us, and then curled her arm around my neck.

Water poured down on us as we finally came to an elevator. I prayed it would take us to the surface.

I smashed the buttons on the wall, and it opened seconds later. Alarms were still going off around us, but I held onto Raiya tightly.

Water flooded into the elevator along with us, and I hit one of the buttons, hoping desperately it was the right one. When the lights for the ground level came on, I allowed myself a sigh of relief.

As the water level inside the elevator went down, I sensed the sky coming toward us, coming close enough we could see it. I looked down at Raiya. My hands instinctively tightened around her.

Disbelief hit me hard all over again. I couldn't believe it. She was alive. And she was with me, here, in this place.

Well, this would be the only place where we would be able to be together, wouldn't it? I thought bitterly.

"You can put me down," she said, jolting me out of my thoughts.

"Huh? Oh, right. Sorry." I carefully released her, and then moved to tighten my wet jacket around her body. "When we get back to the house, I'm going to get you into a warm bath. The last thing I need is for you to get sick."

She shivered as I held her. But it would take more than that to stop her when she wanted something. "Who are you?" she asked.

I tried to shrug off the discomfort. *How am I going to explain this to her?*

"I'm here to get you out of here," I said carefully. "Like I said, we're friends. From … a long time ago."

"Does Rosemary know about you?"

"Who?" I frowned.

"Rosemary. Grandma Rosemary. She's also known as the Matriarch."

Grandma? I decided to ignore that part for now, especially since I recognized the other part.

"The Matriarch is the leader of SWORD, right?"

Raiya nodded. "She was the one who brought me here," she said. Her lower lip quivered. "She was going to hurt people if I didn't cooperate. But she went too far. As soon as

113

I had enough power to overcome my medicine, I woke up. I was on my way out when you arrived."

That explained the inside damage. I was confused by this, but then I recalled what Elysian had told me once: Starry Knight's power was partially dependent on me. Since I was here, maybe that gave her what she needed to get free.

I could only speculate.

And I would have to do it later.

The elevator opened and I put my arm around her waist once more. "We're not out of the clear yet," I said.

We stepped out of the elevator and found ourselves in the woods near the marina. I glanced behind me as the doors shut behind us, only to see just a tree trunk. A normal-looking, nothing-out-of-place tree trunk. Lake Erie was practically within spitting distance.

So this is where they had another black site all along. I couldn't believe how many hours of my life I had walked by this place, walked in these woods, and a secret entrance to a sadistic, power-hungry, control-obsessed organization was within spitting distance.

I was so upset, Raiya stumbled on the ground and fell over before I could catch her.

"No," she moaned as her bags went flying. She scurried around, collecting them again.

"Stop for a moment," I told her. There weren't any other SWORD agents around that I could see; we probably had a few moments, anyway. "Let me help you. You're bleeding."

"It's from the IV," Raiya explained apologetically. She showed me her arms, and I could see she was telling the truth. "There's another one on my leg," she added, pulling up her gown to where I could see a long gash just above her calf. "It didn't come out as easily as the others."

I started to rip at my shirt, tearing the wet fabric into strips. "Here," I said, "let me get them. And then we'll go to the house."

"Thank you," Raiya said. She smiled shyly at me as I wound the makeshift bandage around her knee. For a long moment, I let my hand rest on her skin; I was still in a mild state of disbelief, and touching her, even if it was just to bind up her cuts and clean off her blood, was a remedy to my soul.

There was a shifting noise behind me.

I wasn't surprised to see Dante step out of the darkness.

"I see you found her," he said.

I leapt up at once, stepping between Raiya and Dante. "Are you insane?" I hissed.

"No," he said. "Look, I got you in, and I see you got out. And you managed to do quite a bit of damage in the meantime. There's going to be a good cover story in the news tomorrow."

"You leave me and her out of this." I took a step closer to him. "We almost died."

"Plenty of people did die," Dante said, with enough pleasure in his gaze that I wondered if he'd planned that all along. "And more will continue to die, especially after your power burst managed to trigger a cave-in down one of the main hallways. You should be happy."

"I'll be happy when you're dead," I told him darkly.

Dante turned away from me and gave a cordial salute to Raiya. "Hello," he said in greeting to her. "What a pleasant surprise. It's nice to see you again."

Raiya frowned. "I don't remember you," she said, "but I have the distinct feeling I don't like you."

He smiled kindly at her. "I hope I will get the chance to prove you wrong."

"No," I scoffed, "you won't. Leave us."

"I'll give you some time," Dante said, much as he had when we were teenagers, stuck in SWORD's prison, under his watch. "I'll be back in a few days, when I'm better informed of what progress and recovery SWORD is making from tonight's mess." He smiled smugly. "Thanks for the help in the meantime."

Raiya shuddered as he disappeared from our sight. "He's creepy."

"You never liked him," I said.

"Did you?"

"No. But I thought he was useful, in some ways, so I overlooked some of the problems we had with him."

"We?"

My heart fell all over again. "Never mind. Let's not worry about it. Let's get you somewhere safe."

"I'm tired of safe," she admitted. "I want to go somewhere where I can be free."

I nodded. "I have a place nearby," I said. "It might be a bit of a full house though."

"You have a house?" Raiya looked up at me with sadness in her eyes. "Do you have land, too?"

"Ugh, well … " I didn't actually want to say "My mom does." So I went with my usual methods. "Why do you need land?"

She held out the bags in her hands. "I need to bury these," she told me quietly. "If I can."

"What are they?" I asked. "What's in the bags?"

Nothing could have prepared me for her response. As her tears finally pushed free from her eyes, she answered, "My children."

THE STARLIGHT CHRONICLES

☼<u>9</u>☼
Hurt

I don't remember much about the walk back to my parents' house. It was late, very late—or maybe early, early morning—when we arrived.

I felt like a robot. My movements were strangely mechanical, as though I had to order my brain to give the code to do the task at hand. Everything took twice as long to do, and everything seemed twice as hard to accomplish.

I barely registered walking through the door to my parents' house, and barely paid any attention to the quiet that greeted us. I was only briefly jolted out of my brain fog when I turned on the water in the guest bathroom, and it was more at the noise than at the hot water running down my hands.

Children.

The word rang in my head several times.

I didn't notice much as I dumped Raiya into the tub, clothes and all, taking care to show her the shampoo, conditioner, etc. I tossed her a towel and then went out to sit in the living room, my thoughts consuming me as I sat there.

I'm pretty sure hours passed before I was interrupted from my inner disturbance.

"Hamilton?"

I turned at the sound of my mother's voice.

"Are you alright?"

119

I shook my head.

I'd known there was evil in the world. I knew it even long before I'd rationalized it away throughout my teen years. But coming face to face with it, and to hold the innocent victims of it in my own hands, was harder than arguing over any legal damages.

On top of that, there was Raiya. There had been days when I wanted nothing more than to have her back. And she was here now. But she wasn't. Not really.

She didn't know me anymore. And truth be told, *I* barely knew me anymore. The idea of getting to know her all over again, after forcing myself to forget about her, was almost as painful as losing her.

"Is there something I can do for you?" Cheryl asked. She handed me her cup of coffee, pushing it into my hand.

"I don't know," I told her honestly.

"What happened?"

I forced myself to say the words, knowing she would likely disapprove and I would be less adamant in disagreeing with her. "Raiya's here."

Cheryl said nothing. There was a strange expression on her face as she squeezed my shoulder affectionately. "Tell me what you need. I'll help you."

There was enough coherency about me that registered my surprise when she didn't ask, "Raiya who?" or sigh indignantly.

I'd been up long enough, and done so much, that I was ready to go to bed. I was ready to go to bed and not wake up.

I knew I still had things to do. I needed rest, and it would come in time. I had to take care of Raiya first.

"I need someone to take care of Lyra and Lucas today," I said. "Can you stay home?"

"I took a half day. Your father can watch them, perhaps, until I get home," Cheryl said. "He was going to take Adam to school this morning, so I'm sure he won't have any trouble taking care of the other two kids. I'll help him when I get home."

"Thanks." It was enough. For now.

"You know," Cheryl said quietly, "he called off work today. He was hoping to have a talk with you."

I shook my head. I didn't really want to talk with my dad. "I need time," I said.

"No," Cheryl told me softly. "You need to rest. When you were younger, you always seemed like you could take on the world a thousand times and still win. But you're not the same person anymore, and you need to rest."

"I've never felt this tired," I said, my confession surprising me as much as I no doubt surprised her.

"Perhaps that is my fault. When you were younger, it was so easy to think that one person could change the world. And while I do think that is still possible, I now see that people working together, rather than alone, yield better results."

She patted my hand affectionately as I nodded.

I stood up, her coffee still in my hands. "I'm going to need to borrow some of your old clothes," I added as I headed back up the stairs.

"There's plenty in the guest room," she said. "I keep all my older things there, just in case they come back into fashion. Tell Raiya she can have her pick."

I nodded. "Thanks."

Part of me wanted to go to my room and lie down, and fall asleep there. I didn't want to think about the last day, or day and a half now, and I didn't want to think about the next day, or the one after that.

I knew they were going to be hard to get through.

It was the other part of me that won out in the end. I walked to Raiya's room. I knocked, but there was no answer. I peeked in, making sure she was out of the bath, and I saw she was already lying down on the bed, curled up.

For a moment, I stopped and watched her. I'd seen her sleep before, and I could hardly tell that any time had passed at all when I looked at her.

Her long hair was free, splayed out against the pillow. Her one leg stuck out from the side of the cover. I thought I even recognized the pair of pajamas she was wearing, one of the fluffier pairs Cheryl had barely worn and then tossed out over the years. *Raiya* would *like that one*, I thought with a small smile.

I made my way over to her and brushed a tendril of hair out of her face. She sighed softy, her sleep deep and peaceful looking. Squinting, I could see her dreams were comforting, and I hoped they were providing a soothing slumber for her.

Well, I guess I don't have to worry about her falling asleep in a strange place tonight.

I was just about to leave when she sighed again. "Hamilton?" She rolled over, still half-asleep.

"Uh, what is it?" I asked. I felt awkward, almost like I'd gotten caught spying on her.

Instead of reproaching me, she took a hold of my hand. "Stay."

I had no resistance.

I held onto her hand and lay down next to her, my eyes never leaving her face as I drifted slowly off to sleep.

When I woke up later, she was still asleep next to me. It was hard to tell how much time had passed. There was only a grayish beam of light shining through the slivers of the curtains, and I could hear the rhythmic falling of the rain outside.

Nothing in the house moved. I wondered if we had slept through the whole day, or if it was just that everyone was gone for the day.

I looked up at the ceiling of the room. I felt the warmth of Raiya's hand, still tucked carefully in mine. I watched as the soft light fell on her.

A small twinkle of light fell on her chest; I could see the hint of an old scar cutting down through the middle of her heart.

Dante told me her heart had exploded, I recalled. So what exactly had happened to her?

Adonaias, I decided. A rush of regret and shame ran through me. *He's given her a new heart, rather than a new wish.*

I could still see him clearly in my mind as he protected us during the last battle with Draco. Was I right? I certainly thought I was, but I didn't have a way to prove it. Just yet, anyway.

"Hey." She looked over at me, her eyes blinking back sleep.

Despite everything, I smiled. "You're awake."

"What are you thinking about?" she asked.

I shook my head. "Nothing."

"You're more than just my friend, aren't you?"

She said it was such conviction, I felt the warning flares of hope.

"You know me."

"Yes," I said.

"That's why you saved me."

"Yes." I frowned.

"What is it?"

"There's more. I was told that your power is connected to a black hole, and it can break through Time."

She pulled herself up into a sitting position, releasing my hand, much to my dismay. "I don't know or remember anything about that," she said. "But I'm glad you were able to get me out of there."

"Did they … hurt you?" I could barely ask the question. I didn't need to know whose suffering was greater between us. I already knew.

She ducked her head. "Yes," she admitted quietly.

I reached over, awkwardly, and wrapped an arm around her shoulder. *It's almost like old times,* I thought, pulling her into the nook underneath my arm. "Everything will be alright. I won't let them hurt you again."

She clutched back at me. "Thank you," she said.

For a long time, she let me hold her, and that was just what I did.

The long moment was ruined when her stomach rumbled. She blushed as I laughed. "Excuse me," she murmured.

"It's no trouble."

"You want to get some food?" Raiya asked.

It was a question she'd asked me before, when we were together.

My answer was the same, too. "My pleasure," I replied.

She stilled. "What did you say?" she asked. She frowned and pulled back a bit from me.

"I said my pleasure," I repeated carefully, my heart tingling with hope.

"Oh." Raiya frowned.

"Are you okay?" I asked, trying not to be too effusive as I thought about it. *She has to be remembering me!*

"I have a headache," she said.

My hope died again. This time, I wondered if it was going to stay dead.

I eased away from her. "Let me go see what kind of food we have here," I said. *Or what kind I could order,* I added silently to myself.

Turned out, my mother's French diet was actually bearable. I quickly found a storage container full of croissants and plenty of relatively normal stuff in the fridge.

By the time Raiya came downstairs, I was at home, making an omelet and pulling out the butter.

I stared at her as she came down.

There were bandages on her arms and her leg, but she was wearing an old pair of my gym shorts and one of my mom's more casual shirts, showing off her legs nicely.

After some internal debate, I decided she looked mostly normal; I almost smiled, thinking of how I thought she looked scrawny when I'd first seen her as a teenager. There

THE STARLIGHT CHRONICLES

was no way that she was scrawny back then, especially when I saw her now.

I tried not to think about that.

Her hair was long and free, and if I had been my teenage self, I would've been tempted to run my hands through it. She rarely, if ever, let it hang loose. I had a hard time remembering just how long it was before …

I stopped myself and turned back to the stove. "Omelet?" I offered. "The protein will be good for you."

"Sure." She came and stood next to me. "Can I help with something? I feel like I haven't been in a kitchen in years."

"Do you know how long you've been gone?" I asked.

She shook her head. "No, but I can probably still work in the kitchen without killing anyone, if you're worried about that."

That is probably true.

"Uh, if you want to help, you can." I glanced around, trying to think of something that might help jump her memory. "Why don't you make some coffee? My mother's got the beans in that cabinet over there," I said, nodding toward the machine.

Raiya didn't have any trouble at all. She measured out the beans, ground them up, and had the coffee machine purring like a robotic kitten programed to pee out coffee.

"So … Hamilton. Will you tell me about yourself?" Raiya asked.

"Ouch!" Just as she was asking her question, I managed to burn myself on the stove.

"Let me get that," Raiya said, reaching over. When she took my hand, I felt the familiar stream of her healing power as it poured out of her and into me.

As she dropped my hand, I gaped at her.

"I have healing powers," she explained, almost shyly. She turned back to the coffee machine as it beeped.

"I know," I muttered, more to myself than to her. "I didn't think you did. Not anymore."

"I wasn't strong enough before," she said. "But I've been feeling much better today."

Elysian had told me before that I managed to keep my powers, despite being a fallen Star. I guessed Raiya was still able to heal, even though she had no memory.

Was this what it was like for her while we were dating? I wondered. Falling in love with someone who was supposed to love you back, still recognizing they might not remember what the relationship had once been?

No wonder she'd pushed me away so adamantly when she first met me.

Raiya was blissfully unaware of my existential crisis as she pulled out the creamer and the sugar from the pantry. "You take both, right?" she asked, pouring the coffee into different cups.

"Yes," I said.

She handed me the cup. As she did, my fingers brushed against hers. At the small touch, I felt a rush of caring pour out from her and overwhelm me.

She still cares for me. Even though she barely knows me anymore. Why?!

"Why?"

"Why what?" Raiya asked.

I hadn't realized I asked the question aloud. "Why," I said, "why don't you sit down?"

She looked confused for a moment, and then she said, "I haven't been able to move like this in a long time. I'm sure I'll need some time to build up my strength again, but for now I'd like to push myself some."

"You always seemed to push yourself," I recalled. "Well, you always did more than I pushed myself."

"Have we known each other for a long time?" Raiya asked.

"Uh … yes and no," I finally decided.

"But you came to save me."

I nodded. "Dante needed some help. I don't know yet if he actually meant for me to rescue you like this." I decided not to mention he'd sent me looking for her body. Her dead body, I'd assumed.

"That's the guy from the woods, right?" She wrinkled her nose in disgust. "I hope we don't see him again for a long time. I don't think he's a good person."

129

"He's not," I assured her. "He's not good, and I could make the argument that he's barely a person."

Raiya laughed, catching me off guard. "What?" she replied, seeing my surprise. "That was funny."

"I guess so." I smiled back. "It's nice to hear you laugh."

A somber mood came upon her. "I'm going to need time to heal," she said. "But laughter and joy are healers just as much as time."

"If there's anything I can do to help," I said, pulling the omelets off the stove and skirting them onto our plates, "please let me know."

She took her plate, and then she put it down. "There is something you can do for me."

"What is it?" I asked, grabbing some bread.

"I would like to bury my children," she said. "Would you let me?"

I almost choked on my food. I had to take a large swig of coffee before replying. "In the yard?"

"If you can," she said. "You have a nice place here."

"This is my mother's house," I said. "We'd have to ask her."

"She has beautiful gardens. I think that they would like that."

"It should be fine." I would take the hit from my mom. Surely she would see this as a necessity? I mean, she almost lost Adam when he was a baby. She of all people should be compassionate in cases like this one.

From the size of Raiya's bags, I don't think it was likely any of them had made it that far.

"Thank you," she said.

"We can bury them after the rain stops," I said, aware this was the most bizarre conversation I'd ever had in my parents' kitchen.

"Thank you." She reached over and took my hand and squeezed it. "You're a good friend."

Ouch. I've been friendzoned.

We ate some in silence. Or at least she ate, while I mostly watched her.

I still had trouble believing she was alive.

"So, what else can you tell me about yourself?"

Raiya's new question confounded me for a long moment. I looked at her as I took a sip of my coffee. She looked at me expectantly, and I figured I should try to answer her questions.

"Well," I said, "I'm a lawyer." That seemed pretty basic.

"Really? You don't seem like one. You rescued me from SWORD, after all. Don't you have to go to work?"

"I'm on sabbatical," I told her. "I had some work troubles with one of my … one of my coworkers, and she complained to her dad. He just happened to be the boss."

I felt my heartbeat jump high enough to strangle me. *I can't tell her about Charlotte.*

Dread trickled through me. I couldn't tell her about practically anything that had happened since high school; I'd done a lot of things she would likely cringe at. I mean, *I* was even cringing at the memories.

"You didn't get fired?"

"No." Despite my panic, I laughed. "They wouldn't fire me. I'm good at what I do."

"How long have you been a lawyer?"

"I finished law school a little over two years ago," I said. "I work in Pittsburgh, and even though it's only been a short time, I have a reputation."

"Why did you come here?" she asked.

"Well, I had a couple of unexpected things happen," I said. "A boy and girl came to see me. They wanted me to help them find their parents."

"Oh. I hope you can find them."

"Me, too."

We lapsed into silence again. I made her seconds and insisted that she eat it.

I didn't know the specifics of her time under SWORD, and from what I did know, I didn't want to know anything else. I was already likely going to have nightmares for the rest of my life as it was, and there was little chance I would get sleep knowing Dante was likely going to insert himself back into my life in the coming days.

THE STARLIGHT CHRONICLES

☼10☼
Truth and Light

The rain picked up steadily, but inside the house it seemed as though a different world existed for us. Time passed, both slowly and quickly, and I was uncertain of how to proceed with Raiya.

I'd never really thought about how much she struggled with me when we first met during high school. I knew from our past discussions that she'd retained a lot of her memories from the other side of Time's power, before we became fallen Stars, and before we were reborn into this realm.

Now, I was amazed at her all over again. She used to tell the stories if I asked, but she never pushed. She let me come to terms with it on my own, something I didn't know if I had the strength or the patience to reciprocate.

There was also the matter of how, when we were younger, we didn't have quite so much emotional baggage and scarring. Even if she did remember me, how could she still want to be with me? I had done some terrible things, not the least of which include giving up on her.

That was what I struggled with most with myself. How could I have given up on her? Why didn't I fight Dante harder? Go looking for SWORD? Care enough to make sure she was actually dead?

These questions continued to pummel me as the afternoon transitioned easily into the evening.

Raiya was sleeping on the couch in the den when my dad came home, with Adam, Lucas, and Lyra all in tow. I signaled them to be quiet as they came in.

I was shocked when they all agreed to keep it down—I was not so shocked when Mark told me that he'd filled them in on some parts of the situation.

I was glad to see that Adam had befriended my mini-clients quickly. They ran off to play in his room, mentioning something about video games.

"Times haven't changed so much since I was in high school," I said with a grin.

"Not quite." Mark shook his head and ran a hand through his hair. "Adam's games are much more expensive than I remember yours being."

"I'll concede to that," I said, recalling interest rates and inflation troubles.

"Hamilton."

"What?"

Mark looked at me with a solemn expression on his face. "I need to talk to you," he said.

"I need to talk to you, too."

He nodded. "Let's go to my office, shall we?"

"Alright."

We headed to his office, the smaller one just off to the right of the kitchen. Cheryl had opted for the bigger one, and Mark willingly appeased her. And I knew several of the specific reasons why.

One, it was because it was my mother, and while I couldn't fathom it all the time, Mark absolutely loved her. He was willing to sacrifice to make her happy. And two, it was because Cheryl was the one who would be more likely to bring clients home. Mark barely used his office as it was, and if he did, it was usually just to write up his research proposals and final reports.

When I sat down in the chair opposite his desk and a thin layer of dust wafted up from it, I wasn't surprised.

"Let's go ahead and get this over with," Mark said. At my raised brows, he smiled bitterly. "I don't believe in messing around when it comes to important things."

"Okay." I could agree with that. I knew what it was to have a client go off on some silly tangents before attempting to recall the purpose of the original conversation.

"I want to apologize," he said. "I … I don't really know what happened, all those years ago, during your last year of high school."

I shook my head. "I knew my … activities … were problematic for you," I said. "And I knew how hard it was for you to keep my secrets from Mom. You don't need to apologize."

"Yes, I do." He sighed. "I didn't know how to deal with you after … after everything wrapped up."

137

"I know." I folded my arms across my chest. "I've done a lot of thinking on it myself."

"And I didn't know … I didn't know what they'd done to her."

That was weird. Suspicion rushed through me. "What do you mean?" I asked.

"I had to stop myself from saying anything a million times," he continued. "I couldn't prove anything, and I didn't know. I just didn't know."

"Didn't know what?"

He gazed up at me with sad eyes. "I'm so sorry, Hamilton."

My instincts on matters like these had sharpened over the last several years of training and education. And I hated that I knew I was right about my conclusions.

"You knew she was alive." I barely got my mouth to form the words.

He shrugged. "Well … "

Another day, another shock.

I jumped out of my seat. "You knew?!"

"I was going to tell you when you came back for Christmas your first year of college," he said. "When you stayed, saying you wanted to work on your classwork, I took it as a sign not to push it. And there's also the matter of SWORD. I know from Dante that SWORD has a very tight policy of nondisclosure. I'm sure they'll find a way to punish me for telling you this now, even though you've already found out."

"Why are you telling me this then?" I asked angrily.

"Because you deserve to know the truth." Mark shook his head. "And I need your forgiveness. There's no greater punishment than one that's self-inflicted. The guilt goes down deep; it becomes a cancer to the soul."

I almost squirmed. Did he know that was exactly how I felt? All the years I thought I'd been robbed of something precious, and it turned out I was right. But I didn't even try to find the correct thief. I suffered because of my own mistakes as much as another's.

And my own father played a role in it.

"So you knew she was alive, and you didn't tell me because I wasn't here." I stood up and began pacing. "What else? What else do you know?"

"They continued to ship her blood over to the hospital as part of our old arrangement for a year after everything happened."

"And you took it?!"

Stress tightened on his face. "There's nothing I could have done," he said. "Why shouldn't I have taken it? My research could save lives, Hamilton."

"By destroying others?" I yelled back.

"I *didn't* know what they'd done, exactly."

I fought against the tide of anger inside of me. "How did they even revive her? Dante said that her heart had exploded."

"That's true," Mark said. "He didn't lie to you. I was the one who operated on her myself."

That might explain some of the reasons he didn't want to tell me. He knew I could easily blame him for her death.

Despite realizing this, I was still not willing to soften against him. He'd deliberately allowed me to suffer, and needlessly. I did understand his silence better. And that was enough to ensure I wouldn't go down the path of sweet revenge.

Sometimes, you have just enough sympathy to keep yourself from doing something incredibly stupid. It's a small thing, and something to be thankful for.

"I saw what had happened, and I had them sew her back up immediately. But while we still had her on the operating table, her heart began to beat again. On its own."

"How?"

"How indeed," Mark said. "I had them reverse the stitches as soon as we saw what was happening on the monitor. And when we did, nothing was wrong. All her heart irregularities, the leaks she'd had, the murmur, all of it was gone. A perfect heart had magically replaced her old one."

"More like miraculous."

He nodded. "Certainly. But before we could make the announcement, a lady came in. She said that she was going to take over the case, and we were not to disclose any details to any party."

"A lady?" I shook my head. "How did she manage to get you to agree to that?"

"Legally."

"Legally, how?"

"She had documents showing she was Raiya's legal grandmother—and the marriage license showing that she'd been married to her grandpa."

I paused for a long moment. "Her grandmother?" Raiya had mentioned her grandma. *Rosemary, she called her.*

Mark nodded.

"Do you think she was telling the truth?"

"We had no choice but to discharge her over to her. I knew she was part of SWORD, however, when I saw her talk with Dante in the hallway. He doesn't know I saw them together."

A new thought struck me. "Raiya's grandmother? As in, Grandpa Odd's wife?"

"Yes."

Even while he's trapped in the void, Draco is still making my life miserable.

I suddenly really wanted to see those files.

But instead of demanding them, I just sighed. "I don't want to talk about this anymore," I said. "I *can't* talk about this anymore right now. I don't think I can forgive you for this. I can't even forgive myself for this."

"Hamilton. You know as well as I do that there are no college courses or technical manuals that come with fatherhood. At the end of the day, even after reading all the books and doing all the research, it's a full-time learning experience where you rely on your instincts a lot. Mine were just not as good as I would've liked."

I had a strong suspicion he was using that as a convenient excuse.

On my way out of the room, I turned back to him briefly. "Oh, and Raiya and I are going to dig around in Mom's yard some. No objections. You owe me, especially after this."

Mark said nothing. He only nodded.

I thought I heard him sigh as the door shut behind me.

Well, what did he expect? All things considered, I should've gotten a medal for not ripping his office to shreds or pushing for medical malpractice charges.

Frustration ate at me. I didn't know who I was more angry at. I remembered hating Adonaias at the end of everything last time, and it was too easy to shake my fist at him and demand he punish himself for my pain.

Why did he let my dad do this? Why did he let SWORD do this?

Why didn't he tell me about Raiya?

Why didn't I know better?

And if nothing else, why didn't she at least remember me?

I stood in the hallway, leaning against the wall as I pondered all of this and more, trying to process my guilt and fear and all that other good stuff.

A shimmer of light and Lyra's laughter caught my attention.

"Yes, do it again," she exclaimed, and I wondered what she was so happy about. The noise was coming from the den, I noticed.

"That was so cool," Adam said.

"I want to try," Lucas insisted.

Were they bothering Raiya? I decided it would be best to encourage Adam, Lyra, and Lucas to leave her alone.

But one look at the four of them, and I changed my mind. It was for the better, because I didn't think I would get them to agree with me anyway.

Raiya held onto Lyra's hand, her palm covering Lyra's wrist where the Emblem of the Prince would be.

A bubble of light and music suddenly appeared over their joined hands. Inside of it, I could see a colorful picture of gardens and water, almost like a painting.

The music was haunting and thoughtful, and the light shined in all the colors of the spectrum, dancing off the shadows and shades of the room.

"It's beautiful," Lyra said as the image faded and she let go of Raiya's hand.

Lucas and Adam had identical looks of intense interest on their faces; they began shoving each other as they moved to get closer to Raiya where she sat on the couch.

I watched as Lucas put his hand in Raiya's. "My turn!"

"You know what you want to make?" Raiya asked.

"Yes," he exclaimed.

"Alright, then give it a try. Do you know what to do?"

"I can guess," he huffed, his impatience clear.

A second later, a new bubble of light formed above their hands. This one, however, didn't stay a bubble with a pretty picture inside of it. This one metamorphosed into a dragon, like it was budding out from an egg.

"Awesome," Adam said.

"That's my pet," Lucas said proudly. He tightened his grip on Raiya's hand, and the dragon sprouted wings and went flying around the room.

"You mean like Elysian?" Adam asked.

Raiya frowned. "Elysian?" she repeated.

"Yes. Hamilton's dragon, from when I was a kid."

The look on Raiya's face was painful. Before she could ask any questions—which, to be honest, I was hoping she would, because I wasn't aware that Adam had retained so many specifics of my time as one of the city's superheroes—Lucas interrupted.

"No, my dragon's name is Aeolian," he said.

"Alien?"

"No, *Aeolian*," Lucas said, enunciating carefully.

While they began discussing this at length, Raiya turned her attention to Lyra.

"Your turn," Raiya told her.

Lyra looked nervous. "I don't know how."

"You won't figure it out if you don't try," Raiya pointed out.

Lyra hesitated.

"It doesn't have to be perfect," Raiya said. "There's nothing to be gained by forsaking the good in search of the perfect. Especially when the good is often a stop on the way to perfection."

"Okay." Lyra took a hold of Raiya's hand this time, and I watched in amazement as light sparked up between them.

"It's a simple trick," Raiya told them, "but not always easy. Once you do it enough, you get better at it."

"How do I start?"

"Try thinking of something that gives you joy. Something good and beautiful and true."

As I watched Raiya and Lyra bond over their powers, I stepped back into the hallway, thinking of the times when she would teach me something with my own power. Many times, she worked with me after Aleia had returned to the other realm, and I saw the same compassion and concern etched into her expression as she broke down her instructions for Lyra, using patient words and kind smiles.

Will she remember me? Will she remember us?

Maybe it was better if she didn't. I'd changed since we were last together.

It would be better for her, maybe. But not for me. Not when I want her back this badly.

The pain in my chest prompted me to leave.

I walked outside and felt a sense of surreality fall on me. The landscape that had once been my home still welcomed me, but I was less familiar with it than ever.

Jason had told Mikey that Rachel's was closed, boarded up for sale. I couldn't go there.

I graduated high school, and most of my friends had moved. And even the ones who didn't, I didn't think they would be trapped by the past the same way I was.

So I stood outside my house, watching as the rain fell down from the sky, as the world slowly continued to turn. I didn't notice when my tears began to mix in with the rain.

"This isn't fair," I murmured, angry at the injustice of it all. "Why? Why did you let this happen, Adonaias?"

There was nothing but silence. I slumped down to my knees, leaning against the wall behind me, putting my head in my hands, closing my eyes as I allowed myself to let my pain free.

I felt the words burn in my throat. "I thought you cared about us. About *me*. Don't you care at all? You could at least answer my question, you know."

Before I knew it, I wasn't just crying, I was all out sobbing. My questions turned into the mutterings of a man too caught up in his grief and grievances to give a voice to truth.

What is truth, anyway?

I didn't notice it right away when a hand patted me on the head—lovingly, tenderly, like a parent tending to a child. The moment I did, everything changed. Fear trickled down my body; I was no longer alone.

I glanced up in shock, silent as the Prince of Stars leaned down and wiped a tear from my cheek.

He was the same as he had always been. Fire gleamed like crystals in his eyes as he gazed at me with both compassion and expectancy, calling me to both fear and courage. The white of his hair and the bronze of his skin radiated strength and comfort, all bound up in truth and light.

I grasped onto him, letting the enormity of his power and his embrace wash over me as I wept against him.

I held on for the longest time, fighting for every moment of time and inch of space I could as he held me.

When I was younger, I had looked out across the city skyline and wondered how Adonaias could really be a part of this world. He seemed too far away, too irrelevant. There were problems everywhere, a myriad of obstacles that all required a different approach and a different cure.

Turns out, there was nothing more relevant. As a lawyer, I had little appreciation for medicine, preferring to leave that to people like Mark. Because of that, I often failed to see what the right mix of chemicals and ingredients could do to a sick body.

And I was sick. Sick with grief, sick with selfishness, sick with my own problems and the problems that pushed their way into me.

Nothing was more relevant to me, in that moment, as I held on.

I didn't know how much time passed before I pulled away.

He said nothing still, but he wrapped his one hand around my wrist—the same one that had been marked with his emblem all those years ago—and then placed the other on my heart.

Instantly, my eyes were flooded with a new vision. I could see myself turn away from him, back after the battle with Draco and Alküzor. I saw myself in pain, in the hospital; functioning with walking depression; graduating high school; making mistakes, with alcohol and girls and grad school; driving around on my motorcycle, wondering what would happen if I just let go of control … and then, as I took my eyes off myself, I saw him.

He was beside me—walking with me, protecting me, shielding me, preserving me—through every step and scene of all my life.

Wonder and awe and a bunch of other emotions all tumbled around inside of me, kindling a warmth inside I hadn't felt in years.

I blinked and saw his expression as he gazed back at me. All the wonders I felt and saw and experienced were nothing compared to hearing his voice again.

"You shall know the truth," he said, "and the truth will set you free."

He stepped back and let my wrist go. I looked down to see my mark was back, shining, glowing with restored power. I felt my mouth drop open less than glamorously, realizing just what he meant.

When I looked back up at him, he was gone. But I knew he wasn't, not really. It was only later that I realized he must have been waiting for me all this time.

I had my answer.

THE STARLIGHT CHRONICLES

☼11☼
Healing

Eventually, the rain let up. It was still drizzling out when I woke up the next day. It wasn't too bad, but it was enough to make me depressed.

Of course, I was depressed anyway. I was back in my own room, and my room only made me think of how Elysian used to share it with me.

Thinking of dragons, I thought about Lucas' light dragon. I wondered if, now that I had my mark back, I could make those, too.

I didn't know about my powers as a kid, or as a young teenager, so the idea of using my powers for anything without a need for battle seemed like a good challenge that would cheer me up.

Checking my bank account balance, I was able to think of a few other things which would make me happy, too. Mr. Dahlonega had proven his word was true; I had a nice-sized deposit ready to be spent.

It wasn't like I didn't have anything to buy. I had to go get a wedding present for Mikey. As much as I'm sure he wouldn't have minded it, I wasn't going to opt for cash or gift cards.

Maybe I can convince Raiya to come with me, I thought.

I could even bring the kids, too, if I had to. Which I supposed I did, since both Mark and Cheryl were back at work. Adam had already gone off to school, too, I realized, spying the clock.

I thought it was a good plan, and I planned to present it to Raiya when I saw her.

But when I actually did see her, I forgot everything else.

Raiya was staring out the windows, looking out into some unknown world inside of her mind. Or it was possible she was just looking out the window into the yard. The sun was up, and even though it was still cloudy, there was plenty of light to brighten some of the smaller corners of the yard. Despite the cold of the last few weeks, and the snow in Pittsburgh, Apollo City had yet to see any snow.

"You okay?" I asked.

"Yeah," she said. "Just thinking about how lovely it is outside."

I came up to her and put my hand on her shoulder. It seemed natural to want to touch her, to find a way to comfort her—to find a way to comfort myself.

"I was thinking of going out," I said. "You want to come? We can go shopping for some new clothes for you."

Raiya shook her head. "I have a few more important things I'd like to take care of," she said.

I wondered if she could feel my disappointment.

"But I'll be okay here by myself," she said a moment later. "I know you have to get a gift for that wedding you're going to next week."

Startled, I turned to her. "How did you know about Mikey's wedding?"

Raiya grinned. "I saw the invitation, of course. It was with the stuff you left with the kids in their room."

"Oh."

"You do have to buy a gift still, don't you?" she asked. "Unless that painting you have is what you were going to give them?"

"Painting?"

"The one wrapped up in the brown paper."

The one Rachel had given to Mikey to give to me.

"Oh, no. That was actually a gift for me. I wonder what it's doing here. I didn't think I packed it."

"I brought it," Lucas said as he came down the stairs. "I thought we could get it fixed for you. Since Lyra and I broke it."

"Morning, Lucas," Raiya said.

"Morning," he replied. He came beside her and put his arms around her waist. "Are you going to make me regular pancakes this morning?"

"Lucas," I hissed.

"What? It's not my fault the French have thin pancakes."

"Those are crepes," Raiya murmured.

"Those crepes creep me out."

Raiya giggled. "Well, we can't have you starve, can we? Why don't you see if Lyra wants some, too?"

"Lyra!" Lucas called, so loudly I could feel the soundwaves bounce off of the walls. "We're eating pancakes, so get your butt down here before I eat them all!"

She started shouting back as Raiya came up to me. "Would you like some, too?" she asked.

"I don't even know if my mother has the stuff here to make them," I said.

"I'll go check and see what your mom has. If we need something, you're going out, right? I can give you a list."

"I don't even know how to make them." I really didn't want to bother with it, and I hated the feeling of being overruled. It was part of the reason that I argued against every objection to my arguments in court.

"Don't worry. I remember," Raiya told me with a smile. "It shouldn't be a problem."

You can remember how to make pancakes while you only have my mother's kitchen as resource, but you can't remember that you and I were meant to be together?!

Anger flooded me, fast and vengeful. I knew that life wasn't fair, but I hated when it insisted on being unkind, too. It made it a lot harder for me to be kind. "I'm just going to head out," I grumbled.

"Is something wrong?" she asked.

"No," I snapped. "I'll be back later."

"Are you sure?"

Before I could convince myself it was a better idea to stay and try to smooth things over, I grabbed my coat, put on my boots, and headed out into the cold morning air.

I didn't really have a solid plan of where I was going. I was lost in a world of my own thoughts, and I didn't hesitate to allow myself the time to brood.

I didn't have a job, after all. This was my first real time off in months. When you have to work, when you have to perform, when other people are counting on you to fulfill every one of their expectations, brooding is an unfathomable luxury.

One I could finally indulge in.

Don't get me wrong. I had hope again, now that I'd seen Adonaias and I knew he wasn't ready to give up on me, and he didn't want me to give up on me.

But I was still struggling to find a way to put that into practice. Being stuck is not always a bad thing. Staying stuck—now *that's* the real tragedy. And I knew that one from first-hand experience.

I walked throughout the downtown area, surprised to see a lot of the small shops I'd grown up with were closed or in need of repairs. Some were still open, but I had a feeling Mikey wouldn't quite appreciate me buying him an antique.

Although, I thought mischievously, *it might be fun to buy him something he doesn't need, so completely expensive and extravagant that I can laugh at his face as he unwraps it.*

That was shaping up to be formidable threat when Dante's face appeared in the window behind me.

"If you're really looking for something good," Dante told me, "I'd recommend the new underground mall where Rosemont used to be."

I almost jerked around. In my reflection, I saw myself flinch.

Instead, I clenched my fists and started looking for an excuse to beat him up surrounded by the public and still keep my good standing. And my job. And my freedom.

Dante continued. "The meteorite, and then our lovely battle, really opened up quite a crevice in the middle of the town. Rather than fill it and start over, they decided to keep it and build up from the bottom. Even the subway system just runs their newest platform through it, on a bridge."

"I'm surprised that it's open," I muttered. "Apollo City doesn't have a good record for getting construction done."

"Mayor Dunbrooke—yes, no longer Assistant Mayor Dunbrooke—used tax credits and cut through a lot of regulation. He had it opened officially at the end of his first full term two years ago."

"I didn't like him much," I said. "But at least he's getting things done."

"That's how most people feel here," Dante assured me. He raised his eyebrows. "But I didn't follow you here to discuss politics."

"If you're here to uphold your part of the bargain, you can forget it," I snapped. "I'll get Mom to help me get the kids back home. Or someone else. Anyone else."

"I didn't know she was alive," Dante said. "If it makes you feel better."

"How else would the hospital receive her blood?" I bit back angrily.

"Our arrangements with the Skarmastad Foundation ceased the year after Draco's defeat. The foundation itself has been shut down, since your friend, Rachel, and her mother, decided not to file the yearly registration. If the hospital did get blood, it was likely an older supply."

"Why didn't you know about her to begin with? Apollo City's Flying Angels case was your project."

"The circumstances which followed had nothing to do with me then. And now, I've gone rogue."

"What?" I frowned.

"I'm still working for SWORD," he said. "But after they discovered Starry Knight's shadow power, I began to see that they were no longer in the business of controlling power."

"They want it for themselves," I said, snorting disdainfully. "Isn't that how it always goes?"

"You've been in law for too long." But Dante smirked, and I could tell he agreed.

"Better than running around coercing people into helping you secure power." I crossed my arms. "Especially considering the price."

He caught the insult and let it slide. "How is Starry Knight?" he asked.

"I don't want to talk about her to you," I replied, anger creeping into my voice again. "I don't care if you've gone 'rogue,' you need to stay away from us."

"You should count yourself lucky that I did approach you," Dante remarked. "If I hadn't, you wouldn't even know she was alive."

"You didn't know either until I rescued her!"

"So? It's not like she was the love of my life," Dante said with a shrug.

He said it so causally I started shaking with rage.

"I'd reconsider hitting me," he said. "Because we're still in trouble. The Matriarch is coming. She'll want Starry Knight back. Even with all the damage that was done to our black site, she won't be delayed for longer than another week."

"I don't want to do anything," I said.

"Your hand will be forced in the end."

I had a feeling he was right. "Tell me about the Matriarch, then."

I didn't like talking with Dante; I would've cheerfully shot him, had I been given the chance. But he was the best source—and right now, really my only source—to learn about his secret society/cult.

After what Mark had told me, and, given that I was likely to come face to face with the Matriarch and her agent minions, I would have to be prepared. I'd thought Grandpa Odd was mostly harmless all those months I knew him; I knew that I could never allow myself to be at the mercy of someone else just like him—or someone worse.

Given that the lady was Raiya's grandmother, there was also a personal element to it.

"She's the leader of SWORD," Dante said. "She founded the company close to thirty years ago now."

"Why doesn't she use her real name?" I scoffed.

"I wouldn't know. I have never even spoken to her directly; all our movements were largely coordinated by a board of directors, but most of them have died or been killed off in recent weeks."

"Let me guess; they were fallen Stars?"

"Some of them," Dante replied, non-committedly.

"Why would she kill them now?" I asked. "Why would any of this matter now?"

"Dr. Harbor," Dante said. "The astrophysicist who led the study."

"Jason's dad?"

"Yes. He was the one, along with your friend over at Lakeview, who found the origins of the star's supernova. A lot changed when SWORD and the Matriarch were able to discern that the black hole was connected to your Starry Knight."

Maybe I need to go and visit Logan again.

Between Jason's dad and Rachel's brother-in-law, I was more familiar with the latter. I thought about the mark on my wrist. Would I be able to go and see him as Wingdinger?

Ugh, I hate *that name.*

I hated it even more knowing Elysian was behind it.

"Why did everything change?" I asked.

"She's not the only fallen Star," Dante reminded me. "Why do you think they wanted to kill the others? They were using them to collapse the barrier between this world and the other realm."

"That's right." I nodded. "You'd mentioned that they wanted to be able to drink the bloodwater from the River of Life."

"Yes." He shuffled his feet. "SWORD wasn't able to get any more power from the others, though, and they died as a result of the testing."

"Why didn't Raiya die?" I asked.

"Likely because of her own power," Dante said. "She has healing powers, correct? That would be a factor."

It made sense. It was time to move on to the other area of concern.

"There's also the matter that the meteorite came from Starry Knight. If she had managed to break through Time's power before, that would make her supernova more powerful than the other fallen Stars' supernovas."

"How would they know about the River of Life?" I asked. "I mean, I knew about it because of Elysian, but he's told me before that he only ever mentioned it to Aleia, Alora's sister, and to Starry Knight, but more in passing. Since Draco wasn't working for SWORD, how would the Matriarch … "

She was Raiya's grandmother—the woman who had married Grandpa Odd. Was it possible he had told her? Or he had notes stashed somewhere?

I thought back hard, clawing through the mess inside of my mind. Rachel told me, before, a long time ago, that Grandpa Odd had bonded with Raiya, and she with him, after the death of her grandmother.

Was it possible she knew too much and Draco had to find a way to dispose of her … ?

161

"It's possible other Stars knew about it," Dante said. "Several Stars remembered Draco. His death caused a lot of celebration. I thought at the time it was appropriate, given that he would not work for us. But lately, I have been wondering if the celebration had more of a personal nature to it." He shrugged. "It's hard to recall after all this time."

"Some things you don't forget," I muttered.

"While others wait for you to rediscover them," Dante remarked.

I glared at him. "Such as?" The last thing I wanted him to do was remind me of what I'd lost.

"Your sword."

"Huh?" *That* threw me off.

Dante smiled. "They couldn't move your sword from where it closed up the portal to the realm of the void," he explained. "So the architect decided to make it the centerpiece of his new mall."

I sighed. "Great."

"At least it's still there," Dante said. "You might need to use it."

"I don't transform anymore," I told him.

"You might need to, if we're going to defeat SWORD and its Matriarch."

"*We're?*"

"Yes. I'm already helping you by telling you what I know."

"You might be lying, for all I know."

"I wasn't lying about your Starry Knight," he reminded me.

"A person doesn't tell straight lies *all* the time," I reminded him. "The best liars tell the truth, and then change one small part of it."

He rolled his eyes. "I was hoping you'd become less of a punk as you got older."

"Nope. Now I'm a punk with a law degree." I was tempted to stick my tongue out at him.

"Great." Dante sighed. "When my boss comes after you, you'll see. She won't be held off forever, even with extensive damages. She's cast aside the façade of keeping the world in check, and she's after it all herself."

"Why?" I asked.

"What do you mean?"

"Why do all the villains want to take over the world? It seems like an awfully big job. And if your boss lady wants immortal life, it would just be even more work."

"Pride, for starters," Dante said. "And likely a host of other reasons, too, like revenge and power, prestige and acknowledgment."

I nodded. "I guess so."

He turned away from me. "There are also the tyrants who just want to destroy things," he said quietly. "If a demon is able to take something that has been made and bend it to his own vision, and even gain pleasure from it, imagine how much better he would feel at its destruction."

I nodded. I could understand selfish evil.

"Keep your eyes open," he said. "I'll try to warn you if I hear something."

"Fine." My fists clenched more tightly, and my teeth grinded together, as I once more found myself joined with him in a reluctant alliance.

"By the way," Dante said. "You really should go and see the new mall. Mikey even wrote a blog post about its opening."

I felt a further sting. I'd never read Mikey's blog, and I never would. Not if I could help it. And I wasn't going to do it just to appease Dante.

But, as Dante walked away, I did decide to go to the mall. I figured I needed presents, and there would likely be a better selection. It wasn't a long walk, anyway, and despite my best front, there was no letting go of how curious I was to see it.

Apparently, it had a name, too. I saw its welcome sign at the corner by Main Street, with the words "Rosemont Mall" tastefully crafted in bold lettering.

The mall itself was built into the ground, two layers deep. As I walked down the large staircase heading down to the final floor, I could read all of the twenty or so shops.

I felt an eerie sense of remembrance come over me as I recalled the battle with Alküzor and Draco, and how I lost so much. It was strange that this place, this place I didn't really even recognize, once housed the hole to a hellish realm.

At the center of it, there was a small platform; surrounding it were carefully crafted gardens and pathways of stone and granite. In the heart of the platform was the Sealing Sword. Even though winter had nearly arrived, small rosebuds still kept their vibrant colors.

As I saw it, I thought I could feel its power beckon to me, as if it wanted to say hello, too, after all this time.

I walked up and gazed at it. The blade of the sword had dulled to a dark gray, while the hilt still gleamed with a golden shadow.

I had a strong temptation to try to take it; I was curious to see if I could more than if I should. I already knew, most likely, that I shouldn't. After all, it seemed to be at home in a place where they celebrated the past.

There was a small plaque at the bottom, where the blade went into the ground, but from where I stood I wasn't able to make out what it said. I didn't want to get any closer.

While I stood there, just looking at the piece of my past, I felt a sense of closure I hadn't felt before.

I knew I was a fallen creature, and I knew that I lived in a far from perfect world. It was better that Alküzor hadn't escaped and cut us off from the Immortal Realm. I had lost a lot in that battle, but I would've lost a lot more if he'd succeeded.

Now, I had a second chance—or at least another chance. It wasn't a new chance just for one thing; things like that rarely, if ever, happened. I had a new chance to be with Raiya, I had a new chance to save the world—but I also had another chance to grow, to change, and to be the kind of person who would try and succeed at those things.

A gust of wind whisked by, and I watched as the rose petals danced, all as I felt a sense of peace and purpose I hadn't felt in a long, long, long time. But as I walked away, I knew I had come to a decision: I was going to tell Raiya the truth, at last.

When I walked into the house, I had an armful of bags, and my back was hurting from lugging them from town. I was tired and ready to relax for a bit while I collected the courage to tell Raiya about us and about what had happened to us.

Before I could do any of that, I was immediately aware of how quiet it was. Silence leapt up at me as I stood in the doorway of my parents' home, and I instantly grew worried.

Recalling Dante's visit to my apartment, I hurried from room to room, completely forgetting to drop off the bags.

"Raiya?" I called. "Raiya! Lyra? Lucas, where are you?"

It was only when I passed by the den that I caught sight of them.

They were outside in the backyard. Lyra and Lucas were throwing mud at each other.

"Hey!" I called, bursting through the back door. "What are you two doing? Mom's going to kill me if you make a mess."

"They're helping me," Raiya said from the far side of the backyard.

I turned to see her covered in mud, just as badly as the kids were, and I frowned at her. "What are you—?"

I stopped. She'd been doing exactly what she told me she was going to do—she was burying her children.

I walked over to her as she finished patting down the last of the dirt. It was a small mountain, and one no loving mother willingly traveled on.

I was surprised to see the settled look on her face. As she ignored me, tending to her graves, I thought about how selfish I was.

I was surprised that she didn't remember *that*. It was, apparently, one of the things that hadn't changed about me.

"Sorry," I murmured, leaning over to comfort her.

Raiya nodded. "I would've loved to know them better before they left for the Celestial Realm," she said.

"You wanted to know them better?" I asked.

"Yes." She smiled and put her hand on the grave before us. "This one is Aria. I thought she would like to be over here, where you can see the whole garden easily."

"You named them." I said it as more of a statement than a question. Probably because it burdened me to know she had gone through such trauma alone.

"Yes," she said.

"How?"

"I would dream about them," Raiya said. "Sometimes very vividly." She looked so sad.

I placed my hand over hers. "Hi there, Aria," I said, my voice very soft. I wasn't sure if Raiya was telling me the truth, but I thought it would be something to at least comfort her.

When you lose someone, someone precious, you lose so much more than just the person. You lose the time, the dreams, the fun, the adventure. The friendship, the whole relationship, and the chance to show it to the rest of the world.

I thought letting her introduce me would help her deal with some of that pain.

But the instant I placed my hand on Raiya's, holding her hand in mine over the grave, I felt a jolt of awareness.

I watched, in stunned disbelief, as a small ghost of a girl appeared and waved back at me, before she began to make funny faces. She was clearly laughing, but I wasn't able to hear her.

Raiya just smiled. "She likes you," she said.

I carefully removed my hand from hers. The little girl waved again, and then disappeared.

It was hard to put into words how I felt. Sad, shocked, surprised, fearful—all of those and more. Thankfully, I remembered what I'd brought home and quickly handed Raiya the bag to hide my discomfort.

"What is it?" she asked.

"I bought some rose bushes," I said. "I saw some downtown, and I thought … I thought you would like them."

She counted the pots, which had been less than ceremoniously stacked into my bag. "You have ten of them here," she said.

"Yeah, they were on sale," I said sheepishly, remembering the moment I'd seen them and felt compelled to buy so many. "Would you like to plant them?" I nodded toward the small grave.

Raiya's face lit up. "That would be wonderful," she said. "Do you want to help me? I can introduce you to them as we go along."

Did I want to help her? *No.*

But I would.

Lucas and Lyra came around and helped us, as we used seven of the ten pots of rose bushes as grave markers. I didn't realize how hard it would be on me, personally, but when Lyra took my arm and clung to it with a sympathetic look on her face, I wanted to hug her. Lucas made a big show of scooping up the dirt for me, too.

They really are good kids, I thought.

The rest of Raiya's brood also seemed lovely.

There was Ian, who loved to build things; Patrick, who loved to climb up trees, and whatever else he could; there was a pair of singing twins, Gretia and Sophia; a rabid snuggler named Phoena; and the smallest one, Lee, who loved to tell stories as much as he loved to hear them.

I told Lyra and Lucas they could plant the other three rosebushes, before I excused myself. As I left, they were already fighting over the third one (Adam would come home and plant it later).

Grief hit me hard as I walked inside the house. Raiya's children, the little ghosts I had gotten a glimpse of, were all lovely children. They had passed over this world, and the world was poorer for it.

I was glad that I'd decided to buy the flowers, even if it seemed like such a small and useless gesture to gird Raiya from the tsunami of anguish she was likely feeling at her loss.

My hand—the same hand that had touched the edges of the world beyond the grave, the same one that bore the mark on my wrist just inches higher—rested over my heart as I made the vow all over again that I would protect those who belonged to me.

"Are you alright?"

I turned to see Raiya, covered in dirt stains, standing in the doorway.

A moment passed between us as we stared at each other. Then, before I could ask, or she could offer, we seemed to run into each other. I grasped onto her, my fingers digging into the back of her shirt as I clung to her.

I breathed in the smell of her hair, felt the smoothness of her cheek next to my stubby one, and heard the strength of her heart beating in accord with my own.

I wanted to tell her. I wanted to tell her the truth, to get out all the years of sadness and pain between the two of us, and move on, on to something so much bigger and better than our individual pains.

"Raiya."

She responded at once to me as I pulled her in closer. Her arms wrapped around me, holding onto me. I saw some of her hesitation and the uncertainty, but it was clouded out by her growing desire. I gazed down at her, my eyes meeting hers, until they treacherously lowered to her lips.

"Hamilton," she whispered, and all of a sudden nothing in the world could stop me from kissing her.

Well, almost nothing.

At that moment, there was a loud knock at the door, and I could hear a familiar voice calling out, "Alex! Alex, are you there?"

The magic of the moment was instantly broken. I still held onto Raiya, but I could tell she was more than sufficiently distracted by the continual banging coming from the front door.

"Who's Alex?" Raiya asked.

Ugh. This is not going to be fun.

"It's a long story," I told her, painstakingly stepping back from her.

☼<u>12</u>☼
Return

Opening the door was the only sure way of saving it. Otherwise, I was convinced Charlotte would break it down; she was pretty determined to get to me.

If only she felt this way when it came to presenting her arguments in court.

"Come on, Charlotte," I muttered as I opened the door. "What are you doing here?"

Sometimes, to me, it seemed as though high school never really ended. At that moment with Charlotte, I felt like I was back in high school, trying to get some of the girls to give up on trying to date me.

"I talked to Daddy about his decision," she said, "and I told him that there was just no way that you could leave the company."

She came inside, not even waiting for me to invite her, because manners apparently didn't matter when it came to stuff like getting her way or anything.

I was peeved, especially since she had ruined a special moment between me and Raiya. And since she had come all the way here, I was sure she was going to ruin quite a few more before she left.

Raiya glanced at me quizzically as Charlotte came in and sat down in the living room, almost like she'd done it thousands of times before.

"Raiya," I said, "please—"

She held up a hand to stop me. "I'm going to go clean myself up some," she said. "I'm sure the kids could use some help, too. Excuse me."

At least she'll be out of the way. Maybe I can get Charlotte to leave before she says anything about us dating.

"Alright." I sounded weak, even to myself.

Charlotte didn't even seem to notice that I was with someone.

Until we were alone.

"Is that your new girlfriend?" she asked.

"None of your business," I said. "Next question. What are you doing here?"

"I'm here to tell you not to quit, of course." She seemed surprised that I'd even asked. "When Daddy told me what had happened, I knew I had to come and beg you to come back to work."

I said nothing in reply. I just looked at her, and then I glanced back in the direction of where Raiya had gone.

The same tests had come when I was younger; I remember the difficulty of the choice between my different lives, between the call of the world and the beckoning of the supernatural.

I wondered how I could've ever thought I was smart. Back when I was a teenager, the choice between the two seemed hard. Looking back on it now, there was no other choice for me.

How could I ever think there was?

"I was angry with you during the Wilson trial," Charlotte continued as I barely paid attention to her, "but I fixed it up. I worked out a deal with the judge, and we're going to get another shot before he decides whether or not to take it to court."

"How did you get Judge Lipinski to agree to another round?" I asked, momentarily distracted at the thought of the surly judge who gave me so many stern looks during court, even if he ruled in my favor. "He's always been—wait, I don't want to talk about this."

"It's nothing terrible," Charlotte assured me. "All I did was—"

"Don't care, don't want to hear," I interrupted. "I'm not coming back to work. Not right now, anyway."

"Why?" Charlotte asked. "Look, I know you. I've known you since college. You don't take a free payday like the one my daddy's giving you, Lexy—"

"It's hardly a free payday. And I've earned the time off," I said. "And stop calling me that, you know I hate—"

"But I need your help! The law firm needs your help. My father needs you." She took my hand.

"Your dad can hire new help," I said. *Or, you know, you can actually try to do a better job,* I thought. I wasn't sure how to phrase that in a polite way, though, so I decided not to say anything. "Look, Charlotte, the truth is … I'm helping out my mom with a case. I came here because I'm trying to help a couple of kids find their parents."

"I thought you didn't like kids, though?"

I shrugged. "I like these kids," I said. "They seem like good kids, too. So I'm trying to help them out. I don't want to go back to work until everything is settled."

And even then, I still might not want to come back.

Between Charlotte and Pharris, there was just too much extra drama at work. My clients' lives had enough drama for me, and I didn't need the added pressure.

Besides, I couldn't tell Charlotte the real reason I was lingering around Apollo City. Who would really believe that I was the target of a shadow organization that liked to perform medical experiments on supernaturally gifted beings, all in hopes of ruling the world or destroying the universe?

I barely believed it. I might've seen it with my own eyes, but it was hard getting used to it again after so many years of trying to forget about it.

"Look, I'll call the firm when I get back to the city," I said. "Okay?"

"What about me?"

Ugh. Here it goes.

"What about you?" I shrugged. "We're coworkers. Just go back to Pittsburgh and do your job. I'll see you when I get back."

She frowned. "You won't help me with the cases then?"

"No. That's your job, not mine."

Charlotte jumped out of her seat. "I can't believe I ever liked you. You are a horribly selfish human being."

She waltzed over to the door and added, "You're a lousy kisser, too!" and then slammed it.

"Right back at you," I grumbled, as I got up to lock the door—just on the off chance she might come back.

It was as I turned around that I saw Raiya.

Raiya stood silently, leaning against the wall. Her arms were crossed over her chest. She glanced over at me. "So … who was that?" she asked.

"No one important," I assured her. And that was the truth. "Just a former coworker." Guilt and shame and embarrassment burrowed into me.

"I see." Her lips twitched, and for a moment I was sure everything was lost.

"Please, Raiya, don't cry; I didn't date her for very long," I said. "There's no point in getting upset about her. It meant nothing. She means nothing to me."

I was shocked when Raiya laughed a second later. A second after that, I was angry. This was a serious subject.

"What's so funny?" I asked.

"She called you Lexy."

"Alexander is my middle name," I said. "I started going by Alex at work. You wouldn't believe how many odd looks Hamilton got. But I can assure you I hate that stupid nickname she gave me. I swear, she probably did it on purpose."

She tried to rein in her laughter some, unsuccessfully. "No, that's not it. I just find it funny, considering the issues you had with Humdinger."

I almost laughed myself, before I realized exactly what she said. The moment seemed to stop time itself, as hope overwhelmed me and fear began to choke me.

She remembered! Is it possible … ?

And then she stopped laughing, and I could see the change on her face as it transformed from one of laughter and joy and was steadily, quietly replaced by a look of gradual horror.

"Raiya—"

She shook her head. Her eyes widened, and it was almost as if I could see all the memories come rushing back. Her hands fluttered at her sides, before they came to rest on her belly … brushed against her IV scars … felt the pain of each beat of her heart, knowing she had survived something so terrible, saying the words was too cruel.

She looked back at me, and then at where Charlotte had been sitting. She suddenly stepped back from me.

"Raiya—"

"No." I saw the tears in her eyes, but before I could catch her, she turned from me and fled.

"Raiya, come back!" I called as I ran outside after her. Before I could get far, I ran into Lucas and Lyra, who were both still covered in mud. "It's not what you … please, don't run away!"

"What happened?" Lyra asked. "Did you hurt her?"

I stared at her, trying to find the right answer to that question. *Did I? Did I hurt her?*

Probably.

"What's that?" Lyra asked, pointing off into the distance.

Turning to see what she was looking at, I saw a bright spark of violet light bubble around a dot against the darkening winter sky.

Raiya.

In the distance, I watched as her shadow blazed, her power returning in full, and flew off into the city horizon.

I sighed. "Trouble," I told Lyra. "Stay here and watch your brother. I'm going to find Raiya."

"No," Lyra objected.

"What?" I glared at her. "There's nothing you can do. Stay here."

"Lyra said no," Lucas said as he straightened his shoulders and stood protectively beside his sister. "And I agree with her. We're Raiya's friends, too, you know."

"We want to help her." Lyra pouted. "Besides, she's a Star, just like us. We need to stick together."

"I'm not having this argument!" I pointed toward the house. "Go to your room! I'll be back later."

I hurried off, desperately aware that I had more problems than my body could account for at the moment.

Something told me I should've taken care of the kid problem first. Unfortunately, the something in question was a surge of light, as two winged creatures grabbed me, one on either side, and I was hauled up into the air.

"What are you two doing?!" I shouted into the wind. My head whipped around to see Lyra and Lucas, transformed into miniature Starlight defenders, complete with wings and wingdings, just like I used to sport.

"We're helping," Lyra said.

"After I explicitly told you *not* to?"

"We're kids," Lucas replied on the other side of me. "We don't know what 'explicitly' means."

"*I* do," Lyra retorted. "I'm just disobeying anyway."

"Well, I'm disobeying too," Lucas argued. He stuck his tongue out at Lyra, and I just groaned.

There was hardly anything I could do as they held me in mid-air.

I would just have to punish them later.

In the meantime, I had to get the upper hand.

"Fine," I muttered. "But if you come, you have to follow my orders and listen."

"Fine," Lyra replied, sounding much like me as a teenager.

It wasn't comforting, but I had little choice at the moment. "Fine yourself," I said. "If you're going to help, at least make sure you're flying in the right direction. "She headed that way, to the left of the Time Tower."

"What's the Time Tower?" Lyra asked.

"The big white tower over there," I told her, patiently, even though inside I was ready to shake both of them.

At the same time, though, it was nice to fly again, even if it wasn't the smoother, wild ride on the back of a dragon, and it wasn't on my own two wings.

I glanced at the mark on my wrist, watching as Lyra held her small hand around my arm. *I don't even know if I can fly on my own anyway.*

And, I admitted to myself, it was nice not to have to do this alone, even if it was with two kids who were, by what I knew of their power, limited in their instruction.

"There." Lucas pointed, and we watched as a familiar violet light plunged through the city streets, leaving a large, smoking gash in the cement.

Sirens started going off in the distance.

I heard them, and others, as we followed Raiya where we could see her.

We lost her quickly enough—which, in all fairness, was to be expected, since she had more power and less baggage at her disposal.

I glanced uneasily at the mark on my wrist again.

Dare I press it to see what power of my own I have?

I didn't want to. I didn't want to be Wingdinger anymore. I wanted to be myself, even as merging the different versions of myself seemed impossible.

For the moment, I decided against it.

That probably wasn't the wisest decision. Even I knew I was being selfish. But I thought I could protect her better as myself. Surely, Raiya wouldn't try to harm me. I thought about all the things she'd said and done since we'd been reunited. She was still largely the same person.

A shrieking cry came from a block over, as I heard glass shattering and building starting to crumble.

"Put me down over there," I said, and amazingly, this time, Lyra and Lucas obeyed.

Just as my feet touched down, a terrible force came rushing through the street, sending rubble and debris flying.

Instantly, Lucas rushed forward, and, crossing his arms in front of us, used his power to protect me.

A long moment passed as the dust settled down; Lucas' barrier held, glowing out an ice-blue aura, making me gape at him in unexpected pride.

When things quieted down, I leaned forward. "Good job, kid," I said, reminding myself of Elysian.

The moment came when I was allowed to get a full view of Lucas' Starlight Warrior outfit. The patterns of the outfit reminded me of mine, only his wings burned blue and his armor was navy.

Lyra was a warrior princess if I ever saw one. Her armor was white, with violet trim and a small lacing of stars pinning back her long, chestnut locks. There was a small scepter in her hand; was it possible that was her weapon?

Lucas beamed back at me. "That's my best trick," he said, distracting me from my thoughts and shoving me back to the battle.

Lyra came up beside me. "Look!"

Raiya's blackened shadow landed several yards away. I had to blink and look twice; it was Starry Knight!

Well, sort of.

She was no longer dressed in the same uniform; her armor, once a dark blue violet, had been burned to black; a dark maroon color, like blood mixed with night, accented her armor. Even her wings were no longer the long, white wings I remembered. They'd turned black, like my original set, though I could tell she had no trouble using them to fly.

"Raiya!" I called, hurrying forward.

At the sound of my voice, her eyes burned a blood-colored power as they glared into me.

I nearly fell over as I faltered. *What is wrong with her?*

Before I could ask her that question, her power exploded around her, encasing her in a bubble of darkened light. I was pushed down, my face hitting the cement of the streets hard, and everything around was hurdled into emptiness. Behind me, I could feel Lyra and Lucas cry out in unexpected pain.

This is what you get when you don't listen! I mentally shouted at them.

Gritting my teeth, I was able to pull myself up from the ground enough to see the street had been encased in a large, gray bubble of empty light.

I felt the familiar pull of a familiar panic. *She's going to try to supernova!*

Over the course of the many battles we'd held, both in fighting off demons and chasing monsters, as well as the final battles between Alküzor and Draco, I'd seen her power, and I knew what it could do.

My heart pushed at me, as if it was reminding me I'd always been able to stop it. It was that courage and faith that let me edge closer to her, as the black-colored light pushed back.

"Here," Lucas called. His shield was back up. He edged his way toward me, while Lyra came over and helped me stand up.

"What's going on?" Lyra asked. I could hardly hear her over the wind racing around us.

"Supernova," I yelled back.

Lucas, clearly struggling to maintain his power, called out next. "Can you stop it?"

"I need to get to her," I said. "Can you do that?"

"I can," he said.

"Let me help," Lyra said. She placed one of her hands on Lucas' shoulder. A second later, a blue-violet glow emitted from her, channeling her power to the shield.

With the help of the kids, it was much easier to get to Raiya than I expected.

I came up to her, grabbing her hand just as Lucas and Lyra's power ceased.

"Here," I called, grabbing onto Lyra's hand. She took hold of Lucas' hand, and together, under the extreme duress of Raiya's attack, we managed to stand.

I saw Lucas reach out and take a hold of Raiya's other hand.

Raiya faltered at his touch.

"Please," I said, "please, don't leave me again." My hand dug into her shoulder, gripping onto her for my balance as much as for my pleading.

I was about to lean in and kiss her when her power began to recede.

Instead of flickering out and dying a gradual death, the power burst out all at once, like a lukewarm explosion clearly cut off but confused.

"Augh!" I yelled, angrily, as I was thrust away by the blast. I grimaced as my body hit the ground hard then ricocheted off the sidewalk.

Away from me, on the other side of the street, Lucas and Lyra were also getting up from the ground. I saw Lyra run over to Lucas and give him a burst of her healing power.

Blinking past the dusty debris in my eye, I saw that Raiya had returned to her normal self. Her head was resting in her hands as she stood there. I watched as unrelenting shame and disappointment discharged around her.

"Raiya," I called, my voice pushed back and quiet against the black and burning streets.

She didn't seem to hear me. Or maybe she did, and that was why she turned away and headed off before I could stop her.

I stood up slowly, wiping the dust and seeping blood off me as best as I could.

At least this time, I had a feeling I knew where she was going.

"Are you okay?" Lyra asked, coming up to me as she held out her hand.

I took it and felt a rush as the pain in my body was absolved. "Thank you," I said.

"Come on," Lucas called. "I think we can catch her!"

"No."

The words were frazzled and harsh against the silence surrounding us. Lyra and Lucas both looked at me, surprised and appalled, as I denied them their request for an adventure.

"No," I repeated. "I have to stop her. This isn't just a battle against a bad guy. This is a battle of the heart—for both of us. I need you to go back to the house and stay safe while I get her."

Lucas began to whine, but Lyra nodded. "Alright," she said. "But bring her back to us. We like her."

I smiled. "I will. I like her, too."

THE STARLIGHT CHRONICLES

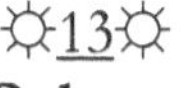

13
Release

When I was a teenager, the back door to Rachel's was always locked, but I found out pretty quickly after I started officially dating Raiya where Rachel left the spare key. I almost never used it, with a few minor exceptions, since Raiya was more often awake in the early mornings when I would come to bother her or to be with her.

This time, I didn't have to use the key at all.

The back door, while it may have once been locked, had been blown in. The wood nailed across the door, boarding it up to easy public access, was splintered open, revealing a small entrance.

I had to suck in my stomach, but I made it through.

It was nothing for me to find my way around the dark house to the stairs. I didn't hesitate any fraction of a second as I made my way to Raiya's room, even though the smell of coffee fumes, sunk into the wood over the years, beckoned me back to a world of happiness.

I sensed her before I saw her. Her room was musty and cold, but I felt the warmth of her soul, and it seemed to make everything more vibrant and lively.

She was sitting on her bed, her legs covered up by her old comforter. There was a quietness about her, an uncertainty; it was a feeling that kept me back, letting me lean into the doorframe. "Raiya."

189

She flinched at my voice, but she managed to find her own. "I guess Rachel didn't do a very good job packing up my room when she moved," she said.

"No, she didn't," I said. I thrust my hands into my pockets, nervously trying to force myself to relax. "It's been seven years," I said quietly.

She only nodded.

"Well, I mean, that means that Grandpa Odd was officially declared dead," I explained, hating myself for rambling. "Rachel and Letty inherited his stuff, or so I heard. It was a lot, too."

"Considering he was an immortal, and he'd been here for centuries, I guess he had a lot of assets hidden around in different places." She tried to give me a smile. "The money probably easily paid off all that debt you were worried about accumulating."

"I know, right?" I smiled. "Mikey told me that Rachel had moved closer to midtown. She's working on expanding her business or something."

"She always wanted to."

A long moment of silence passed between us. I watched, mindlessly transfixed, as she fiddled with her blanket.

"So you still talk to Mikey?"

I shrugged. "Sometimes."

Raiya nodded.

Silence again.

Finally, I broke. "We need to talk."

Raiya arched her brow at me. "Isn't it a little late to worry about dumping me?" she asked.

My temper spiked. "You know that's not what I mean. I want to know what happened to you, and what you know about it. There are more things we're going to have to deal with now that we're here."

"I wouldn't worry about a breaking and entering charge either, if that's something that has you worried."

"I have other concerns. There are other problems that will insist on being more irritating," I told her. "SWORD is one of them. And your grandmother is another."

"You've talked to Grandma Rosemary?"

"Is that her real name?" I snorted disdainfully. "Or does she have some sort of secret dragon name too?"

"She's not a dragon. At least, not literally." Raiya sighed. "I saw her at the hospital."

"Tell me what happened that night. The night that you died." I barely forced out the words.

"I died," she replied simply, and I had to wonder if she was intentionally trying to make me angry.

"What else?" I asked. "Mark told me about your heart."

"Adonaias gave me a new one," she replied, almost dutifully. "What else do you think happened?"

"I might have been able to guess that," I said, "but it's nice to hear it confirmed. There's no need to be snippy about it."

"You're the one who was supposed to find me," Raiya said.

"Well, you're the one who had the gall to leave me in the first place," I countered.

"You can't blame me for that! It took a lot of power to hold off Draco and Alküzor and keep you safe."

"I would've rather died," I nearly shouted. "Especially when I woke up in the hospital and found out you were dead."

She stiffened but said nothing for another long moment.

"They didn't tell me that you came back." I stared at the floor. "Seeing you at the black site the other day was the first time I knew you were alive in seven years."

"I guess it takes some getting used to."

"Some." I hated how unpleasant I sounded.

Raiya slumped forward. "This is terrible. This whole situation has been terrible."

I walked over and sat on the far edge of her bed. "Tell me about it."

Raiya told me how she woke up in the hospital and her grandmother, Grandpa Odd's wife, who had supposedly died twenty-some years before, was there. She had taken Raiya into custody.

Raiya admitted, more than ashamed, that she didn't fight them because she was worried for my safety.

"Why?" I asked.

"Grandma Rosemary told me that you were at SWORD's mercy, and if I didn't cooperate they would let you die."

So she had intentionally kept me from Raiya. That witch.

For Raiya's sake, I decided to hold off on my plans for vengeance—for the moment. "I guess that was easy enough to believe. I know I was in the hospital for several days."

Raiya nodded. "Once I was transported to their research lab, I was able to steal my case file. I knew then I had to fight to escape. But it was too late, and I was so weak."

I was determined to listen, even if I was trying to keep my anger at SWORD in check. I shifted a few inches closer to her.

"Adonaias visited me, at the moment I fainted, and gave me a new heart." Tears welled up in her eyes. "But when I woke up and realized I'd never see you again, that I had gambled my fate away to fear ... and then all the tests and surgeries, all of my babies leaving me before I could hold them, watch them grow ... "

Her voice trailed off as she looked down at her hands, a gesture I had often made myself when I remembered losing her.

Even though the idea of her kids still felt like a weird subject to me, I could sympathize. She had to have been alone, and losing someone she never really met had to have been exponentially devastating.

"Eventually, my body grew weary and stressed to the point where rage and depression were constant, even when I was forced to go to sleep. I wanted justice, but there was none to be had; I longed for comfort, and there was none. It was only recently that I was able to find the strength to begin fighting back. But by then they had me too tightly bound in my own shadows and chains."

I thought of how I'd seen her, huddled in the morgue. I reached out a hand and took hers, squeezing it in my own. Her hands were soft and cold, but I clung to them, willing to impart some of my own warmth.

She tried to give me another smile. "You know, I always wondered if sending out Maia to attack us first was intentional, way back in the beginning. It's so simple to do nothing, even when faced with great evil."

"You *didn't* do nothing," I told her. "You were fighting."

"I might as well have done nothing. I didn't win."

"*We* won," I told her, finally reaching out and tugging her close as her tears finally overcame her strength.

The Raiya I knew was unbelievably strong; I knew she was truly heartbroken if she was crying. And I couldn't blame her. *I* was heartbroken for her, just as much as I'd been heartbroken for myself these past years.

A while passed before I heard her sniffle. "Why? Why give me a new heart, only to have it break?" She closed her fist over her chest, clenching tightly.

I don't remember reaching out; I watched my hands as they extended of their own accord on seeing her pain. I peeled her hand away from her heart and placed it over mine—my own smashed heart, still reeling from the unresolved pain of our tragic parting. While I usually pushed my grief back, or pushed it away, this time I let it sail through me unhinged, let it roll over me like lightning-struck waves, as if I was trying to share it with her, the same as she shared hers with me.

Years ago, I thought that forgetting everything would be the better path; but forgetting only caused me weariness— physically, emotionally, and even on deeper levels. I'd cried out silently, still trying to ignore myself. I'd waited for relief to come, to find an answer to a question I couldn't even bring myself ask—the question of not why or how, but how long? How long would I suffer? How long would I be alone in my own world? How long would I be subject to pain too strong for me to even name?

Looking at Raiya in that moment, I knew I had my answer. I would suffer any time, any pain, anything, all to be near her again. I knew I had never been alone, even as I'd sought to be alone.

"I heard Adonaias say once that you'd been broken," I said. "Maybe … "

Maybe it is my fault you are in such pain.

"Maybe we have been broken for each other, so we can be remade together." I reached up and cradled her face in my hands. "I still need you."

"Hamilton … " Raiya whispered my name as my lips met hers.

How many times is someone allowed a first kiss with the one they love? I wondered, enthralled at the thought as our kiss connected us to the hundreds of kisses before and foreshadowed the infinite kisses ahead of us.

The hand I had placed over my heart tightened around my shirt, and I felt her heated response.

I pushed back her covers and pulled her out of their warmth, determined to have her only cling to me. My hands quickly found her hair, thrusting themselves into their sorely missed softness. Soon I could feel her shiver, but I knew it was not because of the cold.

I tore my mouth away from hers reluctantly, trying to catch my own breath. "I've missed you so much," I murmured, nuzzling her neck.

"I missed you too." She managed to smile this time, and I was more than gratified to see it reach all the way into her eyes.

"We might've changed," I said, "but this sure hasn't. I still want you. I still need you."

"I still love you," she whispered.

Hearing those words from her, the words I had longed for since I lost her, hit me hard. I was shaken from my heart's slumber, as if part of my soul had been dead but was once more alive.

I took her face in my hands and held her, marveling at the feel of her cheek against my palm.

"You are the love of all my lives," I told her, pushing a strand of her hair back from her face. "Nothing has changed that."

"Not even your girlfriend, the one who came to the house earlier?" she asked teasingly.

"She's not my girlfriend. But at least you know that hasn't changed, either," I said. I gave her a quick smirk. "You've always been my pick, even among all my exes."

"High praise, indeed."

"Only for them," I assured her, tightening my grip on her.

"Even if that's the case, I think it's better we don't worry about them again," Raiya murmured back, already falling back under passion's sway.

"My pleasure," I whispered, seconds before I kissed her again.

The spicy cinnamon sweetness of her washed over me, and I was not only comforted, but I felt renewed. She was still there, that girl I'd fallen in love with all those years ago, even if she'd grown into womanhood without me. I was certain of that, and that was just the power we needed to know we could make it—make it despite all pain, all misery, and all darkness.

Raiya sighed contentedly as I cradled her against my chest. "I'm so glad to be home."

I took a hold of her hand and kissed it, catching her eyes with mine. "I'm glad to hear it," I told her. "Because you're never leaving me again."

I was only able to register her soft laugh before I allowed passion to cloud my own mind.

I don't know how long we held each other, talking and whispering and kissing, before we fell asleep. All I knew was that when we woke up, I felt like I was truly awake, as if the smog of the last several years had cleared up, leaving me with the precious gift of hope once more.

THE STARLIGHT CHRONICLES

☼14☼
Fatherly Love

It seemed that I never dreamed anymore, except for very rarely. When I did, it was always frighteningly real to me, and I was pushed out of it wondering just what was real and what was fantasy.

Over the past few years, I'd had only a couple of dreams stick with me to that terrifying degree. One constant dream that came featured a little girl with reddish brown hair and glowing eyes. Sometimes she had a boy with her, too, but this time, as I slept in Raiya's arms, I heard her voice as she spoke to me.

"You're here," she said.

I blinked my eyes, seeing into a dream world. I was in a place that looked just like Shoreside Park at the height of summertime, and I saw her.

The little girl, not much older than five, came running up to me. I caught her in my arms, and she giggled. I felt myself laugh, and she laughed as I twirled her around and pulled her against me. It seemed so natural to hold her, to play with her, to dance with her.

I glanced around to see if her brother was around, but didn't see him.

The little girl clung to my arm. "I'm glad you're here again. I wasn't sure if you would come back."

"Huh?" I suddenly felt cold.

"Ian said he didn't think you liked coming here to see us, since you never said anything or tried to play," the girl said. "But when we saw you earlier, I knew you liked us."

"Ian?" *That's the name … of one of …*

I glanced down at the little girl in my arms. She suddenly looked too familiar to me. "Aria."

Raiya's oldest daughter, the same one I'd seen in my mother's garden, smiled at me. "That's me," she said.

"You're … " I couldn't bring myself to say *dead*, but she was looking at me so expectantly it ushered in my charm reflexes. "Beautiful."

"Just like Mommy?" she asked.

I felt a lump form in my throat. "Yes," I said, "just like Mommy."

"Mommy says I look just like her," Aria said. "Except for my nose. She says I got your nose."

I froze. "My … nose?"

"Yes," she said, pointing to her straight nose, its perky pointedness matching my own perfectly.

"You're mine." Shock hit me hard and fast, leaving me feeling lightheaded.

How is this possible?!

"Of course I am," Aria said, as her arms reached up and hugged me. It was the only thing that kept me together, forcing me to perform.

"And the others?" I asked, barely able to breathe.

"All of them are waiting for you, Daddy." Aria placed her small hands on my cheeks, which were suddenly wet. "We've been waiting for you."

I jolted upright, slamming into the real world.

"They were mine," I muttered. I ran my hand over my face and felt the sweat and tears mixing together. "All of them."

Raiya stirred next to me.

I reached over and ran my hands over her stomach, as if I was trying to find something that had been misplaced rather than lost.

"Hamilton," she snapped. "What are you doing?"

Some part of me realized how irrational I was being. I stopped and slumped away from her, looking down at my hands in something more pervasive than defeat. "They were mine," I repeated, barely hearing her.

At my words, she sat up and looked at me. One look at her, and I didn't need any other form of confirmation.

The lump in my throat from earlier came back with a vengeance. "They were *mine*."

"Yes," Raiya whispered. She leaned against me, trying to offer me comfort in a situation where no amount of comfort could be given.

"How?"

"SWORD was able to get DNA from your blood samples, the ones your dad had scheduled, while you were in the hospital. They wanted to see if they could produce a child Star on their own."

I thought of the small bags Raiya had carried through the site. *Our children.* "It didn't work, did it?"

"No." Raiya's voice nearly broke. "Not the way they wanted it to, anyway. They were all sent to the other realm before they … " Her voice trailed off, and I was left devastated.

"Why didn't you tell me?" I asked.

"You already felt bad about *me*," Raiya said. "I was planning on telling you later on, after … " She shook her head, ducking her eyes away from mine.

"After we were married and talked about kids?" I suggested.

"No. I was just going to tell you later." Even in the low lighting of the early morning, I could see the faint blush across her cheeks. "But if that's something you want, and it's okay if you—"

"Yes." I thought of the little girl—Aria—and how I'd felt having her run into my arms. A new kind of sadness threatened to boil over as I realized I would never hold my little girl in this world. "Yes, that's what I want. God, that's everything that I want."

As I felt the new source of grief swell up inside, I pushed myself into her arms, letting myself sink against her as I released my anguish.

She held onto me, bravely facing the force of my agony, responding to me in love and compassion.

Long, quiet moments passed as I held onto her, trying to work through it all. As I processed my newfound grief on the inside, I barely managed to perceive the world around us. Outside, I could hear the cars passing in the street as the morning bustle began. Through the boarded windows, I could see cracks of dawn creeping up on the distant skyline.

"We really should go back to your parents' house soon," Raiya said. Her voice seemed to echo throughout the room.

"I know," I said, even as I reached out to pull her head onto my shoulder, letting her slide into the crook of my neck. I was glad for the sudden change in topic, even if it was one we would have over and over and likely over again.

"Lucas and Lyra might be worried about us."

"That's a good point, given how they saw us leave." I tried to smile again and found it difficult. "More specifically, how they saw you leave, and left me to chase after you."

"You found me," Raiya said. "Eventually."

"We are in complete agreement on that note. But since seven years is too long to risk it again," I replied, "it's better if you don't leave anymore. Especially like earlier today."

"I'm sorry I rushed out of there, but—"

"No, I can understand that part," I told her. "I'm more concerned with how you used your power. You sort of transformed into Starry Knight again, but it wasn't exactly the same."

Raiya nodded. "I know," she whispered. "And I'm worried about that."

"I think that's a smart position to take on the matter."

"It is. I wouldn't want to end up like my sisters."

That made me worried. "What do you mean?"

"On the other side of Time, in the Immortal Realm, my sisters were imprisoned inside of my star," Raiya said.

"I remember that, and, seeing as how it didn't turn out well, I think it's best to avoid that sort of situation again."

"Good. That's a smart position to take on the matter," she said with a small smirk. "But they weren't imprisoned right away after they decided to join Alküzor and Orpheus. Orpheus wasn't technically imprisoned at all—he was caught up in the supernova, and that's how he more or less wound up in Apollo City, I suppose. The exact logistics of it are a mystery."

"So?" I asked. "What does it mean?"

"Stars—and people—don't always feel the punishment for their transgressions right away," Raiya said. "Sometimes the consequence of bad decisions affect us more on the inside, silently, before surfacing."

"I can see that," I said. "But I can also see it the other way, too. That's how I fell in love with you."

"Charming."

"You weren't, really, when we first met."

"I grew on you."

"That's the point I'm making. You were a surprise I didn't want, and didn't like, but I couldn't ignore you."

Raiya grimaced. "No need to make it sound so terrifying."

"It was." I pressed a soft kiss to her forehead. "But it was a good kind of terrifying."

"You shouldn't distract me," Raiya murmured as I ran my fingers through her hair. I felt her pleasure, though, and I knew she was only half-joking.

Peace and caution settled into me at the same moment. It had been several years since I'd felt this way—like I had something more than a job and career to live for; that I had an actual *life* to live for. The last time I felt this way, my mind couldn't help but remind me, I lost it to SWORD and their scheming. And I didn't just lose Raiya—I lost so much more, too.

I knew I had to take this seriously if we were going to survive together this time. If we didn't survive together, I wasn't going to survive, period.

"Okay," I said, letting her feel the weight behind my word.

"Well then, as I was saying, it takes time for the fruits of our choices to come to the surface. I'm forgiven, but I have to keep my power in check down here," she said. "As do you, of course."

"Otherwise?"

"Otherwise we will need to be stopped, just as my sisters were." She sighed. "The quest for justice often leads to the temptation for revenge."

"I guess, by that logic, that mercy leads to judgment?"

"I'd think you would feel something more along the lines of mercilessness," she replied.

"Makes sense." It was hard for me to imagine *not* killing Rosemary once we managed to find her. I didn't admit (and didn't want to admit) that was the exact temptation I was facing, especially after hearing Aria call me "Daddy" for the first time.

"If I let it get out of control, I could easily transform the way I did and destroy people."

She looked uncomfortable at the thought, and I felt discomfort myself; I didn't know if there was any fallout from her attack on the city earlier. I'd been more worried about her, and about making sure Lyra and Lucas went back to my parents' house.

I gripped her hand. "Everything will be alright," I told her.

She arched an eyebrow at me. I mirrored her look; I'd been right about that before, even if our situation was a pretty terrible way to be right. At least we were together.

"Yes, everything will be alright," she said, "but it might not be that way until we are gone from this world."

"I have more hope than you do regarding that," I said.

"Hope's not going to keep me from hurting other people if my power gets out of my control."

"When it comes to your powers, I'll be here to keep you in check, and you can do the same for me."

"That's hardly going to be enough."

"It's not like we have a lot of other options. Besides, we're good at keeping each other in check. Even if we're a few years out of practice."

"I don't know." She smiled at me. "With all your lawyer training, you might be running circles around me."

"I'll tell you when I get too dizzy."

Raiya gave me a playful punch on the arm, and we finally made the decision, painful as it was, to head back to my home. We had a long day ahead, and between the two of us, at least half of it was going be spent napping.

The other half, for me, would be planning revenge. (Hey, *Raiya* might not have been able to go through it without losing herself, but I certainly had the option.)

THE STARLIGHT CHRONICLES

☼15☼
Agreement

The next few days were nice—almost too nice. There was an all-consuming sense of relaxation around the house, as Raiya was able to remember more, and she worked on building up her strength again.

I was never comfortable letting her out of my sight for more than a minute.

Mark and Cheryl, always up to their workaholic ways, seemed happier, which was odd, because I never thought they would enjoy a full house.

Adam enjoyed getting to make snarky comments as I cuddled up to Raiya, and then he would send suggestive gestures and looks to me when he thought no one else was looking. It warmed my heart to know he was giving me his approval, even if I had to punch him a few times for just how suggestive some of his ideas were, especially for someone who wasn't even a teenager yet.

Lyra and Lucas were happy to see us again. They were especially relieved to see Raiya again; part of me thought that was because she'd been teaching them how to harness their powers, while I generally only served as a short-order cook or a delivery boy.

But I knew that wasn't completely true; while Raiya was napping, I would play video games with them or teach them different games or sports moves. Even I had to admit they were growing on me, and I didn't mind their antics as much as I had when we first met.

Eventually, I even stopped asking Cheryl how her search for their parents was going; she seemed to pick up on this and told me she had found them, but she was still "waiting to see if the parents would respond," promising that I would be the first to know when they did.

I decided not to worry about it at all until they did contact us.

Everything was going really well. It was almost like a real holiday—a real Christmas miracle, even.

So the instant I began to actually sit down and plan a way to ruin all of Grandma Rosemary's dreams and find a way to rightfully condemn her to a small, picturesque corner of hell, it was only natural that Dante would show up again.

Raiya had taken the kids outside to the garden, where, in between marveling at how well the new rosebushes were holding up under the chilly weather, they worked on honing their Starlight defender skills. I was outside, watching them, in half-amusement and half-envy, when I heard a rustling noise behind us.

I turned, just in time to see Dante as he made his way out of one of my mother's neatly trimmed hedges.

"I see you've been busy," Dante said in greeting, nodding toward Lyra and Lucas as they practiced their fighting techniques on each other (with a bit too much enthusiasm for Raiya's taste, I might add, judging from the look on her face).

"Why are you here?" I hissed, blocking him from Raiya's view.

"You seem to be enjoying yourself too much, young Hamilton," he said. "Are you forgetting there's a real world out there, with news deadlines and tabloids waiting for comments on the new superheroes in town?"

I groaned. "But I didn't even—"

He held up a magazine, which had a blurry picture of Lyra and Lucas on it.

"Great." I sighed. "I guess I wasn't thinking—"

"I've noticed," Dante said. "You're lucky I've been able to protect you from the Matriarch. She's upset."

"I can well imagine," I grumbled.

"She wants them, now," he said. "We've been given orders to bring them in."

"No." I balled up my fists. "You touch them, and I'll kill you this time."

"Then you wouldn't have anyone to help protect you from SWORD," Dante countered.

"I'll take my chances, especially since your record is terrible when it comes to protecting me and my family," I snarled.

"Look, for the meantime, let's just agree to the usual terms. We have an uneasy alliance in this. I want to stop SWORD from opening up the space-time continuum in order to gain eternal life and control of this universe. You want to be free, don't you?"

"I'll never be free as long as there is something worth fighting for," I snapped. "My family—and my friends—are worth fighting for."

"Cute, but overdramatic," Dante said as he rolled his eyes.

"We all have our moments," I replied. "I remember some of yours, too."

He frowned. "You still haven't addressed my original claim. We have a common enemy."

"That does *not* make us friends."

"But it does give us incentive to work together."

"I don't understand why you even had me come here in the first place, really. Can't you stage a coup on your own?"

"Like I told you before, it's easy enough. I want you to help me save the universe and stop SWORD."

"How?" I folded my arms across my chest. "How can we even begin to do those things?"

"First, we need to stop the black hole," he said. "That is something your Starry Knight might know more about, considering she's the one responsible for it."

"I'll talk to her about that," I muttered. "She doesn't like you. I don't want you bothering her."

"It's nice to see you want to control the whole situation," he muttered sarcastically. "She'll really like that."

"What about the second part?" I asked. "Stay focused. Tell me how you're planning on defeating SWORD."

"I'll have you know, there are several inside of SWORD who are just as eager as I am to see the current administration fall," he said. "But we are all vulnerable. Remember Martha? Many of us have been coerced into working for SWORD. While I agree family is worth fighting for, sometimes it means making unpleasant sacrifices for them."

I knew he was talking about Mikey when he said it. I doubted Mikey would feel better knowing that. But I could agree that I didn't want to get caught in a situation like that.

"Because of this," Dante said, "it is better that we have someone outside the system that can help us destroy their bases of operation around Apollo City. I couldn't think of anyone more suited to the task than you."

"Gee, thanks." I felt like spitting on him.

"I want the coup to be successful. We can only win if the administration fails in fighting back against us." Dante looked me in the eye. "It's in your interest to defeat them, too. They are looking for your Starry Knight, now that they've caught her radiation pattern once more, and the two smaller Stars, too. Every time they transform, it could tip SWORD off to your location."

"SWORD is getting to be a real pain," I grumbled. "I don't know how it managed to last this long. Surely you guys have other enemies besides me."

213

"As with all things this side of Time," Dante said, "these things which are meant for good can become corrupted. SWORD has seen this tendency accelerated since they won their first big victory at Draco's death."

"He was their original target?"

"One of them, to be sure. There are rumors that he was the reason SWORD had originally been stationed here in Apollo City, even if the company has branched out significantly over the last decades. He was a complex character, with plenty of faces and roles. Now that the Skarmastad Foundation has been disbanded, he and his organization are no longer a threat or competitor."

"I'll keep that in mind," I muttered. "So you want to defeat SWORD before they turn into the business version of Draco, and you want me to help you do it."

"Like I said, it is in your interest to do that. I'm the only one, remember, who knows who you are and where you are, and where Starry Knight is now. And your starlings," he added, glancing over through the bushes toward the kids. "Stopping SWORD means protecting them."

I had a feeling he was right. Martha mentioned to me a long time ago that we were fighting a losing war if we stayed on the defensive. We might be able to outlast the enemy, but we would have to take the fight to them if we wanted to change hearts as well as save lives.

"Fine," I said. "I'll *think* about it. But I want you to leave me and my family alone."

THE STARLIGHT CHRONICLES

"Easy enough," he said, but I shot him a skeptical look. He apparently didn't remember showing up in my apartment last week, I guess.

"And I want Rosemary out of the picture. Sorry, the Matriarch. I want her to pay for what she's done."

He nodded. "What do you know about her?"

"She was Draco's legal wife," I said, thinking of what Mark had told me. "And Starry Knight's legal grandmother." *And she was perfectly okay with destroying innocent lives to further her agenda and gain the power she sought.*

I figured Dante already knew that part.

"So she's the woman he married once he came over to the States," Dante said.

I didn't know much about Grandma Rosemary, and I wanted to make sure Raiya didn't have to recount her time with her any more than seemed necessary. Right now, absolutely nothing was the perfect amount necessary for me. But I was hoping, if I learned more about her, it would help us defeat her.

"It would be best if we move quickly," Dante said. "I know SWORD is still lagging behind in repairs to the black site. It would be an easy strike to take her out."

I glanced back at Raiya, as she helped Lucas and Lyra with their defense techniques. "We might need a little more time yet," I said. "She's not back up to full strength. And I'll have to convince her to help."

"You'll need to see about fixing the hole in the space-time continuum, for sure."

"Yes, there's that."

"See to it you don't take too long. I'll check back in with you soon," Dante said. "I must leave now."

"Yeah, wouldn't want Rosemary to get suspicious of you." I rolled my eyes. "She gives a whole new meaning to 'nanny cam,' I guess."

"She might be an older lady," Dante said, "but she has enough resources to put quite a bit of fear into others. I'm no exception."

I hoped that I would be the exception. So I said nothing as Dante headed out, and I made my way back to where Raiya and the kids were still working and playing. I only stopped when I heard him call out to me again.

"Hey, I have one last favor to ask."

"What?" I scoffed. I didn't want to do him any more favors, especially since I was pretty sure the ones he already wanted me to do were going to be unpleasant and painful.

He tossed me something, something which thanks to all my years on the football team and sports conditioning, I caught.

It was a camera. It was an older model, a bit outdated, and just a little too chunky for my taste. But when I looked at him, I knew it was something that was important to him, not as an agent, but as a father.

"Take some pictures of Mikey and Gwen at their wedding for me this weekend," he said. "I know I can't have a place in his life anymore, but I want to at least know it turned out well for him."

THE STARLIGHT CHRONICLES

☼16☼
The Fabric of Time

It was only after Cheryl and Mark came home, and the kids were in bed for the evening, that I was able to contemplate the matter of the camera once more.

I put it on the coffee table in the living room and stared at it as if it was supposed to be some sort of source of inspiration.

Dante's deal, the one where we get rid of Rosemary, was a necessary one, I supposed. And as for the camera, I wasn't that hardhearted. He had it right; he *had* been the one to point me back to Raiya, even if he'd had some stupid and reckless options for getting me inside SWORD.

That was his trademark, wasn't it? I would never be completely sure of his devotion to anything other than his ideas.

It was a recipe for disaster, and after the fallout from my high school years, I was not looking forward to taking another risk.

Raiya came up to me and kissed me on the cheek. "What are you thinking about?" she asked.

There was also the matter of getting Raiya to agree to this. I looked at her now, and I knew she was too important to me to just drag her into all of this. Besides all the pain from her past she would undoubtedly have to face, there was also the matter of her present concern over her power.

She had to keep her desire for retribution in check. I was supposed to be helping her with that. Not pushing her into a direct conflict which would force her to face that issue head on, largely without preparation.

But we were family. We loved each other, and, knowing her stubborn determination to keep me safe, she would likely follow me even if she objected.

So it was better to just tell her for practical reasons. I could've made a case for not telling her under emotional reasons, but theory is always harder to deal with in practice than in words.

I sighed. "I had a talk with Dante this evening," I admitted.

She frowned instantly. "You really should stay away from him," she told me. There was no love to be found for Mikey's dad in the memories she'd regained, obviously.

"I know," I said. "But he didn't know what had happened to you. Mark didn't tell him about your heart being healed. He thought you were dead."

"He might not have known," Raiya replied bitterly, "but he was still a party to it."

"Rosemary's the one who deserves your anger," I said. "Or at least, more of it."

"We agree with that," Raiya said, "but just because I am angry at her, doesn't mean I am willing to overlook all the pain Dante caused us before that."

"I'm not overlooking it," I said.

"Yes, you are. You're being too pragmatic about it," Raiya said. "It doesn't matter to you what he's done, but you'll help him out here if it means something for you."

"Yes, that's right!" I snapped back. "Because this time, helping him means that I will be protecting you from your heinous grandmother, and Lucas and Lyra as well."

Raiya stilled. I could feel the frustration hanging in the air all around her, entangling itself around me.

"He told me that thanks to your dark transformation, SWORD can track you again. And they know about Lyra and Lucas, too." I began to pace around the room, unsettled. "I can't risk you, or the kids. Principles are all well and good, but they mean nothing if they lead you to a passive front. We have to take a stand on this, and yes, if it means working with Dante to defeat SWORD and save you, and the universe, too, then I will."

Raiya was silent for a long moment. "Alright," she finally said. "But I don't like this."

"If there's ever a written record of this moment, I will make sure that it's included," I retorted. The irritated look on her face told me quite clearly that she wanted to slap me.

I could understand that she wanted to remain philosophically pure, working against evil with the forces of good. But we didn't have much of that at our immediate disposal, and Dante was right; we didn't have much time. But I did still want her on my side. "Raiya … "

"It's fine," she replied curtly.

"Come on, you know you'll do this because it means you'll be protecting Lyra and Lucas." I glanced up the stairs, where I knew the kids were sleeping soundly after their long day of learning.

"I know," she snapped. "But I still don't trust Dante. I don't have to like him, and I don't have to like working with him."

"I don't like working with him either," I argued. "He just seems to know how to make himself indispensable." I crossed my arms over my chest, frustrated.

We were silent for a few moments, before Raiya stepped up next to me. "We're not going to think of a plan if we're arguing," she pointed out.

I nodded, glumly. I took her hand. "I love you," I said, "and I promise you, this would be the last thing in the world we would be arguing about if I wasn't so sure Dante was right about this."

"I'm worried he's right, too," she admitted quietly.

"Alright then," I said. "Let's think of a plan."

"What did he tell you?" Raiya asked, moving away from me. I followed her as she went into the kitchen and began making coffee.

"He told me that your power is connected to the black hole where your star used to be. Rosemary wants to use you to gain access to the River of Life."

"Makes sense," Raiya said. "The supernova ripped through the fabric of Time. It would be seen as a black hole here, instead of an entrance to the Immortal Realm."

"Do you think her plan would work?"

"Easily," she said, sadness in her voice. "It's a good reminder not to indulge in my desire for vengeance. Evil is a choice we face, and with every choice, it feeds it. If I get too careless, it could easily tear open the black hole and devour the world."

I'd forgotten what a talent Raiya had for painting, even if it was just using her words.

"How do we stop it then?" I asked as she handed me my mug. "And then, how do we stop her?"

"We'll have to close it up," she said. "That's the easy part."

"Easy? Taking on a black hole is easy?" I nearly spit out my coffee.

"The fabric of Time is very powerful," she said. "Shouldn't take more than a little blood to sew it up, even though it'll still be a weaker spot in Alora's—"

"So the fabric is a real thing, then?"

"Yes," Raiya replied. "Don't you remember Alora talking about it?"

No.

"When my star exploded, we passed through Time's barrier of protection around the world," Raiya explained. "Instead of just tearing through it, a small patch of it broke off. It was reborn with us in this realm."

"So … you have it?" I asked.

"Yes. I hid it," Raiya said.

Despite the pressing situation we faced, I was intrigued. "Where did you find it?"

"When I was first coming into my powers," she said, "I didn't know what was happening. I was young, only seven when my parents died. Grandpa—sorry, Draco—taught me what I needed to know about my powers. But the first time I used my powers, successfully, I found the fabric of Time."

She stirred creamer into her coffee as she got lost in her memories for the moment. "Or maybe it was more that it found me."

I frowned. "Where is it?"

"In one of my paintings." Raiya glanced over at me. "I hid it under several layers of my power and my paint. Once we get it out of there, it'll be easy enough to call St. Brendan and see about returning it to Alora."

"We'll get to go up and see St. Brendan? And Aleia, and Alora?" When Raiya nodded, I grinned. While I had been desperate to forget my pain, I'd forgotten just how many pleasures I'd tried to throw away, too.

"I didn't see the painting while we were at Rachel's. I was wondering if you could take me over to see her," Raiya said.

"You want to go see Rachel?"

"Sure. I've missed her."

"She'll be thrilled to see you." I glanced over at the calendar. "She'll be especially thrilled, most likely, because she's the one who's catering Mikey and Gwen's wedding. She might need your help."

Raiya's eyes lit up. "Can we go and see her tomorrow?"

"Absolutely," I said. "We'll need to go shopping anyway. I didn't get a gift for Mikey yet."

"That would be wonderful," Raiya said. "And I'll find all my stuff, too. Once we have the fabric, we can call St. Brendan and find a way to protect it from SWORD until he gets here."

"Well, that's good," I said. "See? Plan half-formulated, problem half-solved."

"The other half is harder," Raiya pointed out.

"There are reasons I'm not optimistic," I said. "And you're one of them."

She smirked. "It is my job to keep you grounded."

"Grounded, not ground up."

Raiya shrugged. "Same thing, some days." She took a sip of her coffee, her eyes never leaving mine while she stared at me over the rim.

I laughed. "This is going to get old one day."

"We might enjoy it more when we're older."

It was too much. I plucked the cup out of her hands and then kissed her. "I can't wait to find out."

"In the meantime," Raiya murmured delicately, "we still need to take care of SWORD so we can protect Lyra and Lucas."

"And you, too." I released her and went back to my own cup of coffee.

"I'm more worried about them. How is your mom's search coming for their parents?"

I shrugged. "Don't know. I guess they've grown on you?"

"Of course. They're sweet kids."

"When they're not trying to kill each other."

"Well, yeah." She giggled. "But they do seem to like learning. They're picking up their skills pretty quickly."

"They've been hanging around me for a while now. I suppose it's only natural."

Raiya rolled her eyes.

"In all seriousness, though, I think we're going to have to stop Rosemary, and we'll likely have to do it before we can find their parents," I said.

"I agree."

Her answer came too quickly for comfort. I knew what she was thinking. "We have to be careful about her."

"Make it look like an accident, right?" Raiya joked, but the emotions swimming to the surface told me a different story.

It was time for a different approach. "It's not my preference, but if we can capture her anyway, and give her over to Dante, it will be enough to bring her to justice. He's not happy with her so-called leadership, especially since it includes blackmail against his family and bribery with power."

"She's more powerful than Dante. She could overcome him."

"Even though I am inclined to agree," I said, "I am willing to stake my bets on Dante. He gave me a camera earlier, so I could take pictures of Gwen's wedding."

"What's that got to do with power?"

"So I think he's got his own reasons for wanting us to defeat her and asking us to help. The fact is, he promised to leave us alone—and the kids, too—if we helped."

"Right. What if he doesn't keep his promise?" Raiya asked.

"We'll deal with him then, and we'll teach the kids how to deal with him if he comes back when we're not around," I said. "Believe me, I enjoy punching him. It won't be a problem, if he knows what's good for him."

"So if we capture Rosemary, we'll be able to shut down SWORD?" Raiya asked, clearly trying to get my mind focused on other problems.

"I don't think so, which is the other reason I think working with Dante isn't a bad—okay, completely bad—idea. He told me that Rosemary is old. He suspects that she hated or harbored something against Draco, since they were married. She's here, searching for you, and now Lyra and Lucas, too."

"So?"

"So, even if we capture her, SWORD still has other branches and more agents at their disposal. Dante says there are plenty who want to break free from the Matriarch's grip. Remember Martha—you know, Mrs. Smithe? She was one of the people they coerced into helping the company."

"That means he'll be their new leader?" Raiya frowned.

I shrugged. "If nothing else, he'll be able to set us up in a new life that's free from SWORD."

"I don't like this," she said, staring off into the distance. "This is not going to permanently solve anything; this is just going with the lesser of two evils."

"We are supposed to be the ones who hope," I said. "And I have more hope that Dante will keep his word than Rosemary will repent of her power lust."

Raiya sighed. "I suppose you're right. We can't keep running from Grandma Rosemary."

A rush of adrenaline hit me. It was ever a relief and a challenge to win against Raiya.

She glanced over at me. "How are we going to capture her?"

"Let's talk to Dante again before we have to worry about that," I said. "In the meantime, we have something else we need to worry about.

"What's that?"

"Making you look presentable for Rachel, and Mikey and Gwen's wedding," I said.

"Excuse me?" Raiya put her hands on her hips. "What do you mean, 'presentable?'"

"I love you, and I think you're beautiful," I passionately declared. "But after seeing you waltz around here in my mother's old clothes, I almost miss your Rosemont uniform."

"Hey!"

"Hey nothing," I said firmly. "We're going shopping tomorrow, and that's the end of it."

☼17☼
Reunion

"The end of it" actually ended with me getting a headache. It was well worth it. Raiya cooperated with me, eventually, and I got to guilt her for a few hours as I complained about the bump to the head I sustained while wrestling with her.

And for what it's worth, I had been telling her the truth. I loved Raiya and she was beautiful. But there was something even more magical about her once her hair was trimmed and I forced her into clothes that fit her properly, both in body and in personality. She seemed more confident, and I could tell she was more comfortable.

Which came in handy, since Lyra and Lucas had *decided* to tag along with us, and they were a handful.

"Ooh, I like that," Lyra said, tugging on the new sweater Raiya had on.

"Careful, then," I snapped. "You don't want to ruin it by pulling on it."

"I'm being careful," she insisted. She stuck her tongue out at me.

"We can get you one just like it," Raiya told her, which got Lyra excited again.

"I want a game," Lucas whined. "Can I get one of those games so Adam and I can play together?"

"No," I said. "We're trying to get you home to your parents. You don't know when Cheryl will find them."

"She said she's waiting on them," Lucas huffed.

"It's not our fault you can't seem to get to them," Lyra added.

"We're doing the best we can," I shot back. "In the meantime, you can get along just fine with Adam's stash of games. I know he's got a lot of mine in there, too, so there's plenty to go around."

"Some of them are pretty violent as it is," Raiya added.

I nearly laughed at that, but wisely said nothing.

"I'm hungry," Lucas said. "I want to go eat."

So easily distracted … it's a good thing I didn't give and buy the video game. I shook my head, though whether it was at Lucas' inattention or at my frugality, I wasn't sure.

"Are you ready for lunch?" Raiya asked the kids, and instantly they began hopping up and down with different suggestions.

I stepped in and stopped the argument. "Let's just get there first, shall we?"

"I'm looking forward to seeing Rachel again," Raiya told me as we made our way toward Rachel's new café.

Recalling the awkward parting Rachel and I had reluctantly shared, I could only nod. I hoped Rachel was in a forgiving mood. I wouldn't blame her if she wasn't happy to see me. I knew I'd left her as much as I'd given up on Raiya.

Rachel's new restaurant came into sight as we headed down the street. I was impressed; I had seen the pictures on the Internet, but I hadn't really expected it to make my heart clench the way it did.

I still missed the old familiarity of her previous location. Rachel's café—now titled simply, "Rachel's,"—was a masterpiece of modern construction. It was nearly the opposite of the old house. The new place had simple, bold lines, with patterned glass windows that let in all the winter sunshine.

It might've looked different on the outside, but walking inside was the same.

As soon as I walked inside, the winter air disappeared and the feeling of finding home came rushing at me. The welcoming sensation warmed me all the way through, inside and out. I let it surround me for a long moment, as Lyra and Lucas immediately headed for the confectionary display.

"Dinger!"

I grinned as I saw Mikey approaching. *Even the catcalls are the same.*

I could feel Raiya's hand tighten around mine anxiously; I supposed it had to be hard, reintroducing yourself after you had been declared missing and/or dead after so many years. I squeezed her hand back reassuringly.

"Hey, man," Mikey said. "I was wondering if you would come around."

"You know I couldn't resist Rachel's," I said. "Especially when there are so many good things to celebrate." I glanced over at Raiya.

It was then that Mikey noticed her. His eyes went wide, and then he glanced at me, looking for a confirmation.

I nodded.

"I guess my dad got a hold of you," he said slowly.

"Yep. Several times, actually."

"It's nice to see you again … Starry Knight," Mikey said with a shy smile, which Raiya returned. "I hope Dante didn't cause you any undue trouble."

"He's more of the messenger," Raiya assured him kindly. "It's nice to see you again, too. But please stick to 'Raiya' while we're here."

Mikey seemed to relax. "I'll try to keep it as normal as possible," he said. "Gwen and Tim are coming. Rachel's giving us cake samples today, to see what kind of cake we'd like."

"Tim?" I asked.

Mikey broke out into waves of laughter. "Oh, yeah," he said. "Tim Ryder, your favorite. I forgot all about that. This is going to be hilarious!"

"Who's Tim Ryder?" Raiya asked. I could tell from her expression she was trying to think of the exact memory when I gave her a hand.

"Tim liked Gwen when they were doing *Romeo and Juliet*," I said. "He dropped out of school and went into the army, like, what, ten years ago or something?"

"About," Mikey said. "He finished his tours overseas with the army and got the government to pay for his college degree. He's got a double major in business and theatre from the city college. That's why he's a good business partner for Gwen."

It wasn't hard to regret my teenage immaturity from so many years ago. But it was really hard *not* to think that Tim had accomplished much more than I'd expected.

"Is he Gwen's best man, then?" I asked.

Mikey surprised me by nodding. "Yep." He laughed again.

"I don't get why you think this is funny," I said. "If anything, you're the one who has to worry now."

Mikey laughed. "No, he's married. His wife is military, too, and she's finishing up one of her tours in South Korea right now. But I've met her a few times, and she's more than capable of keeping him away from Gwen. Not that she needs to," he added vehemently, as he saw the teasing look on my face.

"Good to know."

"I wouldn't upset him if I were you," Mikey said. "He's pretty strong."

"I'll take your word for it." I thought about my own forage into kickboxing and karate. *I could take him.*

"Hey," Lucas called as he came bouncing up beside me. "Are we going to get food? I'm hungry, and I know what I want."

I handed him my wallet, perhaps foolishly. "Well, then, go get your sister and order something. Make sure we can see you at all times, got it?"

"Got it." Lucas barely nodded before he skipped away.

Mikey eyed me curiously. "Are those your cousins or something?" he asked.

"No. They're lost, and Cheryl's working on tracking down their parents," I said. "The boy's Lucas, and his sister is Lyra. You've got to be nice. And keep it clean. They're minors."

"Relax, Dinger. I'm better with kids than you are, remember? I'm the one who has to work with them." He grinned. "I gotta say though, for a moment I wasn't sure … "

"Wasn't sure of what?"

He shrugged. "They look a lot like you," he said. "I thought maybe they were related to you."

"I don't think so," I sneered.

"Can we join you?" Raiya asked, turning Mikey's attention away from me.

"Over here," Mikey said, gesturing to a booth tucked into a more private corner. It was at the far end of the bar. "Yeah, come on and sit down. Rachel's going to be finished getting all the cake samples ready."

We started walking over when Raiya stifled a laugh. "That's appropriate," she murmured as we made our way over.

"What?" I asked.

"The painting on the wall, behind the table."

I glanced up to see she was right; hanging up right behind the booth was the painting Raiya had given to Rachel for her wedding all those years ago, the one featuring the tragic lovers. I could still picture Grandpa Odd as he made his speech, telling the story of the Weaver Girl and the Herder Boy, and how they were forced apart, only allowed to see each other one night a year.

It was, I'm sure, pure coincidence that I gripped more tightly onto Raiya as we made our way over.

Another display also caught my attention; Rachel had a bookshelf display for Gwen's *Soldiers of the Stars* series. I decided not to mention that to Raiya for a good while.

The bell above the door rang out once more, and almost as if I knew an awkward situation had arrived, I turned.

And there she was. Gwen came into the restaurant. I hadn't seen her in several years, but she looked a lot like her high school self; her honey-brown eyes were wide with excitement, and her auburn hair was pulled back. She glowed in cheerful anticipation as she looked around for Mikey.

The cheerfulness went away the instant she spotted me. A defiant and guilt-ridden façade, a waterfall of different emotions, spilled over her expression, and I had to wonder if Raiya and Mikey couldn't see it, too.

"Hammy." She reached out her hand to me, like we were business colleagues or something. "Nice to see you again. I didn't expect you … "

To come. At all.

The words were unspoken, but they were clear.

"So soon?" I finished, getting one little, innocent, barely noticeable strike in before I resolved to behave myself. (Raiya caught me and kicked me under the table.) I shook her hand and then turned to face the grown-up version of Tim Ryder.

He'd gotten taller, or at least he stood up straighter. He didn't have acne anymore, and he seemed to grow into his face-shape; if I hadn't known it was him, I might've assumed he was a normal person.

He hadn't lost his instinctual fear of me though, despite all the other changes. Tim seemed hesitant as he waited on me to respond. I quietly decided Mikey had been right; Tim would easily be able to knock me out if he wanted.

I reached out a hand to him. "Hey, Tim, nice to see you again."

He nodded. "Thanks. Nice to see you too, uh, Dinger."

"So, you're Gwen's best man? Or is maid of honor the better term?"

Tim smiled. "Either or."

"Cool. I'm Mikey's best man," I said. "But hopefully we'll be going down the aisle separately. I don't think we'll both be able to fit, with your shoulders and my ego."

I felt much better when he laughed. "Good point," he said, already much more at ease.

Tim came over and I introduced Raiya to him. While I did so, I noticed the look exchanged between Gwen and Mikey. Gwen was clearly just as stunned as I had been. She was one of the few people who knew more of the truth of what had happened to me at the end of my junior year.

She continued to give us odd looks as we settled into our seats.

"So, Gwen," Raiya said, "tell us how Mikey proposed."

Clearly caught off guard, Gwen seemed to struggle to find words. "He proposed to me on the stage at my theatre workshop," she managed.

"I helped with the lighting," Tim said. "She never saw it coming."

Mikey nodded. "I had to surprise her, or I wouldn't have been able to get her to say yes."

We chatted, some of it nervously, but for the most part we were able to keep it going smoothly. Raiya and Tim hadn't crossed paths enough that it mattered, and Mikey and Gwen seemed to have a genuine understanding of each other. He was good at protecting her from her imagined fears regarding me, and she was good at letting him know when she needed help.

I kept an eye on Lucas and Lyra while we ate. For once, it looked like I wasn't going to feel like a bad parent; they were eating their desserts quietly.

"Do you think we should make sure they order something healthy?" Raiya whispered to me.

"Ugh … "

Okay, never mind about that "bad parent" thing.

"They're fine. We're just getting dessert, too, aren't we?" I turned back to Mikey. "You said Rachel was catering for free, right? Does that include the samples?"

"You know it. She's finishing up in the kitchen, with Jason's help," Mikey said. "He's her professional baker now, Dinger, so you don't have to make that face. There's no need to worry about getting off-tasting stuff."

"What kind of cake are you thinking of getting?" I asked.

Mikey grinned. "Whatever which one tastes the best, of course."

"Of course," I said.

Before the teasing could devolve into a full-blown argument (which I would've won), Rachel came out of the kitchen.

She was carrying a full tray of cake slices, and I could just hear Jason's voice behind her as he said, "I don't think you should be carrying that—" before the kitchen door swung shut.

Rachel laughed, clearly still prone to cheerfulness. "My daughter can handle it," she said, still talking to Jason, apparently, even though she'd shut the door, "just like she will for the next four months."

As she turned to face us, I honestly didn't know who had the more surprised expression; Raiya stared at Rachel, and Rachel stared back.

The tray dropped from Rachel's hands.

Mikey's cake samples smooshed across the floor, with several plates smashing.

Raiya and I hurriedly jumped forward. I could hear Jason calling, "Told ya so!" from the kitchen, before I assumed he ran to get a broom and dustpan.

Rachel looked at Raiya as she knelt beside her. "You're back," Rachel said. Her face, framed in braided pigtails, glowed with awe.

"You're pregnant," Raiya said back.

I saw the quick expression of grief on Raiya's face. *Is she going to be okay?*

But before I could worry about it, Rachel reached over and grabbed Raiya, pulling her into a hug over the spilled cake slices. She was laughing and crying and babbling all at the same time. Raiya grasped her back and tucked herself into Rachel's embrace more tightly.

People stared, and I just said, "Hormones, right?" (I don't think they appreciated my humor on the matter.)

It was about forty minutes later that Rachel came out, cleaned up, and joined us. She sat with Raiya and me at a separate table, with our own selection of treats, as Gwen, Mikey, and Tim began tasting a fresh round of samples.

"I can't believe it's you," she said to Raiya. "You look so good, too. Your hair, and those clothes! It's perfect for you."

I sent a smug look toward Raiya as I helped myself to another bit of cake.

"I can't believe that Hamilton managed to find you in a hospital in a Jane Doe mix up," Rachel said. Her eyes were sparkling with added excitement at my fake cover story. "It sounds just like a romance novel."

I recalled how Letty, Rachel's mother, had named Rachel after a character in a romance novel. I never realized before that moment how much that suited her.

I thought about telling her to name her child after a scientist, but decided against it. It was just as well that I didn't; she already had a name picked out for her baby.

"Violet," she told us, after Raiya asked. "I thought you would like it," she said to Raiya.

"It's less weird than my first name," Raiya said.

I gave her a quizzical look, before she whispered, "Violet is my middle name."

"Oh." *Did I really not know that?*

"She's due in April." Rachel rambled on, telling us all about her business and her baby and her general complete happiness now that Raiya was back. I was glad she didn't ask much about me; I didn't have much worth repeating.

Mikey, along with Gwen and Tim, eventually slid out; they had to go back to work or something. I didn't know what exactly, but I did remember that it was a legitimate excuse. I did remember, however, that they picked strawberry cake with white chocolate icing for their cake.

Something to look forward to, you know.

Rachel met Lyra and Lucas after a while, when they started getting fussy about being bored and having stomach aches from eating too much sugar. (Do kids actually get those?)

I got a chance to catch up with Jason, while Rachel and Raiya continued to talk. I could tell Raiya was busy keeping Rachel off more painful or terrifying subjects, and it wasn't easy.

When I finally sat down again, Rachel had just mentioned Logan.

"You should go and see him," she said. "He's graduated with his doctorate now, and he's become a part-time lead instructor at the college, alongside Jason's dad."

"I'd love to see him again," Raiya said. "Hamilton and I were thinking about going to see him again soon, weren't we?"

"Uh, absolutely," I said. "We enjoyed the observatory a lot when we were in high school. Good date nights, you know."

Rachel eyed me carefully. "So, are you two together?"

"Yes," I asserted proudly. "And I'm never letting her out of my sight again."

Rachel smiled. "I'm glad to hear it." She turned to Raiya. "Will you be around in April? I'd love to have you come and stay with us for a while. You'll be able see your new niece then."

I know Raiya loved Rachel, but the thought of a baby right now was more than devastating to both of us. I could tell Raiya was having a harder time in replying, so I answered for her.

"Well, Raiya and I are helping Lyra and Lucas find their parents," I said, before explaining who they were and how they'd wound up in my apartment one day. "Once we've taken care of that, we can certainly come visit more often."

"You're living in Pittsburgh?" Rachel asked.

"Yes," I said again. It was better to keep the story simple. "I have a nice apartment in the city. It's near some of their better museums."

"Oh, really? Sounds lovely." She reached out and took ahold of Raiya's hand. "I'm so happy you're back. I just can't believe it."

"It is hard to believe sometimes," Raiya said. She smiled for Rachel, but I knew there was a darker truth behind her words.

Rachel laughed suddenly. "This must be the week for people coming back from the grave."

"What do you mean?" I asked.

"Well, we got Grandpa's final statements in the mail today," Rachel said. "So the last of his money and assets have been accounted for and they've been sorted out to the recipients." She shook her head. "He must've been losing it toward the end. I can't imagine how he managed all of those accounts and all that money. It was a fortune. And to think, I was worried about paying your medical bills!"

"Grandpa did have his secrets," Raiya said easily enough.

"I'll say. Besides that, I also saw a woman walking around here who looked just like Grandma Rosemary would've, had she lived."

Raiya and I exchanged uneasy glances.

The Matriarch is on the move.

"I don't remember what she looked like much," Raiya said. "Are you sure it was her?"

"Oh, I'm sure it wasn't," Rachel replied, dismissing it. "But the lady had the same haircut—really short, curled in at the bottom, with the one side covering her cheek. She had a similar facial structure, with that perpetually pinched look."

"I remember that look," Raiya muttered somberly.

"I still have the picture Grandpa had of her, the one that he kept on his bedroom wall. But, like I said, I know it wasn't her."

Raiya and I nodded, blandly, but I knew what we were both thinking, especially as I saw Raiya's face, for all its lack of sunlight in the last couple of years, whiten, ever so slightly.

I cleared my throat and took another sip of coffee, trying to smooth over the situation. "Your barista skills haven't changed at all," I said. "Thank goodness for that."

"Still the best of the best, right?" Rachel giggled. "I thought you still liked it."

"I always did," I said. "It was just hard … after … after everything."

She nodded. "Let's not talk about that again," she said quietly.

"There is one thing I have to ask you, Rachel," Raiya remarked. "I was wondering where all my stuff is? Is it packed up or put away somewhere?"

"I couldn't do much," Rachel admitted. "I packed up your supplies, and your clothes, and that was about it. I have a lot of it at my house, but there's plenty more at the café still."

"None of my paintings?"

While I was pretending to check my phone, I held my breath. We needed to know where Raiya's painting was, the one with the fabric of Time hidden inside of it.

"I didn't touch any of them. They were all too beautiful and sad. Sorry."

"Oh." Raiya glanced over at me, nervous. "It's okay, Rachel. I was just wonder—"

"Well, I did actually send one to Hamilton," Rachel said as she suddenly recalled. She turned to me. "Didn't Mikey give it to you last weekend? I know he was going to see you when he had to go to that teacher's union conference."

I recalled the painting I had flung away in a moment of outrage and inner turmoil. "Oh, yeah. I did get that one."

"I had it framed, because I thought Raiya would've wanted that to be done, but … " Her voice trailed off, before she shrugged.

"So it's back at your apartment?" Raiya asked me.

"Oh, well, Lucas actually packed it," I said. "It's at my parents' house."

Before Raiya could chide me for my forgetfulness, Rachel laughed. "Well, it's a relief to know you got it. I know Mikey's excited for the wedding, so his head's been all over the place lately. Last week, he … "

The time we had together went on like this for a long while before I knew it was time to head out. Rachel had to get back to work for the dinner rush, and we were likely driving Lyra and Lucas crazy by staying there for so long; either that, or they were going to bankrupt me for all the money they spent.

Rachel hugged Raiya as we headed out. "I'm so happy," she said. "I'm so happy to see you, and I'm so happy that you and Hamilton found each other again."

"Me, too," Raiya said. As she hugged Rachel once more, she glanced over Rachel's shoulder to look at me.

A rush of longing—not just longing, but belonging—ran over me. "We'll see you at the wedding," I said as I waved good-bye.

THE STARLIGHT CHRONICLES

☼18☼
Double-Crossed

"I can't believe it was here all along," Raiya said, still radiating happiness as we walked back to my parents' house a few hours later.

We'd managed to get some good shopping in, including a gift for Mikey and Gwen that I knew for sure wasn't on their registry list—crystal candlesticks, which I promised Raiya I would put in with a bunch of cash so they couldn't complain we didn't get them a toaster or bread maker instead.

I felt a tug on my sleeve. I looked down to see Lyra smiling up at me. "Thank you for all my stuff, Hamilton," she said.

"No problem," I said, reaching over with my free hand and ruffling her hair. "It's the least I can do. You and your brother must have a lot of patience to be able to wait for my mom to find your parents."

"I miss them," Lyra said. She giggled. "But I'm happy you and Raiya are here. I like hanging out with you."

"Me, too," Lucas said as he came up to the other side of me. In his hand was the bag with his new game in it. (Yes, I gave in. Or gave up. One of the two.) "You're cool."

"Well, I think you're pretty cool, too," I replied.

"Really?" The smile on Lucas' face was huge.

"You sure are," Raiya said as she took his hand. "But let's hold hands as we cross the street."

Lyra reached for mine, and the instant she took a hold of my hand I felt a warm wave of contentment.

For a moment, we seemed like a real family. I wondered at that, floored by the rush of contentment I felt come from my own heart. My hand squeezed around Lyra's as we came up to my house.

"Here," I said to Raiya. "Let me take the bags inside. You can go and get the painting."

It took her less than a second to dump her bags into my hands.

"Do you have them all?" Lyra asked. "I can take some." She reached over and grabbed a couple from the top.

"Thanks," I grunted. *Maybe I did buy too much today.*

I shook off my doubt. Raiya had new clothes, and the kids were happy and settled. Next time, I vowed to myself, we would take the car.

"Can we go play in the backyard?" Lucas asked. "I want to see if Raiya can teach us some more fighting moves."

"I don't know," I said, looking up at the sky. It was getting dark, and I knew it was supposed to storm this evening. For the first time this month, Apollo City was expecting snow.

"How come you never teach us anything to do with our powers?" Lyra asked, as Lucas began pouting.

I sighed. "I don't think I'd be a very good teacher," I told her. I thought of my sword, stuck forever in a place where the world had been wedged open. "Lucas was right. I'd turned my back on the prince when I was younger and in pain. It's been so many years."

I glanced up at the window to my room where the painting had been carefully placed with the other things I'd packed. "Besides, Raiya's the better teacher. She's had a lot more formal training than I ever did."

Even if it was with Grandpa Odd, a psychotic villain who tried to set free one of the most evil monsters in all creation.

"You love her, don't you?" Lyra asked. "I can tell."

"If you can tell, why are you asking me?" I gave her a playful smirk.

"It's just nice to hear it," she said. "My parents always act like that, you know. Lovey dovey, with googly eyes. I'm used to it." She frowned. "I guess I took that for granted."

"We all take some things for granted." I was just about to assure her that Cheryl was just waiting on her parents to contact her when I pushed open the door.

Only to be met with the shock of my life.

SWORD agents, several of whom I did not recognize, and Dante, all stood in my parents' living room; they had their weapons drawn, though some were not aimed at me—they were guarding Adam and my parents, who were bound to the couch.

Raiya was still, but shaking, as she stood by the stairs.

"What's going on?" I asked. Instinctively, I blocked Lyra and Lucas from their direct view. "What are you doing here?"

"They're here at my order, of course."

I jerked my attention toward the far end of the room at the sound of the scratchy, bitter, old-woman voice.

Standing back from the window, I finally came face to face with my enemy.

As she turned to face me, I was instantly reminded of an older version of Pharris. Her hair was white and cut in a bob style, with the longer hair curling in the front and guarding the left half of her face. From all the extra frown-line wrinkles, I could tell she was not the kind of person who smiled or laughed a lot. Unless it was an evil laugh.

Even now, her mouth was pulled down into a severely pinched frown.

"Rosemary," I grumbled.

"*Tsk, tsk.*" She shook her head. "Hardly a proper greeting, young man."

Cheryl took the time to shoot me a glowering look. It seemed that even power-hungry kidnappers deserved some degree of politeness in my mother's house.

"You'll have to excuse my poor manners. I wasn't aware that you kidnapping my family warranted manners on my part."

Her eyes narrowed viciously. "Like it or not, I'm still the grandmother of your soon-to-be bride, am I not?"

"You're not going to be invited to the wedding," I replied. "I wouldn't worry about it."

"Hamilton," Raiya whispered. "Please."

I saw the blatant fear in her eyes, and I tried to calm down. I eased back into the doorframe. Rosemary had us cornered; she might get to me, but she wasn't about to capture Lucas and Lyra. Behind me, I could tell the kids were reluctant to move as I tried to scoot them away.

"So, Hamilton, was it?" Rosemary asked. "Unusual name."

She pushed a new mag up into her gun as she talked, her elderly fingers agile and deadly against the glaring steel. "I'm surprised and rather displeased we haven't met before," she said. "But running a worldwide organization does tend to take priority. Allow me to properly introduce myself. I was once known as Rosemary Johansen, though I am known by another name now."

"'The Matriarch' seems too egotistical for someone like you," I said. "Although I guess it might seem humble from your perspective."

I wouldn't have thought it possible, but she frowned further, driving her lips into her face.

Before I could say anything else, Rosemary swiveled around toward the couch and let off a round of shots from her gun.

"No!" Raiya and I both tried to jump forward; she aimed to protect Adam and my parents, while I wanted nothing more than to take Rosemary down.

Instantly, several guns were trained on the two of us. We stopped short, but only when we realized no one had died.

Rosemary's frowned eased up a bit as she saw the look on our faces. Her rounds ended up flying expertly between my family. I could see the bullet holes on the walls behind them, reading out like a warning.

"After all these years," Rosemary said, "I'm a fairly good shot. I won't miss next time."

"You didn't kill anyone." Raiya's voice was hushed, part in awe and part in terror.

"Not yet," Rosemary assured her. "Now, my beloved granddaughter, let's go for a walk."

Fear of dying suddenly went away, as fear of losing Raiya again swelled up inside of me. "You can't have her," I croaked.

Rosemary cocked an eyebrow. "You can come along, too, Hamilton," she said. "You'll make a nice addition to my collection of agents."

Before I could say something especially vile, I was interrupted.

"No one is going with you," Lyra called out.

"Not as long as we're here!" Lucas added.

Both of them jumped in front of me, pushing me off to the side. They'd transformed into their Starlight defender forms, and I felt the premonition in my gut go from bad to worse. Before I could stop them, they launched themselves forward.

Chaos broke out at once. SWORD agents scrambled to get the two younger superheroes, while Rosemary only stood by with a sense of expectancy.

Raiya also transformed, still in her darkened form. She hurried to cover for the kids, leaving me to hurry to try to free my parents.

I lashed out a few punches of my own as I came up to my parents.

Cheryl's eyes were wide, and I could tell she was frightened. I didn't have time to enjoy how messy her hair was as I untied the knot around her wrists.

"Thank goodness you're here," she said, as I carefully pulled off her gag.

"I'm so sorry," I said as I hurried to free Adam. "I never meant for this to happen."

A SWORD agent reached out to grab me, but I ducked, forcing him to go rolling over me. I grabbed him and pushed him away, just as Lucas came rushing forward.

"Ugh," Lucas grumbled as he flattened the agent against the floor with his shield.

"Lucas," Lyra called, grabbing his shoulder. Instantly, her power flowed into him, and he stood up, refreshed.

"Good work," I said.

Lyra and Lucas each beamed with pride for approximately a half-second, before another onslaught of attacks began.

They dove into action.

As I worked to free my father and brother, I kept one eye on the two of them; they were naturals, both of them, even if I was going to give them a lecture about endangering themselves later on.

"Lyra, Lucas." I beckoned to them, and they came over. "Take the battle outside. See if you can get them to follow you," I told them. "Raiya and I will handle Rosemary."

I glanced over just in time to see Raiya's power managed to knock Dante out with a singular punch. I can't say I didn't enjoy seeing that.

I was also relieved to see her eyes, while determined, were clear. It was nothing like fighting her before; she was not on a blind rampage. She was more like her old Starry Knight self, even if she still didn't look like she had when we were younger.

Maybe getting older prompted a change in color scheme? I wondered.

"Will you be alright?" Lyra asked, interrupting my thoughts.

"Of course," I said, even though I had to wonder myself if I was going to be able to transform. "Raiya will look after me," I finally told them, confident that was the truth. "Go!"

The two of them listened to me only about half of the time, but this was one of the times they followed through. Both of them took off, Lyra out the door and Lucas through the window.

"After them," Rosemary ordered. At once, the remaining agents, the few that were left, pursued them. Rosemary turned my way, her weapon steady as it aimed for me.

"Stop," I yelled, holding up my hands.

Rosemary scowled. "You need to take your own advice," she snapped, before cocking her gun.

"Hamilton!" Raiya cried out as she blasted Rosemary with her power.

The old lady screamed in aggravated frustration as she toppled over. Mark and Cheryl led Adam away, while Raiya grabbed me and pushed me back out the door.

"Run," she ordered. We could see Lyra and Lucas fighting in the distance as we headed toward them and away from Rosemary and her guards.

I grabbed her hand as we ran, pulling her after me. Despite her improvement in the last week, I knew she was not up to running for miles on end. I was certain of this when I glanced over and saw her tired expression. "Are you okay?"

"I was never worried before," Raiya told me as she hurried alongside me, "about fighting SWORD. I thought I could handle them."

"You can," I insisted.

"I've lost too much and too many people," she said. "I underestimated them."

"It doesn't help that your grandmother came back out of nowhere and cornered you into it," I said. "This was a surprise attack on us today, too."

"She knows how to hurt people." Raiya stopped running, ducking behind a small collection of trees. She put her hands on her knees, trying to rest. "I remember her visits when I was at their site."

I squeezed her hand. "I know this sounds bad, but I wish you wouldn't remember things like that," I said.

Raiya gave me a quick smile. "She told me a lot of things. She was unhappy with her marriage to Grandpa Odd."

"I'm hardly surprised. *Two* narcissistic megalomaniacs in a marriage doesn't seem like a good match in the long run."

"She said he abused her."

"The victim often becomes the victimizer," I said. Sadly, working in the law, I saw that a lot. The stats on it weren't good. I also knew it was possible to break the cycle. Rosemary didn't seem like the kind of woman who wanted to do that, let alone the kind who would try. "I'm willing to bet she abused him back."

Raiya grimaced. "It's not for us to worry about now, I guess."

"I'd rather not, anyway. I don't want sympathy for the woman who kept you away from me for all these years." I caught Raiya's eye. "And we can both agree that's the least of all her crimes."

THE STARLIGHT CHRONICLES

"I can agree to that as well," Rosemary said from behind us.

We glanced over to see her as she stepped out from behind another tree.

She smiled for the first time, her perfectly straight, white teeth adding to the overall unnatural aura she projected. "Odd was a smart man, but careless," she said. "When I found out the truth about him, I had to go to great lengths to assure him I was on his side."

"You were just using him," Raiya said.

"Is it a sin to use someone who uses other people?" Rosemary narrowed her eyes. "I already knew about the fallen Stars when I met him. That's part of the reason I convinced him to marry me."

"Why do it?" I asked. "It hardly seems worth it to me."

"That's where you're wrong. Immortality is a grand venture, and one that requires sacrifices of all sorts," she said. "They say death and taxes are the only certainties of life. I've managed to avoid paying taxes; I can certainly avoid death, too."

If nothing else, I thought, *that's enough to get her imprisoned for tax evasion.*

"Once I have Raiya back, I'll be able to open up this world into the next one, and I'll be able to get the bloodwater from the River of Life. All I need is Raiya and the fabric of Time she has."

"How do you know about the fabric?" Raiya asked. She shifted her feet slightly, and I knew she was gearing up to attack.

We just had to keep her distracted.

We can do that.

"You told me all about it, of course," she said. "Including the seal you placed on it."

Raiya's expression was, thankfully, blank as Rosemary continued. "You must not remember our lengthy conversations down in your cell."

I grew more uncomfortable as Rosemary's smile turned more eerie.

"A shame, isn't it? I know I personally will never forget the look on your face when I told you that I was responsible for your parents' deaths."

Before Raiya and I could respond, a small *beep* emitted from nearby.

Rosemary kept her weapon expertly trained on us as she held up a small device. "Yes?" she asked.

"Madame," said a voice I didn't recognize from the device.

Must be a cell phone or radio, I realized. Spy gear.

"We have them."

Rosemary's creepy grin returned. "Excellent." She put the device away and turned back to us. "We have your starlings."

"No," Raiya choked out. She was already struggling, as the truth about the death of her parents clearly haunted her. I stepped forward, trying to shield her.

"Release them," I yelled at Rosemary.

"Oh, I will," she said, "when you hand over the fabric of Time."

Before I could declare that she would never get away with this, Raiya's power turned ominously dark.

She glowed with a blackened aura as she launched herself at Rosemary. "Augh!" she called out, an angry battle cry, one that resonated with my own heart.

Rosemary lost her weapon as she was knocked off her feet, and Raiya was more than capable of holding her own against that vile woman.

But I knew it couldn't last; I could almost see the black hole inside of her heart grow and convulse as it twisted its way toward Earth. And I knew Raiya was supposed to be stopped from indulging in her darker thirst for vengeance.

Despite my synchronous desire, I stepped in. I pushed myself in between Rosemary and Raiya.

"Move," I yelled at Rosemary, who looked shocked I'd stepped forward to save her.

She didn't repay the favor, of course. As I stood, barely clinging onto Raiya's shoulders, holding her back from the fight of her life, she scurried away.

Rosemary turned back to me, briefly. "You have until tomorrow at noon," she said. "Bring me the fabric of Time, or I'll kill your starlings."

Raiya raged even more, her power trying to go supernova as I held her back. Rosemary disappeared from my sight as I focused all my concern on Raiya.

I pushed myself next to her, placing my hand over her heart.

"Come back to me," I called, hoping this would work. It had been many years since I was able to enter into the Realm of the Heart.

Something pushed out from the back of my heart and headed into hers. A second later, my mind followed along, and I got a new glimpse at the secrets in Raiya's heart.

The world around me faded into a new one, one where places and paintings of beauty resided side-by-side. I felt the music of her soul call out to me, though there was another harmony in place.

"Huh?" I blinked and rubbed my eyes, just to be sure that what I was seeing was real.

Raiya's Soulfire had always reminded me of liquid moonlight, with its silvery glow and blueish undertones. This time, as I looked into her heart, I saw two warring powers fighting inside of her. One was a familiar, blood-colored flame, while the other was a black hole.

The two had collided, and in the heart of their battle, I could see Raiya as she fought and fought off their power.

THE STARLIGHT CHRONICLES

The Blood Flame, I realized. She had one now, too. Adonaias had forgiven her.

Instantly, I knew what was going on. She had told me herself, that the choices we made would "feed" our future selves, changing us into a particular way for the rest of eternity.

As a fallen Star, she was destined to fight this, the same way that I was. But with the Blood Flame, we were able to find resolution, even as the war continued.

"Raiya," I called, hurrying forward.

Her eyes were dark, as her internal self glanced over at me. "Almeisan," she murmured, her voice falling over me in caressing waves.

I came up to her, blistering at the battlefront, and took her hand. "You have to stop this," I said.

"How can I?" she asked, helpless. "I'm scared."

"I know it's hard not to be afraid," I told her. Her fear reminded me of the first time I saw the Sinisters and their minions, and of the first time I saw Maia suck out a Soulfire. I knew what it was like to be afraid of things it seemed impossible to understand.

But I also knew that it was a different kind of fear I felt toward Adonaias.

"I *know* it's hard not to be afraid," I said. "But you have to fear the right things."

"What if I don't know which thing is the right thing?" Her voice was soft against the powers fighting around us; I doubted I would've heard it if we hadn't been so close.

"I know you, and I know you know the truth."

Please don't let her get too confused by what I'm saying. This is hard to explain.

My silent plea went unanswered, as she said nothing in return.

"Please," I said. "You told me Adonaias gave you a new heart. He's forgiven you. You have been marked with the Blood Flame, the same as me. I know that sometimes it's harder to have faith in something than it is to fear something, and that those things aren't always mutually exclusive. But you still have to make a choice."

I gripped her arm. "I know life isn't fair. But we still have a choice to be fair or unfair. And this is something we choose, too—who we will follow, and who we will fear."

"I know who I follow," she said.

"Then what would he have you do?" I asked. I gestured with my free hand. "What will do you with all of this?"

She never answered me. The void inside of her pulled in the blood-colored flames, and for a long moment I thought that was it. I thought she was lost.

But when I saw the Blood Flame grow brighter, I realized what was *actually* happening. She was allowing her pain to consume the holy fire, and in so doing, she was giving it up.

I was forced out of the Realm of the Heart a moment later. I woke up to the real world, where we were alone in the woods near Shoreside Park, where Raiya, in her human form, trembled in my arms.

"You did it," I told her, stroking her hair as I held her. "You stopped it."

"It still hurts so much," she whispered.

"I know."

"This won't be the last time."

I sighed. "I know that, too. But I'll be here for you this time to help. If I can."

Raiya rubbed her eyes. "Thank you." She gave me a tentative smile despite her tears. "I feel like I've cried more in the last week than I have in the last several years."

"It's okay to cry," I told her. "I'd be more worried if you didn't, to be honest."

"Thanks. I think." She stood up, sniffling some before she straightened her shoulders. "But there isn't any time for tears now. Rosemary has Lyra and Lucas."

I nodded, solemnly and somberly.

She glanced over at me. "I can't lose anyone else, Hamilton. I just can't."

"I know exactly how you feel," I said. "Let's go and get the fabric. And then we'll take it to Rosemary."

"We can't give it to her!" Raiya said. "She'll destroy the world with that kind of power."

"We'll call St. Brendan," I said. "Maybe we can get some help with this. Alora might be able to do something."

"He won't come in time."

"We'll have to find a way to delay her, then," I said. "Or maybe we can stop time."

"We don't have that power."

I sighed. "We need something to free Lyra and Lucas. Any chance we can give Rosemary a fake?"

Raiya bit her lip. "I don't know. I'm not sure how much she would know about it."

She was still upset, far from peace, and I hated everything about that moment. Once more, she was suffering and I felt helpless to help her. I was out of ideas and nearly out of patience.

I did the only thing I could think to do. "We'll get them back, Raiya. I swear on my life, we will get them back," I said.

Her face crumpled with sadness, but she nodded.

"We have until noon tomorrow," I said. "Let's go back to my house and check on my family. We'll think of something. We'll get a plan together."

Raiya nodded again. She shook off the last of her sadness, replacing it with a righteous determination.

"Maybe Dante will be there," I said, sadistically hopeful all of a sudden. Recalling how he had helped trap my family, with whom he was friends, I knew now more than ever he was among the enemy, and he'd betrayed us to Rosemary. "I can punch him some more."

"I don't know if I'll be able to stop you," Raiya told me.

I cracked my knuckles. "Don't worry. I'll show him mercy. Eventually."

THE STARLIGHT CHRONICLES

☼19☼
Family

I was happy to see several police cars surrounding my parents' house when we returned, even if it did mean that I was going to have to hold off on hitting Dante.

While my parents were busy with the police (they were old friends, most of them, given Cheryl's reputation in the city courts), Raiya and I sneaked inside and made our way up to my room.

"Is this the right one?" I asked, handing her the painting Mikey had given to me, the one that Lyra had so conscientiously rewrapped and Lucas had so haphazardly packed.

"Let me see." Raiya began peeling off the paper. "Yes, it is. But did you have to break the glass?"

"Uh … " I decided not to mention how sad and unsettled it'd made me feel when I opened it up in my apartment. "The kids actually managed to do most of the damage. Lucas wasn't kidding when he said he'd broken it, so be careful."

"I do have healing powers," she said, the slightly teasing tone allowing me to feel a sense of levity despite the desperation of our situation. "I'll be alright."

I snorted. "Just trying to be nice. I suppose it's wasted on you."

"Largely." She smirked as she pulled off the paper. "Goodness, what did you guys do to it?"

I glanced down to see the familiar beauty of Raiya's work—the quick and sure strokes of paint, layered with love and time and care—all shining through the gaping hole in the middle of the glass frame.

I definitely hadn't been paying much attention to how broken it was.

"Wow," I said. "I put it by the door when I left, after getting it unwrapped. I guess Lucas and Lyra really managed to mess it up when they broke into my apartment."

As she finished pulling the painting from its frame, Raiya frowned. "They broke into your apartment?"

"Yeah. I came home from work one afternoon, and there they were."

"Did they tell you anything about how they found you?" Raiya asked. "Anything about when they were born?"

"Well, they're ten and twelve," I said. "I just did the math. Cheryl's talked with them some, too, about everything, but she said she's waiting on the parents to respond." I was about to ask her why when I noticed she was shaking again. "Why? What's wrong? Tell me."

"We're not going to find their parents." Raiya shook her head. "I can't believe it."

"What do you mean? What's wrong?"

"The fabric of Time," she said, pointing to the middle of her painting. "The blood seal I've placed on it has been broken."

Frustration settled into my skin once more. "You know, you and the others do this thing, this thing I remember Aleia and Alora doing on so many occasions, where I feel like you expect me to know the answers, and I really don't know what—"

"They're *ours*." Her eyes lit up as they met mine. "They're our children."

Frustration fell away into shock. Shock turned into disbelief, and then disbelief transformed into raging uncertainty.

Is it possible? How *is it possible?*

I watched, speechless, as Raiya pulled something off the back of her painting. In her hand was something like a small scrap of silvery cloth, made of power and energy so fine it hurt to look upon it.

I reached forward to feel it. It was like touching stymied lightning. There was no electricity, but just this smoothness and wonder at its light sturdiness. "This is … weird."

"When I first found the fabric of Time, I knew it was a powerful object," she explained. "I hid it underneath my painting to keep others from finding it. But it wouldn't stay hidden until I drenched it in my blood to maintain its anonymity."

"Ew, so there's actually blood in your paint?" I frowned. "Gross."

"I never wondered why you didn't become a doctor." Raiya rolled her eyes at my perhaps juvenile but reasonable disgust.

"The important thing is, it wouldn't have been broken by anyone but me. Or … "

"Our kids," I finished. After a moment of thought, I added, "Or at least, your kids."

"They're *ours*," Raiya insisted. "How many times did I have to tell Lucas to listen to me and follow instructions? And how many times did Lyra just sit there and look skeptical, for no real reason?"

"Hey, I have plenty of reasons to be skeptical," I shot back.

"They act just like you." Her hands pressed into her heart, like it was in pain.

"Are you okay?" I asked, my mind scarring itself all over again as I recalled our last battle with Draco. I didn't need her to have another heart attack.

"Are you kidding?" She smiled. "I just found out that I'm a mother, and my children are alive. I've never been more happy and terrified. I can't believe I didn't see it sooner."

"Well, my mom did say … " It was my turn to drift off in mid-sentence, as I remembered exactly what my mother had said. Cheryl said she'd found their parents, but she was waiting to see if they would respond.

Semantics.

Cheryl *would* think it was funny, after all the trouble I caused her in my teens, to have my life interrupted by a pair of stubborn, strong-willed spitfires.

"Oh." The word barely came out of my mouth before I bounded down the stairs.

"Hamilton?" Raiya came barreling after me. "Where are you going?"

I didn't respond. I turned into the kitchen, where Cheryl was still talking to a police officer. Despite the pressing matters earlier in the day, I blurted out, "I need to talk to you."

Cheryl took one look at me and then looked back at Raiya, as she caught up to me. She smiled warmly at the police officer. "Excuse me for a moment, Frank, I have to talk to my son for a moment."

"Do you want me to question him?" the officer asked.

"No, that won't be necessary," Cheryl assured him. "Go and check in on Mark. I know Adam and I have already given our statements, and I am positive we are in the best possible hands."

She waited until he was out of the room before she turned to us.

"Thanks for covering for us," I said, a little unwilling to bring up the other subject. "I didn't want to talk to the police about this."

"I won't make you talk to him," Cheryl told me in threatening tones, "but you owe me and your father and your brother an explanation."

"It was SWORD," I said.

"We know who it was," Cheryl said, "although I wouldn't dream of telling the cops that. We want to know why."

"And I want to know why you didn't tell me about Lyra and Lucas," I countered.

Her eyebrows raised, not in surprise, but rather in slight contempt. She hated to be overruled, even in conversation. "I didn't think you needed to know," she said. "You obviously had enough on your plate."

"I'm their father!" I snapped, and suddenly the enormity of it all collapsed on me.

I have children. Children!

Small people that relied on me for food and shelter and guidance. Tiny humans that needed diapers changed, boo-boos kissed, help with homework, dating advice! Insurance and money for school and doctor's appointments and extracurricular activities! All that they needed, I needed to give to them. And I felt severely underprepared and at a monstrous disadvantage.

On top of that, my kids were Starlight Warriors, just like me. They wanted to study battle strategy, fighting techniques, and the art of war.

That almost brought me down to my knees, as the horrifying thought finally broke me: *My children* were being held captive by SWORD, and I didn't even know how to get to them!

Of course, while I was having the meltdown of my life, Cheryl just marched on, oblivious to my pain.

"Yes, but not for another couple of years, technically," Cheryl said. "You know, you really need to work on your interviewing skills, Hamilton. You would've been able to figure it out much more quickly if you'd asked them better questions."

I was about to begin yelling at her when she smiled kindly. "They're very enamored of you and Raiya, you know. I guess whatever you will do to raise them worked. I don't know how I feel about being called 'Grandma,' though. I think I need something more like 'Gram' or 'Nana.'"

All of my wind came sputtering out as I slammed my fists into the countertop. "Why didn't *they* tell us?" I finally managed.

"I'm not sure they were confident we could handle it," Raiya said quietly. "Especially since, from what I know, they were likely breaking the rules at the time they activated the fabric of Time's power."

"I don't know anything about that, but I would say it's in your genes," Cheryl said, doing nothing to help me at all. "I seem to recall my oldest son neglecting to tell me about his own supernatural trouble, not too long ago."

"Seven years is a longer time than you think," I argued.

"It only is if you're unhappy." Cheryl folded her arms and started toward the den. "Now, I'm going to check in on Adam and your father. You need to get those kids of yours back here and ready for dinner soon. Thank goodness Louis was out shopping when this all happened … "

I almost let myself tell her what happened, but when I saw Raiya shake her head, I shut my mouth. In all fairness, I don't think she wanted to admit in front of her future mother-in-law that we'd lost the kids to SWORD's agents any more than I did.

"It's her fault we lost them," I said bitterly, after I knew Cheryl was out of earshot.

"No," Raiya said as she shook her head. "They're our children. They act like us more than we would like. As nice as it would be to blame your mother, I know I would've done the same thing if I had been in their place."

"You *did* do the same thing," I said. I glanced down at my own wrist, where my mark seemed to mock me. *Maybe I should've done something, too,* I thought, immersed in guilt.

"We'll get them back," Raiya said.

"How are you the one that's calm now?" I snapped. "They're *our children.* The very thing Rosemary always wanted from you, and she has them!"

"I feel a little better knowing they are our kids," Raiya admitted, making me stare at her with what I imagined to be a murderous look. She placed her hands on my cheeks. "Think about it. We've dealt with SWORD before, too. If they are our kids, they'll not only be fine, but they'll take a few of their agents for a ride before they break free."

"They might be ours, but they're still kids, Raiya," I said. "They can be more easily manipulated and coerced and frightened. And we're not there to make it better for them."

"We will be," Raiya promised. "We just need a plan, like you said."

"We need to find them," I said. "Rosemary didn't even tell us where to meet her if we actually were going to be stupid enough to hand over the fabric of Time to her."

Raiya snapped her fingers. "I've got it," she said. "Let's go see Logan."

"Now? Really?" I frowned. "What is he going to be able to do?"

"Dante told you that the kids were on SWORD's radar. They have a radiation signature, just like the other Stars we've known. Maybe he can track down their location."

It was the only idea I could think of that made *some* sense.

"Then what?" I asked, still trying to talk myself out of crumpling into my own despair.

"We can call St. Brendan on the way," Raiya suggested. "I don't think he'll be able to come right away, but if he can come at all, he still might be able to help us find a way to stop Rosemary from getting ahold of the bloodwater and gaining immortality. As much as I want to destroy her, I'd hate to have to open up the world between here and Alküzor's realm again."

"I suppose calling St. Brendan would be a good way to alert Alora, too," I said, as I continued to mull the idea over inside my mind. "I'll call Mikey, too. Maybe he'll help us trap Dante this time."

"I know you want to beat Dante up," Raiya said. "But you'll have to exercise some self-control if you want to get the right information out of him."

"Believe me, I have only known Lyra and Lucas are mine for the last five minutes, but I'm willing to do what it takes to get them back. Even if it means letting Dante live after that stunt he pulled in here earlier today."

"Your dedication is endearing," Raiya muttered dryly.

"I'm hoping that Dante will agree with you on that."

☼ 20 ☼
Logan

"It still stings," I muttered as we walked away from the marina.

"I already healed it," Raiya said. "Stop being a baby about it."

"You know I don't like blood."

"You mean, unless it's animated and coming from one of your video games?"

"Yes," I said. "*Exactly* that."

"We had to call St. Brendan," Raiya said. "Star blood is powerful, and having both of us call him might get the *Meallán* here faster."

"That's the only reason I agreed to give you some of my blood," I told her.

I don't think I was actually that upset about it. I was just overwhelmed. From all I'd found out in the last week, I was almost waiting for the curtain to drop, to awake from sleep, to only just blink, and be back in a world where it was me, me, me, all the time, like a radio station of my emotions and thoughts running all the time.

After a life like that—one I didn't want to return to, even as tired and frustrated as I was—I was exhausted. And now, there was an evil organization to dismantle, a hole in Time to patch up, and a pair of my own children to rescue.

279

How did I manage to juggle everything so well in high school? I wondered.

"We should see if Logan has any of Rachel's coffee," I said. That seemed to be one missing ingredient, at least.

"We're almost there," Raiya said. "Look."

I followed her gaze and, despite everything I was feeling or not feeling, smiled. Lakeview Observatory, unlike the rest of the places in Apollo City I remembered, seemed to have only grown in polish since I left.

Recalling how Grandpa Odd—or rather, Draco—had run a whole foundation dedicated to finding fallen Stars and other mysteries of the universe, I supposed it wasn't something I should've been so surprised about.

"This place has certainly been upgraded," I said.

"I'll say," Raiya replied as we walked into the doors, staring as we passed through the newly renovated observatory.

There was new tech gear jammed into more of the rooms, bulletin boards full of information on bachelor's and master's and doctorate level work; new project schematics and blueprints.

"I wonder how much of Rachel's inheritance went here," I said.

Raiya slapped my arm. "Come on, this isn't a bad investment. The student programs look like they've tripled in recent years."

"Several times over, actually."

At the familiar voice, we both turned. Standing behind us was Rachel's brother-in-law, Logan. Before I could see all of the different changes, he came up to Raiya and embraced her. "I've missed you, cousin," he said.

Raiya grinned. "I suppose Rachel told you I was back, Dr. Reynolds?"

"It's always been just Logan, to you. And yes, Rachel did tell me. But I knew the instant I saw the reports of new superheroes in town," he said with a grin. "It's nice to see you again, Starry Knight. I've missed your visits."

Raiya and I exchanged shocked glances, before she asked, "How did you know?"

"I never believed much in coincidence," he said. "Despite the several theories of that cosmology will present, I've found that things are often more simple and more complicated than we can know or understand. So far," he added, seeing my skeptical look. "After Starry Knight and Wingdinger both died and you went missing, I found that to be too coincidental."

He adjusted the wire-frame glasses on his nose, peering through them at her. "I also thought it was too much of a coincidence that Starry Knight happened to know so much about me, including my favorite selections from Rachel's."

Raiya blushed. "I don't suppose you've shared your thoughts on the matter with anyone?"

"No," he said. "Remember? I keep to myself quite well. We were always alike in that regard."

I used to think Logan might've had a crush on Starry Knight, and I knew that she had great respect for Logan. And even though I knew she loved me, I couldn't help but clear my throat impatiently.

"Oh, Hamilton," Logan said. Instantly, he held out a hand to me. "It's nice to see you again, too."

Before he could bring up my part of the town's superhero past, I said, "We didn't just come to reminisce about the good old days. We need your help."

"We need to know if your radiation device still works," Raiya explained. "We don't have a demonic enemy this time—"

"More like a devilish one," I explained, unable to resist chiming in.

"But they have the two new superheroes, the ones that the news reported on," Raiya said. "We need to find them and rescue them."

Logan rolled up the sleeves of his lab coat. "Alright," he said as he began walking forward. "Let's see what I can do to help you out. Come with me."

We hurried after him, and soon found ourselves in the same room we must've visited a thousand times before. The large telescope was off for the night, but the persistent hum of energy in the large computers and the other equipment buzzed about, almost making a lively sort of music.

"This place hasn't changed much," I said.

"No, not really," Logan said. "Dr. Harbor and I oversee this place, and we are more often hampered rather than helped by new technology. And it's expensive, no matter how much we've had coming in from grants and endowments. Plus the new student interns we get always seem to get more careless as the years go by."

I thought of some of the younger students I met in law school. "I can sympathize."

"Here," he said. "We haven't been as diligent about identifying patterns in the radiation forms over the last few years—there's always a bit of haze around somewhere, but we've been collecting it since Mayor Mills asked us to, back when he was in office."

"I heard he lost his reelection campaign," I said.

"Well, after he was hospitalized, a lot of his supporters found about some of his scandals and more of his half-truths on things," Logan said. "Dunbrooke is far from likeable, but people at least know they're getting someone who tells the truth."

"I can see why that would be appealing," Raiya said. I met her gaze, and I knew she was thinking about the battle at City Hall, where Elektra, the Sinister of Greed, had managed to get a good hold on him.

"There." Logan pointed to a screen. "These are the tracking patterns we've seen since the beginning of the month. Watch carefully," he said.

"There's nothing big there," I said.

"It's coming," Logan assured me. "There," he said as he pointed at the screen. "This is the one from the other day, when the local news station picked up your new superheroes."

There was a cloudy pattern dotting across the area just above Shoreside Park, a blue-violet storm waiting to break loose; surrounding it was a pattern of high-intensity black stripes. Glancing over at Raiya, I knew there was no mistaking her abuse of power.

"I see it," I said. "Can you show me what the machine's picked up today?"

"I'll play it in slow motion," Logan said. "I'll keep my attention on the controls. You tell me if you need me to stop."

"Will do," Raiya said.

We watched the screen for a long moment, before the blue-violet cloud returned.

"There," I said. "Slow it down some more."

"How's that?" Logan asked.

"Can you center it?" I asked. The blue-violet cloud was moving away from my parents' home in Lake County Heights, toward the middle of the city.

I watched as another black blip appeared in the woods between the house and the marina. *Starry Knight's dark power,* I thought again. I watched as it gradually lightened up to gray, and then became more of a maroon color.

Maybe that was when we were together, in the Realm of the Heart, I thought. I could really only guess. Considering we were both more worried about Lyra and Lucas, I turned my attention back to the blue-violet blur.

"It's moving toward the Time Tower," I said. I groaned. "I should've guessed."

"Why would SWORD take them there?" Raiya asked.

"It was owned by the Skarmastad Foundation," I said. "Chances are, it's still pretty clear of any activity. You heard Rachel the other day. She got everything settled recently."

"I suppose. I still don't see why it would make much of a difference."

"This isn't the first time that SWORD has been hanging out there," I said.

"I know they borrowed it when they captured you," Raiya said. "But I didn't think it was special to SWORD so much as the Skarmastad Foundation."

"They've been hanging around there at other times." I thought of the time that Mikey went to go and see Dante there. "I guess even if she hated him, Rosemary wants to make sure she can top Draco at every level."

"That would be something she would do," Raiya said. She turned to Logan. "You can stop the machine now."

He complied with the ready ease of a faithful pet. "Is there anything else you want me to do?" Logan asked.

"That's it," I said. "For now." I noticed the time on the screen. It was getting late. In the winter weather, it was already dark outside.

I glanced uneasily over at Raiya. I was about to suggest we confer together when Logan laughed.

"I see you two haven't changed much in the last several years," he said.

"What do you mean?" Raiya asked.

"I'll leave you alone," he said. He glanced over at me. "I can tell you have things to discuss."

He was right, of course. So I stepped up. "Thanks for all your help, Dr. Reynolds," I said.

I *was* truly grateful for all his help.

"It's just Logan to you, too. And I like helping you guys with this stuff. I've forgotten what a rush it is; sometimes, with science, you forget that it's more like solving a mystery than it is just collecting data," Logan said as he headed out of the room. "Come and visit me again soon."

"We will," Raiya said, before he shut the door. She rolled her eyes after my irritated expression. (Did she have to be so nice to him all the time?)

"Come on, Hamilton. He's been really helpful, and I would like to come back to see if he can show me what else he's found about my supernova and the meteorite from before."

"Uh-huh." I shook my head. "We don't need to worry quite so much about that anymore. We just called St. Brendan earlier."

"Still, this place would be a nice idea for a family outing. It's educational, and there are plenty of things for the kids to enjoy here."

"All you need is the minivan, by the sound of it," I said as I walked over to stand next to her.

"The sooner we get the kids, the sooner we can do just that," Raiya replied.

I almost asked her if she was serious. But since she was right about getting the kids, I decided not to bother her about it. There would be plenty of time to argue about that later (because there was just *no way* we were getting a minivan).

"They're at the Time Tower," I said. "And they haven't moved."

"Did Mikey return your call?" Raiya asked.

"No," I said. "But then he's getting married this weekend, and he's got to get through work yet before the break."

"School should be out already, shouldn't it?"

"I'm sure the students feel that way. But there are still teacher work days." I shrugged. Now that we knew where the Lucas and Lyra were being held, there wasn't much that Dante's assistance, forced or not forced, would do. In fact, recalling the several times that Dante had been "helpful," I ended up being Tasered or something else. "It doesn't matter. We don't need Dante's help."

"I agree."

"I know *you* would agree to that."

She frowned. "Well, if you're going to be like that, I can always say I told you—"

"Okay, okay." I gave her a quick grin. "You know I can't take that."

"When do you want to go?" Raiya asked.

"Now," I said. "But it's probably not the best idea. We should probably—"

"I think we should go now, too."

"Good. That'll save me some time, because there aren't any really good reasons to wait."

Raiya took my hand. "Let's go then," she said as she pressed the mark on her wrist.

Wings sprouted from her back, her armor flickered on over her body, and the Starry Knight I'd come to know as she was now appeared before me.

I looked down at my own mark and, for the briefest moment, I hesitated.

But then I thought of Lyra's smile and Lucas' smug expression. I thought about how much I liked them, and how much I even loved them.

It was time. To honor my past, to prepare for the present, and to protect my future.

I pressed the mark on my wrist, and for a long half-second I wondered if anything would happen at all. Lucas was so sure that I'd turned my back on my power, and even Raiya, in her amnesiac state, was able to tell it had been years since I trusted the power I had inside of me, and that I trusted Adonaias to guide me.

But in the heart of that half-second, I felt the power rekindled inside of me. My heart seemed to let out its own power flare, as blood pulsated and my wings once more spread out from behind my shoulders. I felt the rush of power, the glory behind my sense of self, as it returned home.

The truth will set me free, I remembered. I marveled as my armor appeared, as my hands were half-gloved, and my tunic was made over my regular form.

I even smiled as I felt the once-familiar flutter of wingdings tickling onto my forehead.

Glancing down, I was a little surprised to see Starry Knight wasn't the only one with a color change. My red and black armor was still dark, but the colors were even more muted. In some ways, I saw this as an appropriate change; I had accepted the truth of the evil in the world, and still staunchly stood against it, despite its perverse persistence.

Raiya came up to me. Her hands reached up and stroked my feather-crown. "I've missed your crown of fire feathers."

I groaned. "Did you know Elysian was the one who named me Wingdinger? Apparently he told that lady, Patricia Whats-

289

her-name, that that was my name when she was having that city superhero contest."

"I knew," she admitted. "But not until our last year. He told me once when we were patrolling the city looking for Draco. I decided not to say anything, for very valid reasons at the time." She laughed, no doubt at my annoyed expression.

I was about to reply, quite angrily, when she leaned in and kissed me. "I still fell in love with you," Raiya reminded me. "Even with your goofy name. Which I happen to like."

"I've heard that love is blind, but I never thought it would be deaf, too," I muttered.

She giggled. "Your name's not that bad."

"Come on, I need a new name. Starry Knight is a timeless name. Wingdinger is just lame now."

"Maybe we can work on it while we head over to the Time Tower," Raiya said. "But I doubt it will be easy for a city superhero to rebrand himself."

"Come on, Robin became Nightwing in the DC Comics," I said.

"Do you really want to be on the same level as Robin?"

As we argued and fought and discussed all of these things and more—partially to relieve the tension and the fear we now faced as we raced to get our children back, and partially because it was a valid argument—we made our way out of Lakeview Observatory and headed out for the Time Tower.

☼21☼
Rescue Mission

If there is anything more determined in this world than a father desperate to reunite with his wayward, stubborn children, especially when they've fallen into a web of evil, I wouldn't have been able to name it. As Raiya and I hurried through the night, I felt the simultaneous push of fear and rush of protectiveness alternating inside my heart.

Beside me, I knew Raiya was struggling with a similar divide in her own heart and soul.

I thought of all the terrible things they'd done to Raiya, and all the terrible things they'd done to me. Lucas and Lyra were just babies compared to us.

My fingers were almost numb from my angry, obsessive clenching. *If they've hurt my kids, I'll kill them all,* I silently vowed.

Coming up to the Time Tower, I felt the déjà vu happening all over again. How many times in my life had I come up to this place, only to find a battle being raged?

The eerie normalcy of it all, this time at night, this close to Christmas, made it all the worse. All I could say was at least it wasn't snowing.

"I wish Elysian was here," I said as I pulled Raiya into the alleyway a few blocks up from the Time Tower. "He would've been able to create a good distraction for us."

"We wouldn't want that," Raiya said. "What if they hurt the kids?"

"They'd be stupid to get rid of their advantage."

"They wouldn't have to kill them to hurt them," Raiya pointed out.

I was glad to see that her pain at her own loss had shifted its focus. While I was still hoping she would be able to control the darker rage inside of her, I could understand her desire for revenge. In our case, the line between justice and revenge was razor thin, and there was no getting around the fact we had one big balancing act ahead of us.

"You have the fabric still?" I asked.

She pulled it out, its silkiness like a small waterfall of moonlight. "Maybe I can place a new seal on it," Raiya said as she studied it. "That way, Rosemary would have it, but she wouldn't be able to use it."

"She likely has plenty of your blood in stock," I said. *Or worse, Rosemary could try to capture you again.* "I don't think it would work."

"It could still delay her a while," Raiya argued.

"Any delay could be problematic for the kids."

"You know, you got angry with me when I was arguing with you earlier," Raiya said.

"I know you're just trying to help, but there is just so much that doesn't seem to be helped in this instance," I said, feeling as helpless as I used to when I was a teenager. There was no second-guessing what kind of evil we would face when we were up against those who willingly embraced evil itself.

What can we do? We are afraid. We are unsure. We can't see a way through this.

My mind was racing around inside of me, scrambling to find an answer that wasn't there.

It was at that moment, at that moment of despair and uncertainty, that I felt more than heard a quiet whisper in the back of my heart.

Go.

Peace settled onto me, and the fear crippling me, tearing at me, rendering me stagnant, shattered, as I realized what had happened.

There was more that was said, and yet, at the same time, not said at all. Pictures settled into my head, but my brain couldn't seem to decode them. I only knew I suddenly had a new understanding of Adonaias' power, a new understanding of who and what he was. For the first time, I realized how much *I* belonged to *him*, just as much as Lyra and Lucas belonged to me.

My hand shot out and gripped Raiya's hand. "We need to go."

Her fingers tightened around my hand. "Are you sure?"

My eyes felt watery as my nose prickled. My life had always been touched by the supernatural, I realized, and it was a miracle to feel the miracle of it hit me all over again.

293

Irresistible grace flooded through me, seeming to stop time and render my soul still, allowing me a moment that would mark me many times over every time I would revisit it.

Now, there was no time for doubt.

"I'm sure," I said, nodding. I gave her a small smile. "Remember? Everything will be alright."

"I'm worried about the cost," she admitted.

"I know. I am, too." I squeezed her hand. "But it's the right thing to do."

"Okay." She looked nervous, but trusting. "Where you go, I will follow."

Without another word, we headed for the Time Tower, walking right up to the front doors, our hands still tightly wound together.

As we came closer to the Time Tower, I thought about the battles that had taken place here. There was the one where Gwen and Adam had been captured, and I managed to get to them before I was attacked by Dante, and then there was the one where I'd been captured, and Elysian and Starry Knight came to rescue me.

Neither of these instances made me feel particularly optimistic.

I felt my remaining optimism plummet as we walked into the main lobby.

Rosemary was waiting for us.

How could a grandma manage to look so sinister? I wondered as she frowned at us through the curtain of white hair covering the one side of her face.

If I made it through this, I vowed, I would maintain a healthier respect for old people.

"You're early," she murmured, clearly pleased (for once).

"We want Lyra and Lucas back," Raiya told her. "Give them to us. They're just children. They don't deserve to be tangled up in this."

Rosemary arched an eyebrow. "Do you think I deserved to be 'tangled up' in Draco's scheme for world domination?" she asked. "He was a clever one, you know, and charming and handsome when he wanted to be."

"This is not about you," Raiya said. "This is about them. They're just children."

"Children who have the powers of an *Astroneshama*," Rosemary said.

There was an angry huff from behind her, as Dante and several other agents led Lyra and Lucas out to the lobby. I was gratified to see that he had a black bruise under his eye.

"We're *not* children," Lyra said, staunchly defiant despite her hostage position.

I almost laughed. Relief cascaded through me as I saw them, recognizing them as my children, and wondering, much as Raiya had earlier, how I could have missed that they were ours. Lyra's brown hair had the same copper undertones as

Raiya's, hidden at first sight, but undeniable once they were seen. Lucas had my eyes, blue and sharp and compelling.

In truth, instead of almost laughing, I probably should've admitted I almost wept. Pride, and pain, and love, and recognition all bit at me and my bitter heart. I was so joyful to know them, and to know that they were mine.

Even their foibles seemed to only endear them more to me. I watched as Lucas stuck his tongue out at Rosemary while her attention was on me and Raiya. An agent, one I didn't recognize, caught him by the arm and accosted him.

Lucas only responded by spitting on him.

That kid. He's going to cause a lot of his own suffering in life if he's not careful.

Just like me. A strange mix of pride and pity overcame me as I shot him a warning glare, much as Cheryl had done to me earlier.

I turned my attention to Dante, who only narrowed his gaze. He turned his focus back to Rosemary as she stepped toward me.

"The kids are still not something that you collect," Raiya told Rosemary.

"You didn't enjoy visiting with your grandma?" Rosemary scoffed. "You of all people should know how capable I am when it comes to getting my way."

"I, of all people, know your way can be thwarted," Raiya shot back.

Rosemary's thin lips tightened. "Not this time," she said. "I know how attached you are to children. You would do just about anything to keep them safe."

Raiya said nothing.

I stepped forward, with the fabric in my hand. With its languid limpness, it was almost hard for me to feel like I was holding it. "Here," I said. "Here's the fabric of Time. Give us the kids."

Rosemary nodded to Dante, and he brought them forward.

"If you think of attacking us, any of you," Rosemary said, "you will be shot instantly."

"If you think of double-crossing us," I replied, "you will be destroyed."

"I don't have to think about that at all," Rosemary said as she grasped onto the fabric. Her eyes, old and dim, seemed to shimmer as she beheld its beauty. "Finally, it's mine."

While Rosemary practically drooled over her acquisition, Dante shoved Lyra and Lucas into us.

Instantly, I was completely distracted as my arms caught Lyra, while Raiya embraced Lucas. Their wings flapped excitedly as Raiya and I held onto them.

"Are you alright?" Raiya asked as she looked Lucas over, checking his face for scrapes or bruises. "Did they hurt you?"

"*I* knew you'd come," Lucas said. "I didn't cry."

"Much." Lyra frowned at him.

"You did, too," he argued back.

I cupped Lyra's cheek and ran my other hand through her hair, ruffling the feathers playfully on the small wings on either side of her head. "We're just glad you're okay."

"Why are you giving them what they want?" Lyra asked as I knelt down beside her. "You're not supposed to negotiate with terrorists."

"I'll remind you of that later, when we talk about your punishment for getting captured in the first place," I told her.

She shot me a dirty look as Dante stepped forward.

"It's time for you to come with us now," he said.

"We're not going anywhere with you," I shot back. "All Rosemary wanted was the fabric of Time."

Dante shook his head. "Since when is SWORD worried about keeping its word? She needs you," he said, nodding toward Raiya, "if she wants to bring down Time's power."

"She can't control me," Raiya insisted. But I could see her knuckles whiten as she gripped onto Lucas' shoulders.

"Rosemary seems to think differently," he said, "especially since we have all of you surrounded now."

More agents came out of the woodwork, all armed and looking dangerous.

"This wasn't part of the deal," I said.

"Deal with it," Dante replied.

Something inside of me snapped. I launched myself at him, power swelling up inside of me.

Immediately, Lucas and Lyra conjured up their powers, covering Raiya while she went on the offensive. I didn't have to study her to know she was furious, and she was not about to let SWORD complete their betrayal.

It was for the best that I didn't try to watch her, since I was engaged in my own raging battle, as Dante finally fell under my onslaught.

"What do you think you're doing?" Dante hissed as he twisted away from my attacks.

"I could've asked the same of you this morning when you were holding my family hostage," I shot back. I pounced on him, getting him into a headlock.

"Be grateful that's all we did, under my direction," Dante grunted as he struggled to breathe. "She would've done much worse."

Shots rang out, and I nearly stilled.

"Get them," Rosemary called, and I turned just enough to watch as Raiya managed to knock the smoking gun out of her hand.

"Give me the fabric of Time back," Raiya yelled, reaching out to snatch it from Rosemary's hand.

She was within millimeters of grabbing it when other agents hurried to stop her, and it was only when they tackled Raiya that Rosemary was able to escape.

"Raiya!" I called, frightened for her. I grew even more angry as I saw Rosemary scurry to an elevator and push the button. As the doors closed, I could see a feral pleasure on her crooked face.

Dante managed to slip out of my loosened grip, but he didn't move. "Go and get Rosemary," he said. "She's got a vial of Starry Knight's blood ready. If she can destroy the fabric, she'll be able to bring down Time's power and enter into the Celestial Realm."

Wouldn't she still need a boat like the Meallán *or something, though?*

But then, Rosemary had studied Draco for years. Maybe she learned another trick or two along the way.

"Why should I trust you?" I asked, my voice scathing as another one of my kicks landed soundly.

Dante grunted. "You can't," he said, "but you can trust me more than you can trust Rosemary, can't you?"

I hated—*hated hated hated*—that he had a point.

"Look," he said, "Rosemary told me that if anything went wrong tonight, and it was my fault, that she would kill Mikey and Gwen. You have to stop her if we're going to do this. Go! She's likely headed for the roof. She has a helicopter on standby."

When I said nothing, he sighed. "Please, Hamilton, for Mikey! Don't let the world end because of my mistakes."

It was perhaps naïve, but I didn't think he would lie about Mikey to me.

I shoved him down on the ground one last time, getting the last rush of satisfaction as his head hit the floor, and then hurried off to follow Rosemary.

Several guards, seeing Dante lying still on the ground, hurried to distract me.

"Where are you going?" Raiya asked as she pushed her way through our opponents to fight by my side.

I watched as she unleashed another round of energy at the SWORD agents, careful not to hit Lyra, who was using her scepter to blast guards, while Lucas used his shield to protect her from any oncoming bullets or other weaponry.

"I'm going to get Rosemary," I said, "before she uses or destroys the fabric of Time. Can you handle things down here?" I hit another guard, sending him flying back.

Raiya's hands filled with violent light as she prepared another attack. "I don't like letting you go by yourself," she called back to me.

"It's just for a little while," I said. "And I did say I would be the one to take care of Rosemary. For you, and for our children."

I swiped at another agent's face, before getting hit. I pushed back. "Please, Raiya, just stay here and finish these guys off with the kids. And then you can come and join me, okay?"

She pursed her lips together, and despite the intensity of the battle, I knew she was fighting a bigger war inside of her.

"Alright," she finally said.

After a brief respite in fighting, I reached over and kissed her soundly on the lips, and then headed off. "I love you," I told her before I dashed away and she was pulled back into battle.

"Lucas, Lyra," I called, "cover your mother for me while I'm gone!"

They both whirled around at me, and at the shock on their faces, I recalled they didn't know I knew the truth.

"Keep fighting," I yelled, even as I tried not to laugh at their frightened expressions. "Go!"

Fortunately, they regained their focus, and I saw them as they hurried off just seconds before I burst into the stairwell.

My wings were out of practice, but I knew the moment the fiery feathers caught the wind I didn't have to worry. Apparently, flying was just like riding a bike; it was something you never forgot, no matter how long it had been since your last flight.

Navigating the stairs took more work; it was one thing to fly in a straight line, but it was hard to duck through the different levels, the crisscrossing patterns of stairs and doorways.

I could hear the hum of a nearby helicopter when I arrived at the roof.

Bursting through the door, I watched as Rosemary, startled, turned to face me.

Against the lights of the nighttime city, she was the perfect-looking villain out to destroy the world.

"It's you," she muttered accusingly. "You can't stop me." She held up the fabric of Time in one hand and a small glass container in the other.

"I can see why you would think that," I said. "You've managed to fly under the radar for years, using SWORD to collect government favors, find sponsors and donors, using your influence to wield power for your own goals."

"That's right," Rosemary asserted, her face wrinkling further in the windy night.

"That's the thing," I said. "You're not right. It's a logical fallacy to assume you'll win just because you've been winning for so long."

Rosemary held up the fabric menacingly. As I stepped up to stop her, she poured the vial's contents out onto the fabric of Time.

I watched as the blood seeped into the fabric, and I faltered. From what I knew from Raiya, her blood would only break the seal she'd placed on it, and it had already been broken by Lyra and Lucas.

But when I saw the fabric light up, each of its threads shining brightly as they separated and merged together anew, I wondered if it was indeed too late.

Rosemary laughed at me. "You're too late," she said. "I can now bypass Time's barrier. The bloodwater is nearly mine, at last."

I watched as she stuck her hand into the fabric, shocked to see it disappear. *She's going to use its power to transport herself,* I thought. It had to be something like that, right?

When I rushed forward, I watched as Rosemary sneered at me. "There's nothing you can do," she said as I headed toward her.

Before I could attempt to prove her wrong, the fabric's light began to burn even more brightly; and then, all of a sudden, it wasn't just light, but fire—fire I recognized.

There was a small explosion and an all-encompassing spark of light knocking me down to my knees. My eyes watered and shut at the same time Rosemary screamed in pain.

When I opened them again, I saw the skyline fill up with the dark green outline of a changeling dragon as he burst through the other side of the fabric, breathing down another burst of celestial fire.

"Elysian!" I called, as happiness and hope merged inside of me.

Rosemary dropped the fabric as she fell over. I jumped to my feet and rushed forward.

"Elysian!" I cried again.

My dragon roared back in greeting. "Kid," he called, the wide range of his sharp teeth gleaming as he smiled back. I hurried over to him and grabbed him around his neck.

"I can't believe it's you," I told him. "I thought you died."

"I did," he said. "Remember? I had to repent and be born again. Dragons and Stars have different ways of doing things than humans." He wrinkled his long nose. "Let me assure you, humans have it much easier."

I hugged him harder. "I missed you."

His one claw came around and clasped me to his underbelly. "I missed you, too," he said. "But there are other things we have to take care of first."

"Oh, right. Rosemary." I glanced over at her as she cowered on the ground, using the ledge of the Time Tower to crawl away from Elysian as she clutched at her bleeding arm.

"I wasn't talking about her," he said. "The Prince told me that her time for judgment has come. I was talking about these guys."

He nudged me with his nose affectionately, pushing my attention to where the fabric had fallen behind him.

Seven small shadows of light danced behind me. Instantly, I felt the shock of surprise and recognition hit me.

Each of their faces came into focus as I ran toward my children.

They were light and inhumanly solid, but I touched their faces and ruffled their hair, and I felt the full feeling of love pouring out of them.

I turned back to Elysian. "You brought me my kids," I said.

He nodded. "Yep, and they're yours, alright," he said. "Quite annoying, even if they are capable of being charming."

"I never thought I would get to meet them," I said.

"They live up with me, at Alora's castle," Elysian told me. "They help Aleia take care of Alora. Adonaias himself comes and visits us every so often."

I felt the full emotion rush into me.

Before I could tell each of them how happy I was to meet them, a shot rang out from behind me.

Rosemary had managed to balance herself against the ledge of the building. In her remaining hand, she held her gun steady.

"That's enough," she called, as the celestial fires of Elysian's attack continued to rage on the rooftop, lighting up the tower's antenna like a giant birthday cake candle. "Hand over the fabric of Time, or I'll kill everyone here."

We just stared at her. Elysian looked at her in casual boredom, and I was uncertain of how I could protect my children from her once more.

"I have enough rounds," Rosemary yelled again. "I have enough for each of you!"

Elysian yawned.

Rosemary took that as an insult. She began firing away, and I felt the scream rise in my throat and release itself as the first, second, third, fourth, and fifth bullets burst out of her gun.

By the sixth, seventh, and eighth rounds, I realized that my kids, all seven of them, weren't affected at all by her bullets.

But then, I reasoned, why would they? They were not of this world. Not anymore.

Rosemary gritted her teeth angrily, and I could see her skin tighten so much it seemed as though her head was a skull with hair.

The wind whipped passed, and she dropped her weapon. I saw, for the briefest second, the scars at the side of her cheek. There were four claw marks running down her face, the side normally covered with unevenly cut hair.

And then another shot rang out.

I squeezed my eyes at the sound as it blew from behind me.

I opened them up in time to watch as Rosemary screamed and fell backward, her balance lost, down to her death.

The echo of her cry called out long into the night. Before I could go over and see if I could catch her, the door behind me blew open.

Raiya, Lyra, and Lucas all appeared, sweaty and dirty from their battle down below.

"Hamilton," Raiya called, and then she gasped at the sight before her. "Elysian?"

Lyra and Lucas cheered. "Elysian!" they called, and even I was surprised to see him duck down so they could rub his nose affectionately.

I guess he's already met them.

Raiya came up to me as all of our kids gathered together around Elysian. Lyra and Lucas recognized them, and they began to play and fight like only brothers and sisters could.

"Where's Rosemary?" Raiya asked.

I nodded to where Rosemary had been leaning just a moment before. "I think she's dead," I said.

"You didn't have to … "

"No." I shook my head. "She fell."

I could hear the sirens as they sounded out below, and I finally made myself go over to the ledge and look down. I watched as a team of EMTs came out of an ambulance and picked up a dangerously limp and broken body off the ground.

Raiya took my hand and squeezed it. "Justice has been done," she whispered.

"Are you sure?" I asked. "I mean, it might be possible—"

"You can rest assured, Rosemary is dead."

Raiya and I flinched as Dante suddenly appeared behind us.

"She's dead," he repeated, as if to make sure we understood.

It took me less than a minute to respond accordingly. I punched Dante in the face. He howled and swayed, and I prepared for another round.

"Stop that!" he snapped. I could see a small smear of blood just under his nose, before he wiped his face with his sleeve.

"Why should I?" I asked. "You hurt my family earlier. And you let Rosemary capture my children."

"I know it hasn't always seemed like it," Dante replied with a scowl, "but I've always been on your side."

"I find that extremely hard to believe," I muttered.

"I haven't always been able to show it, but I have always been on your side. I can prove it to you," he said. "Now that Rosemary's gone, I'll give you what you want. You want a new life, free from SWORD? It's yours."

"I want it in writing. Good writing. Writing so well done that my own mother wouldn't be able to find a way to fight it," I told him.

He smirked, making his bruised face look extra twisted. "I'll have SWORD's legal associate write it up," he said. "And I'll personally deliver to Cheryl myself. I owe her an apology for earlier, too."

He walked away from me, pulling his weapon down by his side once more. He shot me a cryptic smile. "Always a pleasure doing business with you," he said.

"We're not finished," I shouted.

"For now, we are … Although, I did want to remind you of our earlier deal. Don't forget to take pictures of Mikey and Gwen's wedding for me. I'm looking forward to seeing them."

I fumed as he walked away.

"Thanks for everything, *Wingdinger*," he said. "Believe it or not, I'm indebted to you."

A feeling of betrayal welled up from within me. I recalled what Rosemary said; she had enough rounds for me and my kids. There had been nine shots, meaning someone else shot at her, sending her over the edge.

SWORD would need a new leader. One who could deliver on Dante's promise to leave me and my family alone.

Suddenly, I had to wonder if Dante had set all of this up to begin with.

As he left, I realized I had no proof, no knowledge of how much he'd actually known, and what was actually true; I only had circumstantial evidence.

Anger and frustration swirled around inside of me. My hands began to shake, and I tasted blood. I nearly jumped when someone took a hold of my hand.

Lyra appeared beside me, battle weary but triumphant. "Everything will be alright … Daddy."

I nearly jumped at her words, but luckily—or maybe skillfully—I remained calm. Even as the temptation to push

Dante off the building after Rosemary was strong, I knew what was really important. I knew what mattered, and what had meaning.

My hand tightened around hers. "You're right," I told her. She gave me a smug look, one that mirrored my own at her age.

"Hamilton?" Raiya asked. She came up beside me as Dante disappeared into the shadows. "What is it?"

"He says this is the last we'll see of SWORD," I said. "But I doubt it's the last we'll see of him."

Raiya shook her head. "We'll be ready when he comes back," she said. "It's all we can do for now."

I grunted, but I was saved from further unpleasant speculation as I heard cries of "Mommy!" calling out.

Gladly, I watched as all of our children—all nine of them— gathered around and began to hug each other, celebrating and playing and singing. I watched as Raiya opened her arms and all of them came barreling after her. She was so happy to see them and hold them, at last.

I glanced down at my wrist, wondering if the Emblem of the Prince would disappear this time, seeing as we'd managed to save the day, overcome the bad guys, and thwart evil's victory. I wasn't surprised or displeased to see it remained, somehow shining more brightly than ever.

I still had a calling. A destiny, a purpose. A job to fulfill, a life to live, and a light to shine. A leader to serve and a friend to walk beside.

You shall know the truth, and the truth shall set you free.

Yes, I did. And he did, too.

Elysian came down beside me, watching the scene alongside me. "I remember that look," he said. "If you're wondering how long you're going to have to deal with the evil that comes your way, the answer's still the same as it was before."

"I was worried about that," I said as I reached up and hugged him again. "I guess the good news is that I'm no longer the same as I once was."

I felt that push behind my heart, and I knew it was true. I had a lifetime ahead of me that would require the battles of the heart to be fought. That didn't mean I would have an easy life, choosing to do the right thing, to stand up for what I believed in.

Elysian nuzzled my hand with his nose. "The good news," Elysian told me, "is that you have an army behind you ready to help. And more help will come, too."

"St. Brendan?" I asked.

"Eh. He'll be coming for you guys in a few days to pick you up for your honeymoon. Don't get too excited; Starry Knight still has to give Alora back her fabric. But Alora will return your youngest kids to their proper time," he said with a teasing smirk. "As for the help, I was thinking more along the lines of other fallen Stars."

I brightened at the thought. With SWORD's setback, chances are more Stars might find a way to cross paths with me and Raiya. Hopefully in a good way, but as far as that went, I could only hope.

"I suppose by now I should have quite the reputation among the ones who are left," I mused aloud.

"Ugh," Elysian groaned. "I did *not* miss your ego, kid."

"Boss," I corrected him.

"Daddy!" More of the kids came clamoring around. I picked them up, one at a time, and kissed their foreheads and asked them questions.

When I came to the last one, Ian, I saw he hesitated. "What's wrong?" I asked.

"I've missed you."

"Oh, Ian," I said as I plucked him up into my arms, thrilled to be holding onto my oldest son. Like the other kids, he had a good mix of me and Raiya, and possibly some of Mark and Cheryl, too. "I've missed you, too. But I'll be coming up to see you in the Celestial Kingdom soon," I said.

He curled his head down into my shoulder, clasping his arms around me. Ian was about half of Lucas' size, though, in all fairness, Ian was technically more than five years older.

"I'm so glad to see you," Ian said. "I thought you didn't want to be with us."

My heart ached at the thought of his misery. "There's nothing further from the truth," I assured him. "I'd give anything to be with you, all the time."

I shot Elysian a teasing look. "I know we only have stolen moments on this side of Time. So while you're here, let's teach you how to ride a dragon."

As my children, relentless in their enthusiasm, began to climb on him, Elysian shot me a hard look. "You'll pay for this later," he said.

I was tempted to tell him that I had a feeling I'd already paid enough.

But instead, I just laughed and enjoyed the beauty of the moment, knowing that despite what problems might arise later, there was no price I could pay that could possibly match how much I would treasure the time I had with my family, all of us together at the same time, in the same place.

☼ 22 ☼
Onward

Thankfully, it wasn't the last time I got to see them. Nor was it a long time before I got to see them again. Elysian was true to his word, which, considering he had been reborn, I shouldn't have been so surprised about, and St. Brendan came the following week.

It was early New Year's morning when Raiya and I, along with Lyra and Lucas, boarded the *Meallán*. It was so nice to see St. Brendan again. I think he missed us, too—he picked me up into a hug so fierce I thought I was going to be squeezed in two.

We went up through space, heading up to Polaris, where Alora resided. She was still in the heart of her castle, in her pool of Time, but she was very happy to see us—even Raiya.

My children, from Aria down to Lee, were attending to the care of her castle. All of them played in the Gardens of Time as we visited.

Aleia welcomed me just as enthusiastically as St. Brendan, and I felt my heart truly regenerate at their kindness.

Raiya was my home, but these were friends I had missed more than I realized.

Elysian, the new river guardian and one of Alora's protectors, also came down to give his welcome. I was, like always, as happy to see him as I was to fight with him.

When the fighting calmed down some and we made our way to Raiya's Star to patch up the hole in Time's power, he asked me how Mikey and Gwen's wedding was.

I told Elysian the truth; I honestly didn't remember a lot of it, other than all the red and green party favors, because a week later, I married Raiya. At last, she was mine, in all senses of the word.

Hearing this, rather than his congratulations, Elysian gave me his largest, most soulful eyes. "So you didn't bring me any of Rachel's cookies?"

I laughed and promised him I would bring him some next time we came to visit. That seemed to settle him some, even if I saw him moping about it later as he complained to Alora.

We fixed the fabric of Time, placing it back where it belonged. Somehow, as the tear mended itself with the help of our power, I felt—just like that—the pieces of my life had come together, and everything clicked into place.

It was a miracle, a miracle made out of many small and seemingly inconspicuous miracles as much as larger ones, with nothing short of divine providence guiding me home.

☼<u>Epilogue</u>☼
Bedtime and Beyond

"And that," I say, as I tuck the bedcovers around my young children while they lie in their small beds, "is Daddy's story, about how he not only found truth, and how he found Mommy, but also how he fell in love with her again and again and again, and how he fell in love with so much more."

Their eyes flutter shut as I kiss them goodnight. I realize how much time had passed, and it was much later than I thought. But I let it go. Some stories are well worth the time they take, both in the making and in the telling.

Soon after I turn off the lights, I hear Lyra's gentle breathing and Lucas' quiet snoring, and I know sleep has taken ahold of them.

"Don't you think you overdramatized it just a little?"

I turn back to see my beloved as she leans against the door to the kids' room. I know Raiya had been standing there for a good while as I told our kids their favorite bedtime story, the one which happened to be my own.

I grin at her. "Come on, you enjoyed it. And what's wrong with a little poetic license here and there?"

There is a small pause before she answers. "I suppose I'm the last person who should be saying something about that," she finally says.

"I love it when you argue against yourself," I tell her, heading over to kiss her forehead and hug her. "Anyway, they're young. I don't think they're ready for the more graphic version at their ages. Two and four are a bit young for all the violence."

"I thought you did pretty well with that part."

"Then what was the overly dramatic part?"

She puts her arms around me, welcoming me with the same rush of affection she always had. "We knew—we *know*—everything is going to be okay in the end. There was no need to make it sound so dark and hopeless at some points."

"It's close enough," I say. "Remember? 'You just can't live with some decisions?'"

"It might scare them. I don't want them to have nightmares."

"Fear is the beginning of wisdom," I remind her.

"Fear of the *right things*, Hamilton," she says. "The right kind of fear only comes when we understand it properly."

"We may never understand the prince properly."

Raiya frowns, but when she remains silent I know I've scored a point.

I laugh. "You can tell the story next time. Or you can take that one up with the prince if you're worried about it."

"I have nothing to be worried about," she says as she leans in and kisses me. I pull her in close, breathing in the smell of her hair as my hands run down her back. Beneath her nightgown, I can feel the strength of her heart above the

THE STARLIGHT CHRONICLES

softness of her belly, where the marks my children have left on her remain, making her all the more strong, all the more beautiful—all the more mine.

"It's late, and we have a busy day tomorrow," she says. "Your parents are expecting us for dinner. Adam's going to be there with his new girlfriend."

"Yeah, I know. Mikey and I are going to meet up later on, too," I say. "He has some big news, apparently."

"Hopefully, it has nothing to do with his father," Raiya mutters, and I heartily agree. Dante, along with SWORD, had dropped off the map, and we were nothing short of grateful for that.

Pushing the matter aside, I reach over and kiss her, and then kiss her again. "Let's go to bed," I say.

She smirks at me as she takes my hand. Without another word—shocker, I know—I follow her.

Years Later …

The tender morning light echoes off her face as I silently, peacefully watch. All these years, and I still wonder at the thought that she belongs to me.

I've watched her as she walked down the aisle on our wedding day; as she graduated from college; as her belly swelled with our children, first Lyra and then Lucas; at every

319

Christmas, where she laughingly makes cookies with the kids and me; as the silver fairylights pop up in her gingerbread hair, even as my own begins to gray.

It's hard for me to believe she's the same girl I hated, sitting behind me all those years ago in Mrs. Smithe's class.

After everything that has happened, I wonder at all the normal routines of our life. How she yells at me for leaving my socks on the floor. How I growl at her for leaving the toothpaste cap off. How she reads to the kids every night before bed. How I kiss her deeply each morning before work.

When she farts I laugh at her, and when I pick my nose she scolds me.

We give to charity. We pay our taxes. We have a house near the 'Burgh, and I find it's nice to know my neighbors and have their kids play with mine.

Raiya goes to work at the nearby hospital—fitting for her, a natural healer. I teach law at the university, always careful to emphasize ethics and morality, though even they are not popular.

I periodically recognize my own depravity. What I would've missed if I'd stayed in a world dedicated only to myself. I think of how life is so awfully wonderful, and how I don't deserve anything I have.

When I have fears at the thought of losing Raiya again, or even my children, now that I see how reckless they truly are—I think of the one who reigns over all the realms, how he both subdues and transcends death. He promised to keep me safe when I promised to trust him, and I make sure I keep believing that he will. In the many conversations we have, this is a reoccurring theme.

My life has been speckled by the supernatural, and on this world I will get both the good and the bad. But I am able to see beyond this life's troubles to the overhanging picture of grace, love, and joy which awaits my fuller scrutiny on the other side of Time.

This doesn't mean I have an easy life, or even a normal one.

"Hey." She looks at me now, her violet eyes glowing like springtime violets.

"Hey," I say back, smiling.

"It's too early to be that contemplative," Raiya tells me with a teasing smile. "What're you thinking about?"

"How our crazy children are going to ruin the pretty morning picture you make," I say matter-of-factly. I hush Raiya's whispery giggle with a kiss. She snuggles in closer to me and takes my hand.

As if on cue, something smashes to the floor, and the pitter-patter of our offspring can be heard running in the opposite direction. We laugh, even though we know we will both be yelling shortly.

"Shall we face this fate together then, my love?" she asks me quietly.

My answer is ironic and immediate, born out of habit and continually renewed by love. "My pleasure."

C. S. Johnson is the author of several young adult sci-fi and fantasy novels, including *The Starlight Chronicles* series, the *Once Upon a Princess* saga, and the *Divine Space Pirates* trilogy. With a gift for sarcasm and an apologetic heart, she currently lives in Atlanta with her family. Follow her on Twitter at @C_S_Johnson13.

THE STARLIGHT CHRONICLES

THE STARLIGHT CHRONICLES

AUTHOR'S NOTE

Dear Reader,

Praise the Lord, the God of our fathers, and his son Jesus Christ, in whom we find everlasting redemption. As this series comes to a close, I pray you will see that it never truly ends.

Redemption and fatherly love are no small matters in this book. I started writing this book series as a way to channel my pain over my high school experiences. I wanted revenge when I left. Now, only a clearer vision of redemption remains. I was an innocent idealist, and then a failed idealist, and now I am a redeemed idealist. What had hurt me, I now see led me to great healing. Where I saw pain, great pleasure now flourishes. The scars on my heart have become symbols, both of the past and providence, pointing to a greater story even as it tells my own.

I can see more clearly than ever that God truly does work all things for good for those who truly seek him (or maybe in my case, those who can't avoid him). It is not a happy thought, truly, but a staying one. It is a reality that will guide me through the ups and downs and all arounds this life has to offer. In accordance with this, I fail to see the irrelevance of fatherly love to redemption, especially since I live in a world where such humanly love seems to have failed us.

Someone once told me that God revealed himself as the father, rather than the mother, to show there was nothing natural about his love. It is all supernatural, superseding this world and the limits of this life. In fact, I do believe that this force, this love, is the very thing that will carry you to your final home.

In the believer's journey, home is our final destination. We need to keep the focus on that more than we might think. The Bible's story is all about that: God does what it takes to get his family home. My stories, on the other hand, are more on the other side of the relationship DNA; we are called to head out for home, seeking out truth and reaching out in love, despite pain, despite joy, despite all things.

I hope that you have enjoyed this series. I have not always enjoyed writing it, but it is a part of my life I could never, would never, separate from my soul or my self.

My thanks continually goes it to Jennifer, for her patience in editing my work, and for being nice about correcting me, even when I insist on getting it wrong. I am also indebted to Amy, for her friendship first and her work second. Such beauty can only come from a beautiful soul like yours.

Other names will top my list. My mother, Ryan, and my family; but most of all, I need to thank Sam. Ever since high school, I have smuggled you into my imaginary audience, and I have never let you leave. I am a fallen, imperfect, sputtering soul, always second-guessing myself (or trying not to), and this book has taught me that all over again. It is my second greatest wish to meet you again one day (I suspect you know the first).

Lastly, I need to thank you, beloved reader. While I do not have another book in this series planned, I do hope to see you again in my other work (read on for a sample from *The Heights of Perdition,* the first book in a new series I'm working on).

I write with God, but I write for myself, and now for you. As ever, I will continue to trust him to do what he thinks is good.

Until We Meet Again in Paradise,

C. S. Johnson

THE STARLIGHT CHRONICLES

AUTHOR'S ACKNOWLEDGEMENTS

EDITOR

Jennifer C. Sell

Jennifer Clark Sell is a professional book editor and proofreader. She works from her home in Southern California. With her years of professional and personal experience, she offers several quality packages for authors. Find her at

https://www.facebook.com/JenniferSellEditingService.

Photo Credit: Savannah Sell

AUTHOR'S ACKNOWLEDGEMENTS

COVER ILLUSTRATOR

Amalia Chitulescu

Amalia Iuliana Chitulescu is a digital artist from Campina, Romania. Raised in a small town, this self-taught artist has a technique which is delineated by the contrast between obscurity and enlightenment, using dark elements in a dreamy world. Her areas of expertise include the use of theatrical concepts to create a macabre and surrealistic world that still maintains a highly recognizable attachment to reality. Bridging a diaphanous environment with light elements, an eerie view, she creates a dream world of dark beauty, done with a blend of photography and digital painting. Find her at https://www.facebook.com/Amalia.Chitulescu.Digital.Art

Photo Credit: Amalia Chitulescu

Chapter 1 *from*

THE HEIGHTS OF PERDITION

BOOK ONE OF *THE DIVINE SPACE PIRATES*

◆◆◆◆

C. S. Johnson

♦<u>1</u>♦

At just the right angle, the dark blue and white orb, suspended in a sea of invisible shadows, held in place by a faith as impossible to believe in as it was to see, fit nicely between his fingers. Outside his window, Earth looked small and fragile, seemingly innocent, and mostly harmless. A hollowness slipped between his thumb and forefinger as he squashed them together, crushing the blueberry-sized circle.

Amused by the irony of the forced perspective before him, a rare, genuine smile formed on Exton Shepherd's face.

It was, he decided, almost a shame no one else was around to witness such an unusual event. He smooshed his fingers together, imagining the world completely decimated into dust.

But then, he recalled, he'd given plenty of smiles earlier, as all the hubbub went on about the ship. Surely the crew, his hodgepodge of adopted family and coworkers, would have been satisfied with those, even though they were inauthentic at best and mocking at worst.

Duty sometimes demanded playing happy. Exton knew that, and he followed it, even in instances he loathed.

Like today.

Between the thirteenth and fifteenth sunrises of his day, he'd watched the only other person he truly cared for in all the world—no, he mentally corrected himself, in all the universe—pledge her love, heart, and life to another man.

It was heartbreaking on some levels, but strangely freeing, too.

332

The wedding had been quaint, warm, and sweet. Its simplicity suggested nothing of its socially taxing nature.

Exton had no regrets about ducking out as soon as the bride and groom finished their vows and the Ecclesia had pronounced them husband and wife.

Once he had successfully slipped out of sight, Exton proceeded to the Captain's Lounge, the small room he'd claimed as his the day after launching the *Perdition* into space. There was little to be said of the room's comfort; it was more like a tall elevator shaft than a room, empty of everything but the coldness of space and a small window hidden up near the far end. More than once, Exton wondered if he'd found a kind of kinship with it; hollow and bleak, with a tiny view looking out toward the fleeing horizon.

It was there, on a window seat built into the windowpane, where Exton tucked his legs under his chin and entered into his own world of privacy, where he was free to be who he wanted, even if it was for only a moment.

As captain of the ship, he didn't want his crew to see him in one of his more melancholy moods.

His frown returned when he opened his fingers again, only to see Earth was still hanging in space before him, its silence mocking and spiteful. Rearranging his hand, he made it seem like he was carrying the earth in the palm. Fleetingly, he toyed with the idea of pretending to toss the small pearl away into the dark recesses of space, into an imaginary hell.

But he knew that would not work.

Exton knew two things with startling clarity and unshakable certainty: The first was that hell was real, and the second was that it was his home.

"Having fun?" a voice asked from below him.

"Huh?" Exton jerked around in surprise, nearly falling off the window ledge. "Come on, Emery, don't do that," he groaned, while the young woman dressed all in white only laughed. His balance, already compromised by the pull of the starship's gravity, faltered again as Exton tried to adjust himself. "You know I don't like it when people interrupt me, especially when I'm here."

"But it's my wedding day," Emery insisted. "And I'd like to have a dance with the ship's captain before the night shift starts. Come on, we're up first."

Exton gave up on staying by the window and jumped down as gracefully as he could. "All the shifts up here are technically the night shift," he grumbled.

"Some would say we live in perpetual day up here on the *Perdition*," Emery offered, her voice gentle even as she maintained her stance. "Sunrise and sunset are only ninety-two minutes apart for us now, when we're this close to Earth."

"Sunrises and sunsets do not make day and night up here," Exton told her, touching his forehead.

Emery reached out and took his hand, before she placed it over his heart. "I think your problem is too much night in here, not out there." She turned her attention back to the window, where six inches of steel-grade glass separated them from the vacuum of space.

Exton followed her gaze, wondering if she was looking for any sign of familiarity from their old home. He watched as the end of the ocean braced itself against the shore of the Old Republic; he felt his memory pull him in, and he could see it clearly inside his mind.

The chill of the old mountains where he would go work and play with his father, the spray of the salt water on his

THE HEIGHTS OF PERDITION

transport module, the warmth of his mother's arms as she welcomed him home from school—all of it embraced him, surrounding him and penetrating into the deep recesses of his heart.

And then there was pain, and then it was gone.

Exton shook his head. "I know it seems like a long time has passed, but it's time to cause the URS some trouble. It's almost the anniversary, you know."

"I know," she replied. A sudden sadness appeared in her gaze, and Exton wondered if she had been reminiscing as well.

Pushing aside his grief, he straightened his shoulders. "I have a plan that will really make them sorry this year, Em."

"I know you're a man of your word," Emery replied, "but I'm not sure it will be enough to convince them to give us what we want."

"They already cannot give us what we want." Exton shrugged. "Our game was never for power. It was for meaning."

"It's not a game, Exton."

"I know it's not!" Out of the corner of his eye, he saw Emery flinch. "I know it's not," he repeated carefully, reverting to his usual, detached tone. "It's not our fault that it became a quest for survival, Emery. I know that even more than you do."

"If it's survival you want," Emery scoffed, "there's no point in selling your soul in the process."

Before Exton could assure Emery he had no soul left that was worth saving, let alone selling, he stopped. Happy times, he reminded himself.

Emery's wedding was a special occasion, one that had excited her for the past several months, offering a glimmer of hope on a horizon of gloom and turmoil. Exton was determined not to let the past rob him—or her—of anything else, so long as it was in his power. "You're right," he acquiesced, momentarily giving in.

Emery smiled brightly, and Exton suddenly had a hard time believing she was only two years younger than he was. At twenty-two, she seemed much more innocent than the figure that gazed back at him when he looked in the mirror.

He slipped his hand out from under hers, before taking and squeezing it. "Are you sure you wouldn't like to have the first dance with your new husband?"

"Tyler is my heart's desire," Emery told him firmly, "but you will always be my hero."

Exton grimaced. He knew he was no hero. "It would be a shame to waste your time with me."

"Time with you is not a waste."

"Did Tyler approve of changing up the dancing order? The man might be in love, but there's no need to make him prove to be the fool."

"Hey, Tyler's your commander, and your best friend," Emery objected. "You know he's not a fool."

"Not where it concerns you. He would be smart to correct that, and I have been telling him since he received approval from the Ecclesia to start courting you," Exton told her. He gave her a devious look. "Should I make him walk the plank?"

Emery frowned and searched the darkened shadows of his face. "That's not funny, Exton."

"I know."

They walked in silence for a few moments before Exton spoke once more. "I don't want to dance. No offense, Em."

"Traditionally, it was the daughter's duty to dance with her father, first." Emery smiled. "But that's more of a cultural thing I've read about from the Old Republic."

"Yes, I remember that," Exton agreed. "Ironic, how the Revolutionary States would be appalled by it now."

Of course, he recalled, even the idea of using the term "father" might have some of the more militant protestors up in arms, as the beloved Daddy Dictator of the URS, Grant Osgood, did not encourage familial relationships, unless such feelings were directed toward government.

"If the URS is against it, you should be more inclined to appease me, then," Emery contended.

There was a breath of silence and stillness before Exton responded. "I'm not our father," he scoffed.

"You're more like him than you might wish."

As Exton scowled at her, Emery pointed her finger at him accusingly. "See? You even have the same exasperated look he used to get when he was frustrated."

"I'll have to take your word for it." Exton shrugged, scratching his head. He frowned as he realized it had been some time since he'd gotten a haircut. His father used to do the same thing, especially when he was planning his next engineering endeavor. Exton suddenly wondered if it was his own scruffy locks that had been making him shrink back from mirrors of late.

He missed his father too much to want to see him staring out of the mirror from the other side of the grave.

Emery chuckled again, drawing him out of his thoughts. "Well, I know at least one trait you share with him. He had a hard time telling me no to anything I wanted, if memory serves."

"You look too much like Mom for me to say no," Exton admitted. "I'm sure he had the same problem, but that's one I'm more willing to share with him."

With her dark brown hair, blue-green eyes, and petite form, Emery was the living memory of their mother. She even had the same dimple hovering above the left corner of her lips, a trait Exton knew was the extent of their common features. Their father's blue eyes, as clear and sharp as ice, had passed to him, along with his height, broad shoulders, and black hair.

"He always did want me to follow in his footsteps," Exton muttered as they headed out of the Captain's Lounge. "But I'm not sure he would have enjoyed the ghost of Captain Chainsword, the infamous space lumberjack pirate."

"I don't think he would have liked it, given how much he derided you for enjoying those fantasy adventures you used to read."

"It seemed fitting at the time, to create a new role for him to play, along with the rest of us."

"I suppose." Emery shrugged. "But Papa was a brilliant engineer, same as you, and a good man. I'm not sure he would have liked your emphasis on piracy and power."

"For the most part, I think you are right," Exton agreed. "But he was too idealistic by far. That was what got him killed." He looked out a nearby window, where, even as he could no longer see Earth, he still felt the pull of its shadow.

"In hindsight, you would prove to be correct on that point."

"That is why I will not make the same mistake as he did. While *Paradise* is out of reach, *Perdition* will do what it can to ensure a better life for us."

"And others, too," Emery added proudly.

"Maybe." Exton shrugged. "I only have a duty to you, and you're technically Tyler's problem now. Anyone else is just extra."

"Your duty to me hasn't ended."

Exton rolled his eyes. "I'm going to dance with you, aren't I? What else is there?"

"Your duty to me might include a dance tonight, but I wish for you to find someone you would love as I love Tyler." She smiled. "Someone you can spend your life trying to make happy."

"Even as life makes me miserable?"

Emery frowned and sighed. "I don't know why you do that."

"Do what?"

"Make it impossible for yourself to be happy."

"Happiness is fleeting, remember?" Exton rolled his eyes. "Even the leaders of the Ecclesia would agree with me there."

"They don't often agree with you, especially when it comes to your mandates," Emery concurred. "The only reason they would on this account is because the phrasing is vague enough to seem to agree on the meaning." She narrowed her gaze. "And the practice."

Exton wrinkled his nose. "We've been up here for too long if you know me so well."

"I still prefer this to when we were off at different universities, working on our studies," Emery admitted with a thoughtful smile. "But as for the argument, you don't seem to agree with the Ecclesia a whole lot, either. You don't share most of their beliefs. I find it hard to believe that you would try to garner support from among their teachings."

"Their teachings on wisdom and life, and how it should be, I respect. But it's different when you're trying to manage a pirate starship and ruin an empire."

"Not to mention when you insist so stubbornly on remaining miserable."

"I *am* going back to your wedding celebration, aren't I?" Exton groaned. "Please don't push it, Em. You know how I feel. If God would grant your wish for me, if he wanted so much for me to be 'happy,' he could have let me 'fall in love' with someone on the *Perdition*, like you and Tyler. But even when we send our smaller ships down to Earth for supplies, see Aunt Patty, or attack the URS, there's no one there for me. There are only people there who want the protection *Perdition* can offer to political dissents or refugees such as themselves."

After a moment of thought, he added, "Besides, my job is to protect and lead aboard the spaceship. The last thing I need is to be led around by the whims of a woman."

"There's no need to make it sound so deplorable," Emery scoffed, arching an eyebrow at him. "Do you honestly think dealing with the moods of a man are any easier?"

He flashed her a charming grin.

"You don't need to set yourself up for failure like that. We have only been up in space for six years now, hiding in the shadows of all the toxic clouds while playing war games with the URS."

"Not to mention watching destruction of all other sorts go unchecked," Exton added, his voice grim.

"It's not all 'unchecked,'" Emery reminded him. "Exton, you still can't lose hope. God is a supposed to be a god of miracles, remember? We have time."

Exton wondered how his sister could be worried about his heart, when his life, as well all the lives of his crew, faced the bigger risk. It was one thing to be aware of danger, but another to disregard it, especially for something as silly as true love.

He studied Emery's daydreaming smile in silence and decided he had the right of it: As much as she was ever his practical and precise sister, Emery's wedded bliss was affecting her judgment.

Exton was surprised at the sudden stab of jealousy. He squashed it down as he caught sight of the approaching Earth through the galley windows.

Didn't Emery see the coming battle? Exton wondered. *Didn't she feel the haunted air about the starship, with specters of the past lurking around every corner of the* Perdition?

They couldn't outlast the URS forever up in space. While Exton and the Ecclesia had established the *Perdition* a safe haven over the past few years, it was only a matter of time before the URS would come for them, and he knew it would not be to make peace.

"What is it, Exton?" Emery asked, jolting him out of his gloomy thoughts.

Exton sighed. "It's not like God's just going to dump someone into the ship just for me. You might as well save your breath for dancing, Em."

Thank you for reading! Please leave a review for this book and check for other books and updates!